BLUNT FORCE

BLUNT FORCE

JB ROTH

Blunt Force

© 2024 by JB Roth

Editors: Josh Owens, David J. Remy
Cover Design:
Interior Design: Emma Elzinga

Indigo River Publishing
3 West Garden Street, Ste. 718
Pensacola, FL 32502
www.indigoriverpublishing.com

Ordering Information:

Quantity Sales: Special discounts are available on quantity purchases by corporations, associations, and others. For details, contact the publisher at the address above.

Orders by US trade bookstores and wholesalers: Please contact the publisher at the address above.

Printed in the United States of America

Library of Congress Control Number: 2023918030
Paperback ISBN: 978-1-954676-66-4
eBook ISBN: 978-1-954676-67-1

First Edition

With Indigo River Publishing, you can always expect great books, strong voices, and meaningful messages. Most importantly, you'll always find . . . *words worth reading.*

To Penny.
You make everything worthwhile.

PROLOGUE

He was laughing so hard he never saw death coming. By the time the mass of metal connected with his skull and silenced his laughter, he was dead.

But death never comes at once. Time slows down when you die. In the split second it took for the Grim Reaper to do his job, William Morrison felt searing pain as the skin on the side of his head split open. He felt a warm flow of blood on his cheek. He felt his skull shattering, sending shards of bone into his brain.

Then he felt nothing. Ever again.

CHAPTER 1

The headlights reflected on the concrete wall ahead of me as I pulled the shiny, nearly new 2021 CR-V into its space in the parking garage. Black block letters marked the spot: *COOPER MALONE. PRIVATE INVESTIGATOR.*

I locked the car and took the elevator up to the eighth floor. My office suite door had the same words at eye level on the frosted glass. It had no logo or intricate font. I was Malone. I was a private investigator. No point getting fancy about it.

I pushed my way through the unlocked door, finding Courtney already behind the front desk. She knew it was me barging in from the camera outside the door. Otherwise, her hand would have rested on the .38-caliber Walther PK she kept just out of sight and knew how to use, not on her keyboard. We saw all kinds come through these doors.

"Hi, Coop," she said. She sounded cheerful. She always sounded cheerful, even on Mondays. She could have passed for a South Florida beach bunny with her bleach blond hair, perma-tan and big tits she liked flaunting. Problem was, she had way too much brains for a beach bunny.

"Hi," I said.

"We already got a call for you. CJ took it."

"Okay, thanks."

I walked past Courtney's desk. It was just a few steps to CJ's office, right across from mine. I leaned against the door frame and leered at her while she worked on the computer, unblinking, in the zone. Her face, with its high cheekbones and framed by the long, jet-black hair she had inherited from her Grandma Vinh, glowed under the light of her oversized, flat-screen monitors.

"Your friend, Heather, called," she said, looking up. "And stop staring."

CJ and I had dated for a short time before we realized we made better business partners than bed partners. I figured our history gave me license to stare. And who wouldn't stare? I shrugged.

"Heather? Why? She has my cell phone." I stepped into her office, my eyes narrowing. I took in the familiar art on the walls as I walked in. It was oriental and tasteful. It fit CJ without opening too much of her to the random people who walk into a PI's office.

CJ stopped typing and looked at me. I'm barely over six feet and still had the lean figure I had in the Army. I wasn't exactly blocking her light. She was simply ready to talk to me.

"She didn't say, but she sounded out of sorts," my partner said.

"Is it work-related?"

"I wondered about that and asked. She mumbled something I couldn't make out, and I let it go. She asked if you could meet her around nine at that martini lounge you guys like."

"Nick & Nora?"

"That's the one."

"Weird, but okay, I'll be there."

I did paperwork most of the day before driving out to meet Heather. Shuffling paper is about all I cared to do while I wondered why my oldest friend in Miami had called my office and not my cell. It was work for the sake of work, anyway, the kind of cases that paid the bills but didn't exactly make my heart pump faster. There were background check interviews, trailing a disgruntled employee who may or may not have taken trade secrets with him, and more just like them. The only criminal case lately had been a missing-person case that ended badly. I'd found the kid stoned out of her mind in a drug den, a needle sticking out of her arm.

I still had time to kill when I was done. I stopped by one of the Cuban cafés that dot Miami's streets. Black and white pictures of the old country covered the walls. I traveled back in time on my way to the counter. Old cars were parked in front of grand buildings, showgirls strutted on stage, shoppers milled in the streets, and workers stooped in the fields.

Striped bench seating lined the walls, with matching chairs on the other side of the tables. The restaurant was half-full with diners hovering over food piled high in bowls or sandwiches too tall for the human mouth. The whole place hummed with conversation and smelled of coffee and bread, enough to make my mouth water before I even ordered.

I ate a Cubano at a table in the corner. I munched quietly, focusing on the food and the crowd. Patrons pointed at the pictures of the old country, smiles on their faces. Memories flowed along with coffee and *pastelitos* around here. I tried not to wonder too much about what Heather could possibly want that wouldn't fit in a phone call to my cell. It wasn't as if we didn't talk.

I got to Nick & Nora right at nine. Its neon sign bathed the dark parking lot in cool blue light. There was no logo, just the name. Maybe it honored the old characters from the 1930s. Maybe it came from the filigreed Nick-and-Nora glasses in which the bar served their martinis. Either way, it was old and simple, a little like me.

The moment I walked into the place, familiar sensations surrounded me. I breathed them in. I took my appreciation for the old-world feel from the hardwood floor underfoot, the dark furniture, and the low lights more than I did from the name. I might as well have stepped back in time and landed in the Roaring Twenties. That was part of the charm, and I loved it.

I walked to the tune of classic jazz, looking for Heather on one of the soft benches that surrounded low tables. I half expected to smell stale cigarettes and walk through a smoky haze. But it was still the twenty-first century outside the walls. Wood varnish fought with a layer of perfume for my nostrils' attention.

Heather and her husband, Doug, were already there with drinks in front of them. Heather looked up from hers, and what I saw worried me.

Her light red hair did not have its usual bounce. Her full lips were devoid of her trademark red lipstick. And she wasn't wearing a dress. Heather the fashionista always wore a dress. That night, she was wrapping herself in a loose top and plain, run-around-the-house jean cutoffs.

Doug stood up first and shook my hand—a quick touch of the hand, a vanishing smile as if he didn't have time for words or a firmer handshake. I'd met him not long after they started dating and liked him right away. As always, he had overdressed for the occasion and showed up in a blazer and dress shirt. His hair was unruly despite being cut short—at least that was par for the course. It looked like cowlicks racing each other that could not decide which side of his head they were racing to.

Heather stood up and put one arm around my waist. This wasn't a real Heather hug. She usually hugged like she meant it—tried to crush your ribs. Her one-arm attempt barely deserved the name.

We all sat down, and I ordered a rye. I let small talk last long enough for the waiter to come back with my drink. I left it on the table.

I put my hand on my knees and leaned toward Heather, trying to take the edge off my usual bluntness. "What's wrong?"

"I'm sorry," she said. "I don't know what to do." Her voice was raspy.

So much for me taking the edge off. It's not that Heather would have expected anything else from me, but I never knew what to do in these situations. My brain goes blank and I can't come up with two words to string together. Forty years on this planet, twelve of them in the Army, and I still didn't know what to do when a woman looked anxious.

Our waiter appeared again, his hand gesturing toward Heather's empty glass. She looked up and ordered a vodka tonic. She returned her attention to me, trying to smile and beat back the tears. "I know. Not my usual fruity cocktail."

I filled the void with small talk. I hated small talk, but better wait for Heather's drink to appear. When it did, the vodka tonic hardly hit the table before Heather took a gulp.

"What's going on?" I asked in a whisper, leaning forward again.

"Somebody died," Heather blurted out. "I . . . it's . . . ." She was choking, words stuck in her throat. Maybe it was anger, maybe distress, or maybe a little bit of both.

Doug took her hand and looked at her with a weak smile. "Do you want me to start explaining?"

Heather nodded.

Doug went on. "Every year, Heather and her two best friends from college take a girls' trip."

"Jen and Amy," Heather said, dabbing her eyes with a Kleenex she'd extracted from her shorts' pocket.

Doug continued, "They call it their 'Girls Gone Wild' trip. That's just because it's fun saying it, really. They drink too much, go dancing, flirt with the boys, and renew their college days bonding."

He looked at Heather, smiling the way people in love smile at each other. "Either liberal arts majors have way more fun than architecture students, or I went to the wrong college."

Heather chuckled and squeezed Doug's hand. "I'm okay," she told him, then looked at me and continued, "For this year's trip, we booked a cruise with Mardi Gras Cruise Lines. Have you heard of it?"

"I have." Cruises were big business in Miami, and I was as familiar with the industry as the next guy.

Heather ran a finger along the rim of her glass. Silence lingered for a moment.

I filled it, keeping the conversation going. "They're a new player in town. They run adults-only cruises and are unapologetic about being a party boat. There's even a strip club aboard if I'm not mistaken. Sounds like just the place for your girls' trip."

"You're right," Heather said softly, "and it should have been." She took a deep breath and a long drink. She put the glass back on the table and looked back up at me.

"In fact, it was perfect for most of the cruise, glorious even. We were on last week's cruise, by the way, the one that came back into port yesterday.

"We had all piled into the suite we'd booked together and started bar hopping across the ship. It was great—exactly what we were looking for. We made friends with this group of guys, bankers or Wall Street types of some kind, but from here in Miami. They were partying hard and throwing money around."

"What do you mean?"

"Buying rounds or bottles at the bars and the clubs on board—and the strip club, for that matter. Things like that. Anyone who wanted to could end the night in the row of VIP suites they had on the top deck, and the booze kept flowing on their dime.

"There were a lot of people around them, not just us, but us too. We drank champagne we could never have afforded and danced into the night. The flirting was a bit touchy-feely but nothing crazy. Not with me anyway. It was like we were in some reality show or a movie or something. We . . . ."

The group in the booth next to ours got up, loud and a little drunk. Heather looked up and smiled. We waited as one guy needed a bit of convincing it was time to go. They exited to the sound of forced chuckles and a groan.

"Sorry," Heather said, her attention back on me. "Where was I?"

"No worries. You were partying with the bankers."

"Oh, yes. And party we did. Then we'd have a hair of the dog in the morning and hang around the pool or in port in the afternoon. Rinse, repeat. There were drugs, too. I didn't do anything more than pot, but I could have, and lots of people did. It was like a scene from *Wolf of Wall Street*, except on a cruise ship."

There was no stopping Heather now. Her story had been burning her from the inside. Now it was coming out, come hell or high waters.

"Come Saturday," she said, "I was actually a little nervous. Strip clubs and champagne in the guys' suite? That was a bit wilder than our 'Girls Gone Wild' trips usually were, even if only by a little bit. It was kind of crazy. I had a little pang in my gut about that night . . . you know, the last night on board."

"Why is that? Did anything happen to put you on guard?"

"No. But they seemed like the type of guys who'd want to pull out all the stops for the last night, you know. So, I went looking for them, just to chat, get an idea of what they were planning. But whatever my gut was telling me, that's not what was weird. It's that I couldn't find them anywhere. They weren't even at dinner, not that we could see anyway. After we ate, the three of us all went up to their suites, but the whole floor was cordoned off. There was a sign about a private party, but those guys' parties were never private. The more people, the more they loved it. I started thinking something bad had happened.

"We went back to one of the bars, just the three of us, and had a few cocktails—more than a few, actually. We had plenty of laughs reminiscing, but it was a bit subdued. There we were, three party girls on our last night, sitting at the back of the bar, by ourselves, speaking in low voices.

"When we got back to our cabin, I opted for a late disembark and told the girls I felt like walking around for a while before leaving, but that they should go ahead and get going whenever they felt like it in the morning. I was upset. I felt certain something had happened. I spent the morning roaming the ship with a big purse on my shoulder like I was looking for last-minute souvenirs. But I was really floating from one group of security guards to another while they watched over emptying the ship, and eavesdropped on their conversations."

Heather's gaze had been lost somewhere in space as she revisited her memories and put them into words. Now she stared straight at me. Her cheeks were as red as her lips usually were. Her eyes, swelling with tears a few minutes ago, were shooting daggers now.

"Coop," she said, in case looking straight into my soul wasn't enough to get my attention, "I swear I'm not crazy. I know I only heard snippets of conversation, but from everything I overheard the security guys say, one of those bankers we were partying with was murdered. There is no doubt in my mind. And I'm pretty sure they didn't even call the cops or whomever else they should have either. At least I heard nothing that would make me think they did. If I'm right, they're trying to hide what happened."

Then, Heather leaned back into her chair. She ran a hand through her hair. She even had a hint of a smile. I smiled back. It was good to see—and not overly surprising. The enormity of someone being killed overwhelms everyone. It's not supposed to happen. That's something you read on the news. Now, she'd let it all out, even if that was only by talking to me. That had helped.

I'd been careful to interrupt her as little as I could. I wanted to let her get her story out. Now, I went ahead and made our talk a two-way street. "You're doing the right thing talking to me," I told her. "Is it okay if I ask you a couple of questions?"

"Yes. Yes, of course."

"Those Wall Street types, they have names?"

"William, Walt, and Cabe." She looked down, speaking the next words in a whisper. "I . . . I don't know their last names."

"Don't sweat it. I didn't expect you to have checked their IDs between bottles of champs."

That brought a bit of a chuckle back, and she looked up again. "William was the one flashing his Beads Card the most—that's what Mardi Gras calls their door key that you also use to pay for everything. He acted like the leader of the band—brash and flashy. I'd guess he was in his thirties."

Heather took a break and closed her eye for a few seconds. "Walt was quite a bit older, but he still partied hard. Cabe seemed younger than William, but I'm not sure. He was more subdued. I don't know for sure or even why I think so, but I think William was the one who was killed. I'm probably going on too little information for that. My mind's gone crazy."

"Nah. You're not crazy. Take it from me. Now, you said it wasn't reported. You're probably right about that since no one with a badge came to see you. They'd have been there when you arrived in port. And since we're all sitting here, I'm guessing you'd rather I took a look into it instead of the cops. Am I right?"

Heather shrugged. "Yeah, because we're involved—Amy, Jen, and me. But if you think I should go to the cops instead, I'll go. I know I didn't know those guys well. Hardly at all, really. But I can't just let it go. I can't."

"I know. I know you. And I didn't say you should go to the cops. This is what I do. Did you share your suspicions with Amy and Jen, too?"

"Amy, yes. She's a good ole girl, strong personality, lots of common sense, and smart as hell, so I ran it by her. She said it fit, and I could tell the wheels started turning. We didn't have much time to talk about it, but that clinched it for me, and I called you."

"And Jen?"

Heather's smile widened. "We're all artsy, the three of us. Jen's the artsiest of us all, the sensitive soul type—a little like me, I guess. I left her out of it for now, but I know you'll need to talk to her, and it's okay."

I sat back and took a sip of my rye. I didn't really want it—I was working. I was looking for something to give me time to gather my thoughts. The glass made a thump when I put it back on the table.

"Heather, I believe you," I said. "You're smart and you have a good eye. You notice things." Heather had parlayed her artistic talents, love of fashion, and drive into becoming a power buyer in the industry, buying for a big retail chain. Saying she had a good eye was the understatement of the year. I felt like I was insulting her with faint praise, but this was not the time to split hairs.

"Still," I went on, "we don't actually know that someone died, let alone was murdered. So, if I do this, I'll start there. You need to be cool with that. No ego about being right."

Heather laughed out loud for the first time that night. "Hell, no! Tell me they're all alive, and I'll be beyond a happy girl."

"Good. And if your suspicions prove right and someone was killed, I'll find out and I'll get to the bottom of it."

Heather nodded. "Thank you."

Doug chose this time to chime in, leaning in toward me. "Just one more thing. We want your help. We need your help. This is an awful weight on Heather. She's pissed. You can see that. I don't think I'm talking out of turn here by saying she's kind of spooked, too, that someone she spent the week with may have been murdered. That means we want to hire you, emphasis on hire."

He pointed a finger at me as he kept talking. "I'll do anything for friends, and I know you're the same way. If you ask me to design a house for you, I'll give you a friends-and-family rate, but I'll charge you for it because it's my work. You're an investigator. This is work. Treat it like work and charge us. I'm not kidding. This is important to us."

"You'll have a harder time convincing CJ than me," I said. "Friendship is everything to her, doesn't matter if it's hers or mine. Let her pick the rate, okay? I promise you this is work, and my bill will reflect it."

"So long as it's not unreasonably low," Doug said.

"I'll talk to her." I knew where Doug was coming from. Part of it was him not wanting to take advantage, but there was something else to it. If I charged him, what I did had value, the kind you could measure. There was something reassuring about that.

"I have more questions," I said after Doug leaned back into his seat, "but let's not do that here. Can you come to the office tomorrow morning? Say nine-ish?"

"Can we make it eight? I have meetings the rest of the day," Heather said.

"As early as you want. I still wake up on Army time. I was trying to give you your beauty sleep."

"Buy me another drink instead. With Doug and you by my side, I feel better already."

I downed the rest of my glass and ordered another round now that Heather was feeling better. I barely touched it and left as soon as it was polite to do so. I sat in the car, staring at the parking lot, watching people walking to and from their cars. *What the fuck did you just do, Malone?*

I hadn't seen a dead body since my Army days. What did I know about solving a murder flying solo? Heather was a friend, a good friend. But was I really helping her by taking on a case like this? Sure, I hated the corporate work we had. It made my eyes bleed. But the occasional break-in or missing-person case kept me happy. I was good at those. I didn't need this.

Or did I? I wanted to feel important. I wanted what I did to matter. That's what I missed most from my days in the shadows with Army Intelligence.

What I did then changed lives. And if my life was going to matter again, I needed to solve crimes, real crimes, big crimes, crimes with blood dripping out of them. Well, I had one. But it didn't only matter to me. It mattered to someone I cared about. What was I thinking?

CHAPTER 2

CJ was already there when I got in the next morning. I'd called her from the car on my way back from Nick & Nora and asked her to come to the office early the next day. That's all she needed to know. We were partners. We trusted each other.

We sat in the two blue chairs in front of her desk, and I briefed her on the case.

"I told Courtney she could come in a bit later so you and I would have a chance to talk first," I added when I was done with the facts and just the facts.

"About what?" CJ asked.

"I told Heather I'd take the case. I'm not sure it was the right thing to do."

"She's a friend!" CJ sounded horrified by what I said.

"That's exactly why. She's a friend and I've never handled a murder case without a team of Army specialists around me. Just maybe I shouldn't handle this one. Just maybe I owe her better."

CJ shook her head, a smile on her face. Her shoulders relaxed. "I've seen you work cases, Coop. You've got this. Don't you back off. This is the right thing to do."

That wasn't quite enough to make me stop worrying, but it was enough to keep the case, at least for now. I had my partner on board. I reached over and squeezed her hand. "Alright. We'll start working, then. Speaking of which, I'd like you to interview Heather if she's okay with it. You have a softer touch, and it will put a second brain to it."

"Of course, no problem."

When Heather came in, she was back in one of her trademark dresses. Color had returned to her lips and cheeks. I hugged her a little tighter for it.

"You remember CJ?" I asked after we let go.

Heather smiled. "Yes, of course. How are you?"

"I'm well, thank you."

"I'd like her to be the one interviewing you," I said, "so she can look at everything with a fresh pair of eyes. I'll start working other angles."

"No problem," Heather said.

"I'll be in my office if you guys need me."

I went to my desk and got busy on the computer. I did not have Courtney's cyber-sleuthing skills, but I knew where to start.

I logged on and started checking out Mardi Gras Cruise Lines. They had just the one ship in Miami, the *Mardi Gras Rio*, that ran the usual Caribbean cruises, alternating between western and eastern routes. Their website was all promos, specials, and pretty pictures. Fair enough, that was to be expected.

I opened a new tab and moved on to Dun & Bradstreet. I may get frustrated at all the white-collar work we do, but I liked the D&B subscription it justified. The company offered every business data imaginable—for a price. I'd used it enough to know my way around it, and gleaned all they had about Mardi Gras Cruise Lines, jotting notes with pen and paper as I went.

Once I got what I needed there, I checked what public information there was to be had from the federal alphabet soup that had their fingers in the cruise industry: DHS, Coast Guard, Federal Maritime Commission, those kinds of people. That took a bit longer and only gave me so much. No one ever accused the government of being user-friendly.

I stopped working long enough to talk to Courtney when she got in. She took one look at me and didn't bother to say, "Hi, Coop." She knew my business face. She greeted me, tablet in hand, with, "What do you need?"

She sat down, and I started talking a mile a minute. "I need the manifest from last week's cruise on the Mardi Gras Cruise Lines ship. They only have the one right now."

"Legally or not?"

"Since when do I tell you how to do your job?" I never had, and we both liked it that way. This was our own Abbott and Costello routine.

"What else?"

"See if there's any report of a death on board. Check everything—local law enforcement, FBI, even the Coast Guards. Check with FDLE, too," I added, referring to the Florida Department of Law Enforcement.

Her eyes got a little bigger for a second when I mentioned a death, but her fingers kept flying on her tablet.

"Got it," she said.

I thanked her and headed back to my office.

Once I had enough to get started, I unlocked the safe and stuffed my short-nosed .38 special in a holster in the small of my back. My untucked shirt covered it.

CJ was still talking to Heather. I stuck my head in and announced I was leaving. They said "bye" like I barely existed. That was fine with me. I waved at Courtney on my way out; she half waved back, lost in her work.

I took the company CR-V, feeling as conspicuous on the road as a ham-and-swiss on a lunch counter, just the way I liked it. Nobody wants to get noticed while tailing someone. The little SUV ran well and blended in, so we'd bought two in the company's name.

My research had given me a name and revealed that Mardi Gras Cruise Lines had offices attached to a warehouse a couple of blocks from the airport. They were smaller offices, probably running logistics in support of their operations in port. The man I wanted to see would not typically be there. He'd be at the company headquarters in Bayonne, New Jersey. But if Heather was right, if someone had died, let alone been murdered, he might just have come down in the field.

I pointed the car away from the morning sun and headed out.

I made it reasonably quickly for Miami traffic and pulled into one of two spots marked "guests." I checked my phone before getting out. I found a text from Courtney confirming there was no report filed with law enforcement, and saying she was still working on the manifest. CJ had texted too. Heather had been great, her message said, and I should call when I could. I acknowledged both and got out of the car into blinding sunshine.

Mardi Gras' name and logo confirmed I was in the right place. The cruise ship profile superimposed on a parade of floats, musicians, dancers, and confetti was uniquely Mardi Gras'. The single door into the stucco building branded the place as a secondary office. This was no gleaming tower of steel and glass.

I walked in, squinting as I entered. Mardi Gras didn't have a booking office at this location, but I wouldn't have known that from the woman behind the front desk. She was a short Asian lady, her black hair pulled into a bun and a practiced smile on her face. There was no warmth to it. Her eyes were empty and heavy, as if she had already looked at too many strangers asking about types of cabins, drink packages, and excursions. *It's barely ten*, I thought.

I slapped my business card on the counter. It identified me as a private investigator with a Class-C license issued by the State of Florida. She looked at it. She looked back at me, expressionless.

"I want to see Mr. Morant," I said.

"Is he expecting you?"

So, he was here. "No. He'll want to see me, though. Tell him it's about last week's cruise. And remind him that the first word in PI is 'private.' It's the opposite of 'public.'"

She nodded to the security guard who had appeared at the other end of the room, then stepped through a recessed door behind her. She was gone long enough to pass the message to Owen Morant, the man I'd identified as the company's head of security.

"He will see you," the bored woman said when she returned. She motioned for me to follow her around the counter. She dragged her feet as we crossed the doorway and walked down a corridor with dark gray walls and dark gray carpet tiles.

The gatekeeper waved me through an open door halfway down the corridor. Morant rose, never moving from behind his desk, extending his hand across the furniture. He was a tall black man with short-cropped hair and a thin, trim physique. He stood ramrod straight, which made him look even taller and gave him a military bearing. His eyes were set deep into his face. They were small, inscrutable, with barely any white around the iris. This guy was probably used to intimidating people just by standing up.

I shook his hand, neither of us saying a word, and we sat down on our respective sides of the desk. The room was small and purely utilitarian, with rows of metal file cabinets on either side of us. There was no window and the floor lamp in the far corner did not give off enough light. There were not even any pictures on the walls, which felt like they were closing in on me. I wondered if that was the point. This could be Morant's office, especially since he wasn't here full-time. Or it could be an interrogation room.

"You were asking about last week's cruise?" Morant asked without preamble.

"That's right."

"How can I be of assistance?"

"You can tell me if somebody died."

If I took him by surprise, he hid it well. His posture did not change. I was starting to wonder if he ever blinked.

"What would lead you to think so?" he asked.

I had no reason to play coy. "I represent a passenger who socialized with . . . shall we say the possible victim. My client seems to think something happened to him. From what I've heard, I agree."

"Which passenger did you say you represent?"

"I didn't, and I can't tell you."

He leaned back in his chair and joined his hands together, forming a steeple with his index fingers. "Then I am afraid I cannot tell you anything."

"That's where you're wrong. I can't tell you because my client's identity is confidential. It's part of the terms of my engagement. You, on the other hand, you can choose to work with me if you want. You should want to. I'm a lot easier to work with than a gaggle of federal agents."

Morant stared at me. He still hadn't blinked. I stared back. He'd spoken with only the slightest of accents, but by the way some consonants came through, I figured him for a childhood in Jamaica. As we stared each other down, I saw someone who came up through the ranks from the bottom rung up. He would have had to put in a lot of work to get where he was now, hard work, smart work. I was not intimidated, but I did not have to be an asshole about it.

"Look," I said, "I'm being straight with you. I'm not interested in making a name for myself by throwing mud at you or Mardi Gras. I realize the kind of risk this represents for a company selling good, clean, dirty fun if that fun ends up killing you. I know how public opinion tends to overreact. That's not my goal here. But if there was a death, I will find out and I'll get to the bottom of it, because that's what I was hired to do. I will do that with or without you. That's just a fact. I'd rather we worked together."

"You do not seem to fully grasp the situation here, Mr. Malone."

Morant still had not moved. He spoke in a matter-of-fact manner. I, on the other hand, was already feeling aggravated. I worked hard at keeping it out of my voice.

"Why don't you explain it to me, then?" I asked.

"Nothing bad ever happens on a cruise—and certainly not on a Mardi Gras ship."

"I read you loud and clear. And I just told you I am willing to keep that fiction alive. But I need you to work with me for that to happen."

He eyed me for a long time, or at least it felt like a long time. He was working out our quid pro quo. Then he pushed back.

"If your client is so concerned," he said, "they could have gone to the police. Whatever reason she had to call you instead, she may still reach out to the authorities. You make assurances of discretion that you cannot guarantee."

"I know my client, and I know me. I'm the closest thing to a guarantee you have."

"That is assuming that anything happened. In fact, I will go one step further with that statement—it is assuming that anything happened that would be of any concern to law enforcement."

"A death usually qualifies."

"Usually, perhaps. But let us also imagine, strictly for the sake of a hypothesis, you understand . . . ." He let those words hang between us.

"Strictly," I said with a sneer.

"Let us imagine then that someone died, quite a leap of our imagination, of course. If that were the case, Mardi Gras would negotiate handsome settlements with that person's family and others who might be harmed by that person's absence, and there would be no need to involve law enforcement."

"Unless it was not a natural death. Then there'd be a need to send the perp to jail and throw away the keys."

"But that is unlikely to be your client's motivation. My company has very apt negotiators who I am certain will be able to come to a satisfactory understanding with you and with your client."

So that's where Morant was leading. He thought he could buy us out. I tried to remember he was doing his job and not sound too disgusted when I answered. "You don't know me, and you don't know my client, so I'll throw you a bone and not walk out right now and slam the door in your face."

His eyes widened—just a tad, just enough to notice if you were paying attention. "Are you telling me arrest is the object of your engagement? By some person who met another on a cruise, who has known them for all of a week?"

"Some people are like that," I said, not breaking eye contact. "Some believe all that shit about evil triumphing when good people do nothing. Some simply can't live with an unexplained death in their vicinity. It's not your concern. It may not even be mine. I was hired to look into it, and I'm going to do my job."

He started talking. I raised my hand and interrupted him. "I'm also starting to think that I misread you. I thought you were the kind of person who put in the work over the years, in and out of uniform. A person like that would care about someone dying on board, especially if it was suspicious. Maybe I was wrong about you."

Morant leaned forward at the hips, his shoulders still square to me. He was pushing back at me by reducing the distance between us.

"There is not enough discretion for my company to live with under any scenario involving an investigation," he said, his voice barely above a whisper.

"That's too bad," I said, keeping my voice low as well, "because I am going to find out what happened. If there was a murder, I'll turn the killer in when I find him—or her. Please make no mistake about that.

"From where I sit, that leaves you two options. You may have had more before, but you only have two now. If you work with me, I won't call the press or pick up a megaphone. I'll even try and turn the case over to a prosecutor who's not out to see their name in the papers. If you don't, I will wash my hands of Mardi Gras and let the chips fall where they may."

Another moment's silence passed while Morant thought everything through. I passed the time putting myself in his shoes. He faced a conflict between wanting the case solved, whatever case that was, and loyalty to his employer. Or maybe he just faced a conflict between making waves and keeping his job. Either way, he faced one key question: could I be trusted? He never took his eyes off me. He never blinked. It was as if he was trying to look into my soul. Let him. I probably blinked a dozen times.

He got up without a word, and I thought the meeting was over. But he raised a hand, bidding me to stay put, and closed the door before sitting back down.

"You did not misread me, Mr. Malone. I am impressed you did not, as a matter of fact. So, I will help you, because I believe it to be right and because I think it will ultimately be in my company's best interest. I will help you if I can, but it will be in my private and personal capacity, and in that capacity only. Do we understand each other?"

"Crystal."

"Very well."

"Can you give me the basics?"

"Again, you need to grasp the greater picture here. This is not being investigated. This will not be investigated. Settlements will be made, non-disclosure agreements will be signed, and the ship will keep on cruising. I may not agree with it, but that is the way it is, and all I know is what little I found aboard the ship two days ago."

"Understood," I said.

"The decedent is one William Morrison, age thirty-two. He was the founder of something called StarQuest. It is some sort of hedge fund, the kind where Mr. Morrison was immensely rich last week and could have been bankrupt tomorrow. He was an impetuous young man, from what I have been told. One officer said Mr. Morrison struck him as the kind of man who would buy an island if he could, just to say he owned one."

So Heather was right. It was William, flashy finance guy, who died. This time, I kept my poker face up while Morant continued.

"He was there with two other finance men," he said. "They were our whales on this cruise. That is what we call rich and exuberant people throwing lavish parties that celebrate nothing more than their own existence. They spend a lot of money and attract a lot of people around them. Like most whales, these three stayed in the top-deck VIP suites, which have a valet assigned to them. That is who found the body on Saturday morning around 9:30.

"The door was open. He found Mr. Morrison on the floor with his head split open. There was no blood on the floor. There would have been had it been an accident, so I am afraid we have a killer on our hands who took time to clean up his mess. Ship security found traces of bleach. That is something you can find in every other janitor's closet on the ship, however, so it does not help us. The ship's doctor estimated that death occurred several hours before the body was found, maybe two or three in the morning."

"Where's the body now?"

"A morgue in a private clinic."

I winced. "Here in Miami?"

"Yes."

"I am guessing there is no chance of performing an autopsy. Or talking to the valet."

Morant sighed. If he moved from his ramrod-straight posture, it was nearly impossible to tell in the dimly lit room.

"You are guessing correctly," he said. "As a matter of fact, the valet is in the Philippines at the moment. He flew out on Sunday night. The only action taking place about this unfortunate occurrence is taking place above my pay grade or, it may be more accurate to say, outside my chain of command. I hear that many people in legal and public relations have been extremely busy making private contacts where they needed to be made."

I nodded, feeling grim. I felt out of my depth, taking on a murder case solo. Morant may have been willing to help, but his hands were tied. I still did not have the first clue who was involved, and now I had Big Business trying to make sure I never would.

"Is there anything else you can tell me?" I asked.

"I will try and provide you with information—it can only be general information, in the absence of any investigation. And I cannot do it here or now. We may meet tomorrow, somewhere private, if you'd like. I would rather it not be your office."

"That's fine, we can meet at my home." I wasn't in the habit of broadcasting my home address, but coffee shops were too public for something like this. I made a split-second decision on location.

Morant nodded. He pulled a Post-it pad from a desk drawer and scribbled something on the top sheet before handing it to me, his movements precise and economical.

"This is my personal cell phone," he said. "You may text or call me at any time, and I will do what I can."

I took my phone out of my pocket and texted my address to the number he'd written down. His phone beeped in his pocket. I gave him the Post-it back. He turned around and a shredder whirred. We understood each other just fine.

"Zero-six-thirty tomorrow," he said.

"Are you willing to have my team there with me? In my book, the more brains we have, the better."

Morant turned back to me and only hesitated a moment. "I am sure we must now trust each other a little bit more than we did an hour ago. Very well, Mr. Malone. Your team may attend."

He extended his hand—his way to tell me the interview was over. I shook it and nodded to him. I had a feeling I was going to need all the help I could get.

CHAPTER 3

I headed back toward the ocean and stopped at the first decent lunch spot I found, a Mexican joint squeezed between a nail salon and a flower shop in one of a dozen strip malls within a two-block radius that all looked the same. The architecture of nowhere is strong in Florida.

I walked around plastic tables on a Formica floor. I wouldn't be paying extra for the decor around here, so maybe the food was good. I had them swear their shrimps were Key West Pinks, and from this morning's catch, before I ordered some tacos in a mix of English and tentative Spanish. "Just the shrimps. No filling. With some hot salsa on the side."

"Corn tortillas," the man behind the counter said with a smile and a nod. It was a statement, not a question.

"Yeah," I said as I went to find a place to sit.

Old habits die hard, so I looked around for anyone snooping, someone who might come in and sit too close to me when most tables were empty, someone staring at me or being a little too still, not doing anything—except maybe trying to listen in. There were no snoopers, not unless they were too well-equipped and organized to notice. Hell, there was barely anyone in the place. Paranoia was one of those old habits clinging to life.

The shrimps came in still-warm tortillas with a Coke. I called CJ while I munched on my food. I gave her the basics of my conversation. Her keyboard clicked on the other end as she entered draft notes in the file that I'd beef up later. When I was done, she said she'd be at my house at the appointed hour to meet Morant, then she updated me on her interview. Heather had been great, focused, giving CJ direct answers to direct questions.

Once CJ and I went through what we had, we agreed I'd start the afternoon with Heather's friends, Jen and Amy. They were the logical next steps. She'd also suggested we contact the police now that we knew a murder occurred. I'd promised both Heather and Morant I wouldn't do that, so she relented. I also thought it would be a waste of time anyway, but I didn't go into that. CJ would have disagreed.

I had a hard call to make before I could put that plan into action. I stared at my phone as if it were a scorpion about to sting me. I dialed anyway.

"This is Heather," came the familiar voice on the other end of the phone.

"Hey. It's Coop."

"Hi, Coop! You have news already?"

I could not tell if her voice sounded more excited or nervous. "Yeah, I do."

"What is it?" she asked when I did not offer more details.

"Are you somewhere you can talk privately?"

A few seconds elapsed. A door closed and voices in the background receded into silence. "I am now. I just stepped into an empty office. What is it?"

"Heather, you were right. Someone died. It was William."

"Oh, my God!"

"I'm sorry, hon. I don't know how to give news like that except to tell you straight up."

"No, no, that's good. I'm good. No worries. I'm sure I wouldn't expect anything different from you anyway."

"Probably not. There's one more thing, though. It was not an accident. You were right about that too. There's something fishy about the whole thing."

More silence followed. I listened carefully. There was no crying or sobbing. When Heather spoke again, her voice was strong, determined.

"You're working this, right, Coop? You've got this."

"I do," I said, "assuming you still want me to."

"Of course, I do."

"Give me a second here." I took a deep breath and scratched my head. What I was about to say had to make sense to her. "Yesterday, you didn't know what happened. You needed to know. I get that. Now you know. It's murder. And maybe that's enough. There's no shame in that.

"Things are different now. Murder means at least one person knows what happened and wants very badly for no one to find out. There's a whole big cruise line out there that does not want anyone to know either. That's a lot of opposition. It's my job, but it's not yours. You're under no obligation to spend money finding out who killed Morrison. Not to mention that, if it comes out you hired me, you could be in danger. They won't find out from me or CJ, but you never know."

Heather had the good sense to think about all that for a minute, nothing but soft breathing coming back at me from the other end of the line. Then her voice came back, loud and clear.

"I can't let it go," she said. "You're right, I didn't know William that well, and maybe it's none of my business what happened to him, and I'm being stupid or reckless. I don't care. It's not really about him, anyway. I want the bastard who killed someone on my cruise. I'm pissed and more than a little freaked out. I still don't know *why* this happened. I want you to keep working on this."

"Then, I will."

"Thank you. And thanks for letting me know."

"You got it. We'll talk soon."

We hung up, and I took another deep breath, letting it out slowly through my lips. I'd just given Heather my word to figure this out. It was the second time I did, and the second time I thought maybe, just maybe, I shouldn't have.

I shook my head and forced myself out of my own mind. *You have a job to do, and you better get to work, Malone.* I focused on the next steps, tapping the plastic table rhythmically as I gathered my thoughts, starting with Heather's friends.

Amy was the writer of the group. After college, she started writing ads. Like Heather, she'd turned a liberal arts degree into a corporate career, writing copy for a big ad agency. She bought back the soul she'd sold to big business—Heather's words—by building a house on an acreage on the edge of the city.

I called the number Heather had given us, knowing I'd catch Amy at work. I only needed enough of her time to make plans to meet later. I told her as little as I could about why I was calling. She did not sound surprised Heather had asked a private investigator to look into things. She told me I could catch her at home after 7:30 and gave me the address. I didn't tell her I already had it, and promised to be there.

I had tapped half the digits to Jen's number when I changed my mind. I thought I'd better approach her in person. Heather had said she was the sensitive type, did not know anything yet, and she was working odd jobs. I took the chance she'd be home.

Jen still lived in glorified student housing not far from Miami Dade College. It took me a while to get there. A monument sign and good landscaping made promises the three-story buildings in the complex could not keep. There were four of them, with several apartments on each floor. The walls were streaked with dirt and mildew, and the paint on the front doors was peeling.

I drove slowly, craning my neck, looking for the right building. An early summer crowd hung around the parking lot here and there, chatting and laughing, a mix of students and those who wished they still were. I found building B and parked. There was a shadow of a B on the wall, anyway, where the letter had once hung above the door.

There were no doorbells, and the door into the building did not lock. I entered and nearly choked on the smell of sweat and mildew in the 90° heat. I guess air conditioning was a luxury too far for the slumlord. I climbed a narrow set of stairs to the second floor, which smelled just as bad and looked just as dirty as the first.

I found Jen's door and knocked. It opened less than an inch, and a single eye looked at me from under an arched eyebrow behind a security chain.

"Yes?" asked the person hidden behind the door.

"Name's Cooper," I said. "Cooper Malone. I'm a friend of Heather's and a private investigator."

I slid my card through the opening. Two manicured fingers reached for it. The door slammed shut so fast I took a step backward, then it reopened wide just as quickly. The face looking at me was framed by dark curly hair falling in a broad cut from shoulder to shoulder. It was a round face with big eyes that made her look even younger.

She spoke very loud and fast. "Did something happen to Heather?" Her eyes were getting even bigger. They were pretty eyes, I couldn't help noticing, dark eyes that looked like they were reflecting the vastness of space.

"No, no," I said. "She's fine. I saw her just this morning. She's well. The reason I'm here is she asked me for help with something. Is it okay if I come in and talk to you for a moment?"

She nodded and moved away from the door. She had decorated her apartment with taste. She'd hung lots of understated art. The pictures were all in brown tones that played nicely with the landlord-white paint on the walls without clashing with it. The rug in the living room served the same purpose. A mismatch of armchairs and a sofa around a makeshift coffee table gave off that student-living vibe. Somehow, they all coordinated. Nothing looked out of place.

She sat on the sofa, sitting straight, hands on her knees, looking at me while I was still looking around her place. When she allowed herself to sit back, the couch nearly swallowed her. She was wearing a loose T-shirt over sweat pants, the kind of thing she'd wear if she was planning to be home for a while. I could picture her on that sofa getting lost in a sketchpad, busy with her art, losing track of time. I took a chair near her and sat down.

I didn't tell her Morrison had been killed. There was no need, and it wasn't my place. I just said Heather thought something weird had happened and hired me to ask around. It was weak. Maybe she bought it, maybe not. Maybe she bought it because she wanted to buy it.

I asked general questions about the Morrison trio and about life on board. It was a short interview that matched what Heather had told CJ earlier that morning.

Heather had said that Cabe was a kind of math genius. Jen told me she liked Cabe (a lot) and Cabe liked Scotch. She had his last name—Roper—and his phone number, which she gave me. Heather had said Walt was older and always impeccably dressed in three-piece suits. Jen said Walt did not touch meat but ate sushi like it was The Rock's last cheat meal. Heather had said William threw money around. Jen spoke of all the women around William, some of whom looked like they regretted their choices the next morning.

I thanked Jen and left before giving her occasion to worry too much. At least, I hoped I hadn't. She was a sweet kid. With some time to spare, I called CJ and asked her to meet me at one of those little cafés in South Beach, the kind where you can sit outside and talk without being overheard, the kind where I could have a beer and a snack, clear my head before heading to my third interview of the day. It was just like my days in the field. You eat when you can.

It took me an hour to get there from Jen's and find parking. I fought the crowd that was already gathering, jostling for shade in the June sun. CJ was waiting for me. She'd picked a good table at the edge of the café's patio. I sat down next to her.

We updated each other with more details on our respective interviews. We had a pretty good picture of the cruise. This was a party boat and there was a party crowd gathered around the three finance guys Heather and her friends had met. William Morrison was the leader of the gang and partied the hardest, but everyone went along. So did the rest of the crowd.

"They both said things could get rowdy," CJ said.

I shrugged. "Rowdy, but not out of hand."

CJ leaned into me. "Drinks and rowdy mega millionaires can make some women nervous—men too, but especially women."

"And men jealous," I said, building on her point.

I took a long sip of my beer and put my glass down. It hit the table a little too hard. CJ sat back in surprise.

"It's not that," I said, raising a hand. "Yeah, I'm frustrated we don't have anything more concrete, and I hate it, but I know it's early."

"What, then?"

"I'm worried about Mardi Gras. They're not investigating at all. They're stupid but fine. The real problem is that I don't know how actively they might want to dissuade *us* from investigating."

CJ shook her head. "You know me. I like corporate. It's my first love in the security world. Otherwise, I wouldn't have done it for ten years before taking my big leap of faith and partnering with you."

"Your point?"

"My point is that, even then, I hated when the people in charge made boneheaded decisions. I hate it even more now, and Mardi Gras is definitely being boneheaded. But seriously, this is not a war zone or even war zone adjacent. You're not back in the Army, Coop. They're not going to start shooting at us."

"Maybe, maybe not. Always assume the worst."

CJ took a deep breath and patted her clutch in response. She had several of the same size, just right for her gun and her cell phone.

"Just in case," she said.

"Just because you carry does not mean I want you to have to use your gun."

"Nor do I. And I'm sure I won't have to, but I'm ready for the worst, like you said."

"Be careful, okay?" I said, "I'm less optimistic than you are. There's no telling how reckless Mardi Gras may get to protect their reputation."

"Probably stupid enough to honor the reservation for that suite on this week's cruise," she said, deftly changing the topic. "How do you plan to resolve this case without a body or a crime scene?"

It was a fair question, the very same one I kept asking myself, the one that made my muscles tense and my jaw ache. I rattled out the first thing that came to mind. "With witnesses. We have to—that's all we got. Maybe Amy will have seen something Heather and Jen missed. And I have Cabe's number now, so I'll talk to him, too, and he may lead me to Walt. Besides that, I'll ask Morant if he can get us on board on Sunday with a forensic team. You never know. They may have cleaned the suite with post-pandemic fixation and honored the next whale's reservation, but there can still be trace evidence."

"You make it sound like a plan, but you're gritting your teeth."

"You're only noticing because you know me."

"You're still doing it. You said yourself it's early."

"I also said I hated it. I don't like that four witnesses are all we have. I don't like that two interviews–three, counting Morant–led to diddly squat. I need more to move this fucking case."

CJ shot me a look, not at my language but at my impatience. It hadn't been twenty-four hours yet since I met Heather at Nick & Nora and she handed us the case. I knew that look and raised my hands in surrender again. I kept my thoughts to myself.

It's twenty-four hours too many.

CHAPTER 4

CJ indulged me and kept me company until it was time for me to go back on the road. It felt like I was driving west forever. Heather's friend, Amy, had built her soul pad in a patch of nature as far away from the city's center as she could, commute be damned.

I pulled up to the house. The art world had struck again. It looked like two white cubes, one higher than the other and with its edge digging into the other's side at an odd angle. I leaned forward as if having my eyes closer to the windshield would make guessing where to park more obvious. A driveway would have disfigured the art.

I figured out that the space below the higher cube doubled as a carport and coasted that way. It did. I glided in next to a purple Wrangler I took to be Amy's car, my foot barely touching the accelerator pedal. Once at a stop, I killed the engine and got out of the car. I took a wild guess that the red door to my right was the front door on a house like this. Bingo! There was a doorbell. The button was one of several blocks in what looked like a Tetris board. I rang.

A pretty woman with a pale, freckled face, blond hair sun-bleached into something closer to platinum, and striking blue eyes filled the doorway. She smiled as she opened the door, showing perfect teeth like this was a toothpaste commercial. I wasn't used to people looking that happy opening the door to a stranger.

She leaned against the door jam. She was barefoot, wearing loose jeans and an old T-shirt.

"You're Amy?" I asked.

"And you're the PI who called."

"That's me." I handed her my card.

"Cooper Malone," she read aloud. "Coop! You're Coop! Heather's Coop!"

Her voice had gone up twenty decibels, and her smile widened. I smiled back. Hers was infectious. I'd never really been "Heather's" anything, and Doug may object, having married her and all, but I let that go. "Yeah, that's me."

"I hadn't put two and two together on the phone. Show yourself in already." She walked in without looking back and pointed to her left. "Straight that way through the sliding doors. I'm on the patio. I'll meet you there."

I pulled the door closed behind me and followed her directions, walking down a short corridor, past the living room to my right. The walls were so white and the furniture so colorful I had to squint my way through the place and was a little afraid to touch anything. I walked out onto Amy's slice of paradise. The patio was more of a broad wraparound balcony some fifteen feet deep, overlooking untouched nature. I stood there, looking at so much greenery it was easy to forget we were still in Dade County.

I looked for somewhere to sit. Her patio furniture was nicer than most people's living room set. Two wicker loveseats with plush cushions flanked a matching table. Amy had put the sofa further down, facing another corner of her happy place. A bottle of wine in a chiller and a half-drunk glass of white sat on the table between the loveseats. I walked around and sat on the opposite side as Amy came out with a second glass.

She served me a pour without asking and topped off her own. "Please tell me you don't have a rule against drinking on duty," she said as she sat herself back down, legs tucked underneath her.

"I have a rule against not drinking."

She raised her glass to that. I followed suit, we touched rims, and took a sip. It's not like I knew anything about wine, but it tasted fine to me.

"Do you think Heather's right?" she asked, putting her glass back on the table. "It seems pretty far-fetched, even if I have to admit that finding the whole floor off-limits was a little weird."

"She's right," I said. Heather had told me Amy was sharp as a tack and cool as a cucumber. I saw no point in sugar coating it.

She froze for a moment, staring at me. "You're sure . . . ."

It was half a question and half a statement, maybe a lifeline for me to say, "Nah, I was kidding, everyone's fine." I couldn't do that.

"I'm sure," I said. "I'm also sure it was no accident."

"Who?"

"William."

"Fuck! He's an . . . . He *was* an asshole, but he was a fun asshole."

"Enough of an asshole for someone to get angry? Or jealous?"

"Enough to kill? Come on!" She threw her head back and rolled her eyes. "You'd have to be dumb as a box of rocks to get mad or jealous at anything William did. William is . . . *was* the kind of bad boy you screw on a cruise precisely because you'll never have to see him again. There's nowhere to attach strings at sea."

"You did . . . ." It was my turn to leave things hanging with something halfway between a question and a statement.

"Screw him? Hell, yeah! I was there to have fun, and I had fun with him too." She looked up at the clear sky, smiling. "With Heather and Jen, I was always the 'wild' in our Girls Gone Wild trips. Jen's too sweet for shallow sex. And even when Heather was single, she always seemed to have someone. She gets into it, don't read me wrong. She'd flirt and let the guys get away with a little grab-ass here and there, maybe flash her tits, but there was always a line. She makes a great wingman."

"Got it, and good for you." *And remind me to go on my next vacation with you.*

I pressed on. "Did you notice anyone around William getting upset? Somebody who came aboard a party boat but didn't know the score, or didn't like the way William played the music?"

"You just said it, Coop. It's a party boat. They brag about it."

"Can still happen."

Amy looked up at the sky again and took a moment inside her head before answering, as if she were looking for an answer in the clouds. "There's this one woman . . . I don't want to make too much of it. She was never threatening, never made me feel uncomfortable, me or anyone else."

"But?"

"She was hanging around William a lot more than just hanging with our crowd at random." Amy closed her eyes now and kept talking. "Tall. Brunette. Her party outfit of choice was a microskirt and a button-down top opened low enough to advertise she had no bra, to make up for the fact she barely had any tits."

She opened her eyes and looked at me.

"I have the opposite problem," she said, squeezing her own in case I hadn't noticed. I'd noticed.

"No-tits has a name?" I asked.

"Linda, I think. Yes, definitely *Linda*. I heard people call her that. As I said, she was kind of always there. She was even there once when William and I were going at it. I figured she liked to watch and gave her a good show. I don't want to throw her under the bus for it, though. She had her thing. She never creeped me out. She never acted obsessive or weird, unless you think watching is weird."

I shook my head, filed that factoid away, and moved on from Linda. I'd have to find her later, just in case Amy's creep radar was off that week.

"Anything else you can tell me?" I asked. "Fun facts from pillow talk? Anything can help."

Amy laughed a happy laugh, loud and unguarded. I put my empty glass down, and she refilled it without asking before she answered.

"I told you William was a fun asshole, right?" she said. "Emphasis on his backside? I don't mind saying that—he'd own it. All he could talk about was himself and his company. Good thing he was good at the fun stuff."

"What did he say about the business?"

"I tended to zone out when he got talking too much about it, but, best I remember, Walt started it as a real estate investment company—way back—long before William met him. William came in a few years back with Cabe. Cabe is a math genius who figured out something about the stock market. William's role was to bring in big money on top of Walt's stable real estate business. Imagine that, William hobnobbing with the rich and famous. Their roles fit them, and things had taken off. That's where things were at when we met them on the cruise."

I groaned on the inside. Rich bankers, real estate deals, and now stock market shenanigans. Like I needed this case to get more complicated.

I brought the conversation back to the victim. "Anything about William I might not know? I have a pretty good picture of the flashy party guy." I'd asked the question often enough in this case, but it made sense to keep asking. You never knew. And I was enjoying the wine, even if I'm more of a whiskey and beer kind of guy.

"Nope, that's pretty much it, at least it was last week. That's who he was, and he loved it, loved being the center of attention. He could have cruised on a yacht, but then he'd be one of several super-rich guys. On the *Rio*, he was the one with the fattest Beads Card. That's the way he liked it. He was never mean, though. He just liked going fast, and slow cars better get out of his lane."

I took my time finishing my wine. I didn't need to drink it slowly, but I was enjoying Amy's little slice of heaven. Truth be told, I was enjoying her company. She was a breath of fresh air—unassuming, cheerful, and sexy all at the same time.

She did not seem to mind me hanging around. She was sitting across the table, her gaze back toward nature. I allowed myself to think for a moment that, if I weren't in the middle of a murder case and Amy a witness in it, we might just have ended up in her bed because we could and it would have felt good. But I was, so we didn't.

I put my empty glass down and stood up. She unwound from her seat and walked me to the door. She hugged me tight, her arms wrapped around me and her hair tickling my cheek. She pulled back just enough to look me in the eyes. "Find the son of a bitch who did this."

"That's the idea."

She sealed my promise by planting a kiss on my lips, one just long enough to hold promises for later, too, maybe for another day.

When I got home, I poured myself a bourbon and brooded. The team would be here a few minutes before Morant was to show up at 6:30. Then I'd look for William's partners. I didn't brood too long. I had a plan, or something that sounded like it. The bourbon helped dull the voice in the back of my brain shrieking about plans never surviving contact with the enemy. I didn't even know who the enemy was.

CHAPTER 5

CJ arrived fifteen minutes early the next morning. As I'd expected, she came in straight from her run, all sweaty, her long hair tied in a single braid down to her waist, a gym bag in hand.

"Shower's all yours," I said as she rushed in behind me. There were advantages to having parted on friendly terms.

I saddled up to prepare the classics—coffee, eggs, and bacon. This was a business meeting, but I could still be civilized. CJ emerged before I was done, a transformed woman, perfectly put together in jeans and a Malone Agency polo.

Courtney rang the doorbell a minute later and walked right in, laptop in hand. I brought the food to the table, and we all sat down for a hot minute. I recapped my meeting at Mardi Gras from the day before amid the clatter of silverware from CJ's post-run munchies. I ended on a note of caution.

"I don't know what Morant will have for us since he can't investigate. We'll need to figure out what to make out of what he brings, whether it's about what happened, the execs from StarQuest, or the people around them. I also want the two of you to make your own opinion of him. My first impression was favorable, but yours count as much as mine. I'm not infallible."

That last part was meant more for Courtney than CJ. My partner already went through life assuming I was fallible. That was her job. It was my job, too. We questioned everything.

Courtney nodded. She had her laptop powered up, eyes on the screen. "Do you know if what he'll bring will be in electronic format?" she asked. "No idea," I said.

I was about to add something snarky about dinosaurs in the twenty-first century when the doorbell saved me. I glanced at my watch. It was 6:30 on the dot.

Owen Morant was standing as straight as ever on my front porch. He had the corporate dress uniform on today: suit and tie, navy blue and perfectly cut to his frame, with a Mardi Gras pin on the lapel. I'd expected him to show up with a banker's box of documents or at least a bulging satchel. He turned up empty-handed. Maybe what he was bringing was in electronic form. Maybe he wasn't bringing anything at all.

He extended his hand. We shook, then I ushered him in and made all the introductions.

"You eat breakfast?" I asked as we sat down. It's not like everyone did. Courtney had already declined anything but coffee. You couldn't work with me and not have coffee.

"Indeed," Morant said, "I have had breakfast already, but I never say no to coffee or bacon."

I poured him a mug. He picked up a strip of bacon with two fingers, taking small bites at one end and working his way down.

"Thanks for coming," I said.

"Thank you for welcoming me into your home."

"Were you able to get anything for us?" My patience with small talk had already evaporated. Morant chewed and thought as if he was still putting his thoughts in order. He nodded slowly, if only to let me know he'd heard my question.

"The matter of Mr. Morrison is not being investigated internally," he said, even though he'd made that clear to me the day before. "Nor has it been reported to law enforcement, nor will be it investigated or reported. While I opposed that policy, I am now beholden to it in my official capacity."

Morant behaved no differently that morning than in his office the day before. He spoke slowly and carefully. His jaw moved, and he turned his head both ways to include all of us in the conversation—not that including everyone was especially hard around my small breakfast table. Besides that, he sat straight against the back of his chair and did not move a muscle.

"And unofficially?" I asked.

Morant turned to me, his eyes focused on mine. "Mr. Malone, your comportment leads me to believe you may have served in your country's uniform. Am I guessing correctly?"

"You are."

"So did I, both in military and civilian forces. I always respected my chain of command. This is something I brought with me into the corporate world. I may believe, and indeed I do, that my superior's policy is unlawful. Even so, even acting unofficially, I will act in my employer's best interest. Which is to say that before I act, I will warn you that I shall hold you to your promise of minimizing any harm to Mardi Gras Cruise Lines."

"You have my word. That goes for my team, too."

Morant took in CJ's and Courtney's nods from the corner of his eye and went on. "Unofficially, then, you will understand I am in a most delicate position, caught between an utmost duty of loyalty and what I concluded is illegal conduct by my Board of Directors."

"I understand." I did, in a way. Tensions between orders and what's right happened in the military, too. CJ would have been the more experienced and understanding voice about Morant's dilemma, but she was leaving me the floor for now.

"I have been putting much thought into trying to resolve this internal conflict," Morant said. He paused—a pause that made him look like a statue, silent and unmoving. Then he went on. "And do understand that, without an internal investigation, I have nothing of immediate value in any event. I have no actionable intelligence, as you and I might have once said."

I squinted at Morant as he spoke. My face hardened. I started to think he had come all this way just to tell us he couldn't help us. He proved me wrong.

"What I did, then," he said, "which I believe is consistent with my position, is to give you limited access to our corporate computer system. I created a log-in that will give you access to all the data we have that is connected to last week's cruise on the *Mardi Gras Rio*."

"The internal databases?" Courtney asked. She was glowing, cheeks brighter than the light from her computer screen.

"That is correct," Morant said.

"Searchable, right? What search language do you use? SQL, XQuery, LINQ?" The dam had breached—Courtney was unstoppable.

Morant laughed. It came in short bursts like he wasn't used to letting it out. "I can tell you this is all raw data. It is also only the raw data since no one has used it for investigative purposes."

That seemed to trigger something in both Courtney and CJ. Courtney's eyes narrowed. CJ's head tilted toward Morant, if only by a fraction of an inch, which is all the reaction she would ever allow.

"Access to static raw data requires special access," Courtney said.

"And every company I've ever worked with tracks this very carefully," CJ added.

"You are both correct," Morant said. "However, my position as the head of security gives me, shall we say, certain privileges. Bear in mind that I am sometimes called upon to perform internal investigations, which may in turn require surreptitious access. I have every reason to believe you should not be discovered so long as you take appropriate precautions."

My team nodded. CJ assured Courtney every company in her experience made their databases searchable. Courtney couldn't stop grinning. And I was at a complete loss.

"What exactly do we have?" I asked. The words "corporate databases" alone made my head hurt. "I know what 'raw data' means. I think. I know it will only be actionable when properly analyzed. But what kind of data are we talking about? What good can it do?"

CJ leaned in. It was her world. Even her body language was corporate appropriate, arms before her, locked at the elbows, speaking with her hands but without exaggerated movements. "Think about what you would want to know if you ran a cruise line and wanted to keep people coming and make money from them. Where do people go on board—what are the heavy-traffic areas? Where do they shop? Where do they go in a port call? Are the people making up your clientele shoppers or drinkers or art collectors? Do they shop for clothes or jewelry or trinkets? All that kind of stuff."

"Ms. CJ is correct," Morant said. "We use an electronic card as both a door key and a wallet, as well as to get on and off the ship in a port of call. We call it the Beads Card. We collect quite a lot of data from it, I understand, as well as from our reservation system and the points of sale on board.

"We also have surveillance footage. However, there are no cameras on the VIP deck, and the rest does not show anything useful. Some faces become familiar faces, perhaps your client's among them, but we cannot put names on those faces without a painstaking comparison to the booking system."

"Okay, I get it. Beads Cards and points of sale and shit. I still don't know what good that does for us." I asked.

Fortunately, I had smart people around me. Courtney was beaming, eyes fixed on Morant. She had all ten fingers wiggling in the air.

"So, every time someone buys a drink, it will be in the database?" she asked.

"Yes," Morant answered.

"Including where they bought it and when?"

"Yes."

Courtney turned to me with a shit-eating grin. "How would you like to know the names of the people hanging around William and his friends?"

"I'd call that actionable," I told her.

"I can build a query for that. I can identify who was buying drinks or whatever else at the same place and time that William and the other two were buying theirs. I mean, William can't have bought every drink for everyone all the time, could he? That should tell us who was sticking with them like white on rice. It won't even matter if they were creeping or partying. If they bought a bottle of water around William, I'll know. And that will narrow down what to look for on the surveillance footage if we want to do that."

"How quickly can you put that together?"

"If it's a query language I know, just long enough to understand how the database is structured. I might have it this morning."

"Do it," I said. "Morrison was throwing money around and buying a lot of drinks, but you're right, probably not every single one. This will give us something to start from."

"One Morrison Groupies List, coming up," Courtney said, barely able to keep still on her chair.

Morant took a piece of paper from his coat pocket and handed it to Courtney.

"These are your access credentials," he said. "Your access will be logged, should anyone look. As I handle security, the chances of someone looking are low. Nevertheless, be careful as we would not want anything to trigger an alert in IT. I have no influence inside that department."

"Thank you," Courtney said, plucking the paper from him. "I'll be careful."

"You will keep me posted?" Morant asked, turning back to me.

"I will. But I have one more favor to ask before you go."

"What is it?"

"The *Rio* will be back in port on Sunday, right?"

"That is correct."

"I'd like to go on board with a small forensic team. I don't care if it's official or not. And yes, I'm sure the scene was compromised in a dozen different ways, but you never know. I still want to take a look."

Morant glared at me. When he spoke, the rolling consonants of his native Jamaican accent came through a hair clearer, the only sign of emotion from him. I wasn't sure what he didn't like the most—my question or that he could not investigate the scene himself.

"It will most definitely have to be unofficial," he said after a few moments, stressing the *un-* in *unofficial*. "And it may turn out to be an impossible request altogether. However, I will see what I can do."

"Thanks," I said.

Morant was already getting up. He might have been eager to avoid addressing any more requests for favors. Or our time was up, and the business

44

suit was needed somewhere else. I showed him to the door, shook his hand goodbye, and went back to sit down with CJ and Courtney.

"No wonder you like him," CJ said with a smile. "He's as warm and cuddly as you are—and as devoid of bullshit."

"'Doesn't matter if I like him or not. Can he be trusted? What's your gut saying?"

"I don't listen to my gut," CJ said. "That's your thing. But I have no reason not to trust him, at least until Courtney dives into those databases and we see what kind of access we have."

"What about you?" I asked Courtney.

"I feel for him. Those higher-ups at Mardi Gras put him in an impossible position. I think he really wants to help us, and, if anything, he's frustrated he can't do more."

"Good enough for me. I'll consider him on our side for the time being. Can you log into their system before you go, Courtney?"

"Sure."

She was in a few seconds later. I got up and looked over her shoulder. There were a few windows opened on her screen and a menu bar at the top.

"It doesn't look like much," I said.

Courtney started pulling drop-down menus quicker than my eye could follow.

"Looks can be deceiving," she said in a soft voice. She might as well have been talking to herself.

"Can you get to the manifest?"

"Give me a second to get my bearings here."

I gave up figuring out what she was doing and sat back down. I poured myself another cup of coffee while Courtney clicked and typed, eyes glued to her screen, a small wrinkle just above her nose. It didn't take her but a couple of minutes.

"Yeah, I have it," she said.

"Can you confirm the last names of Morrison's friends? They should be in adjacent cabins on the VIP deck."

"Yes. William Morrison, Cabe Roper—that's the name Jen gave you, right?"

"Yeah."

"And Walt Rosling. Heather and her friends were right. I have a DOB on the reservation, and he's twenty-some years older than William."

"Got it. Is there someone named Linda? I'm guessing she'd be about Morrison's age, but I can't be sure."

"Why do you ask?" CJ asked as Courtney looked.

I gave her the basics from my talk with Amy the night before. I'd put it in the file, but CJ had not read it yet. That was a rare occurrence. Had I not dragged her in right after her run, she wouldn't have needed to ask.

"There are several Lindas," Courtney said after a few seconds. "Maybe try a more common name?"

"Alright, smartass, point taken. Let me know if any of them shows up in that Groupies List or whatever you're building from all that data."

"Okay."

"And get me the full manifest."

"I will." Courtney was making notes somewhere on her screen. "Anything else?"

"Yes. Once you have the list, start trolling social media. Let's find out who those people are."

"Will do."

"And send me that list as well," CJ said. "I'll start making calls, interviewing the most ardent followers of William and his clique."

"You sure?" I asked. "You're already doing three people's jobs on every other case. Not that I've ever known you to be afraid of work, but everyone has their limits, even you."

"Thank you. It is to be expected with a murder case on our plate. I'm fine."

CJ in business mode used fewer words, not more. "I'm fine" is all I'd get out of her, but it meant more than some long speech about time management and sleeping when she's dead. If she said she was fine, then she was.

"Anything else?" I asked.

No one spoke up.

"Very well," I said. "I'm going to try and see Cabe Roper this morning, see if Morrison's younger associate has anything useful to say. I'll report back after that. Let's get to work."

Twenty seconds later, CJ and Courtney were out the door, and it was just me and my contacts list. I started the rest of my day with a tap on my phone.

CHAPTER 6

texted my contact info to Cabe Roper. I said I was a friend of Jen's and asked to meet with him and talk. I re-laced my boots to keep my hands busy and my impatience in check while I waited. Seconds later, my phone dinged with a return text. Roper named a coffee shop in Miami Beach and said he'd be there at nine o'clock. I checked my watch. I'd have preferred earlier, but that would work.

I knew the place where Roper wanted to meet. It was one of those storefronts off the beach with good coffee, fair food, and astronomical prices to pay for the rent within reach of an ocean breeze. I got there early and ordered a double espresso and a pastry. I didn't much care for the sweet, but I thought I might need something more than my espresso to look busy while Roper and I talked. A plate would do.

There were no out-of-the-way tables in places like that, so I picked one in the middle of the room where our conversation would be drowned out by all the others. I sat down and started scanning the room. A young man entered just after nine. He was craning his neck, looking in every direction like a submarine with its periscope up.

"Cabe!" I called out in his direction.

He smiled a thin smile that barely moved the corners of his lips. He pointed toward me, nodded, and walked to the coffee bar. He made it to my table a few minutes later, carrying a giant cup of something that smelled of flavored milk and spices. I wrinkled my nose despite myself.

Roper sat down in front of me with a shrug. "Yeah," he said, "I admire people who drink the straight stuff. My coffee order has more ingredients than a Real Housewife's fruity cocktail."

I laughed with him. The guy was alright, at least at first blush. Maybe Jen had taste and good instincts.

"You should try Army coffee," I told him.

"You're Army?"

"Was."

"My father was in the Navy. He was a radio operator. Then he got into code breaking. That's what started my love affair with math."

I didn't feel like opening up about my Army career to him or sharing war stories, so I nudged the conversation back to where I wanted it to go.

"You drink your coffee all prettied up but your scotch straight?" I asked.

"Jen told you that?" The way he smiled, I figured he was sweet on her. Maybe those two would have more than a cruise romance. Weirder things have happened. I'm just not sure what.

"She did."

"She's mostly right. But you always add a few drops of water into the dram after the first few sips. It opens it up and lets the more nuanced flavors come through the barrier of the high alcohol content."

"Huh . . . ." I guess I'll have learned something this morning.

"Is Jen okay?" Cabe asked.

"Yeah, yeah, she is. She likes you, you know."

"I like her too. I'd like to see her, but I want to keep her out of . . . out of everything that's happening. She doesn't know, does she?" He was moving his cup around the table, looking straight at me, forgetting to blink.

"No, she doesn't. Not from me, anyway—at least not as of yesterday, unless she's one hell of an actress."

"I don't think she is, so that's good."

I let the silence hang over us for a spell.

"I thought that Mardi Gras wanted to 'move forward,' as they put it," he said less than a minute later, breaking the silence. "Walt and the attorneys are the ones working with them, mostly."

"I don't work for them."

He nodded to himself several times. "I thought the odds were against it."

"What did Mardi Gras tell you?"

"That William died."

"Did they say how?"

"No, but I analyzed their behavior, and I'm pretty sure he was murdered."

"I'm pretty sure you're right."

"That's what I do, you know, analyze behavior." He was leaning over the table and speaking fast, like a child too excited to share his adventures to slow down. "People think I spend my days running financial information through spreadsheets. I don't. Financials do not drive the market, not much anyway. People's behaviors do—what makes them decide to buy or sell or sit on their stock. I've created a mathematical model of that collective behavior that's crazy successful at anticipating market movements. And . . . that's not a formula that will fit on a spreadsheet."

I could have sworn the kid blushed as he sat back, shoulders squared, a smile lighting up his face.

"Can you use your model to get an idea of what happened?" I asked.

He deflated, looking down, playing with the sleeve around his mega coffee cup. "I didn't pay enough attention. There's not enough data."

"Don't beat yourself up. Nobody ever pays that kind of attention. No one ever expects something like that to happen."

"I guess not."

"You've thought about it since, though. Anything come to mind, maybe something you didn't notice then, but it's bugging you now?"

"I wish there was." He was still looking down. He was gripping his cup so hard I half expected the lid to fly off and the coffee to spill all over the table.

"I really wish there was," he said again.

I danced around the previous week with him for a while longer, pestering him with general questions to which he gave general answers. He didn't say anything I didn't already know. He did not mention Linda, so I didn't bring her up.

I asked him if he knew where I could find Walt. He reached for my napkin. I handed him a pen—I'm old-fashioned enough to still carry those—and he wrote down an address in Key West.

"He's holed up there," he said. "The house is probably titled under one of his LLCs, but he's there."

"Thanks. Why is he 'holed up,' as you put it?"

"That's just who Walt is. He's better with land than people and always comes out grumpy at first. He wouldn't want to socialize with anyone while everything plays out between Mardi Gras and StarQuest."

We exchanged pleasantries for another minute. We both sucked at it. Then Cabe Roper left and disappeared into the blinding sun on the other side of the door.

I figured I'd better check in with the team and put the info from my interview into the file before I did anything else. Out the door I went, tossing my uneaten pastry in the trash on the way.

Once back at the office, which took longer than it should have thanks to South Florida traffic, I waved Courtney a hello she barely saw, lost in her screen, and went straight to CJ's office.

"You have impeccable timing," she said, looking up from her screen.

"How's that?"

"Courtney's already done with her Groupies List. I was spot-checking it, and it passed my tests for far."

"Spot checking how?"

"It matches what we know. Heather, Jen, and Amy are all on the list, although Jen barely makes an appearance, and we already knew they hung out with the trio from StarQuest. And Cabe and Jen are at the same place a lot, though again Jen doesn't pull out her Beads Card that much, and she told you she liked him and that they spent a lot of time together."

"Yeah, he confirmed that this morning."

"What else did he say?"

I sat down across from her desk, folded my hands in front of me, and gave her the four-one-one. She typed as I spoke, saving me the trouble of doing it myself later, twice as slowly.

"How many people are on Courtney's list?" I asked when I was done updating CJ.

"There are sixty-seven people in forty-seven cabins."

"Did we get lucky and get down to one Linda on it?"

CJ grinned, her face illuminated by her screen. "Yes, as it happens. Let me pull her up."

She focused on her screen. A few seconds passed that felt like minutes. "A Linda Mayak," she said, frowning. "It's odd though . . . . It's mostly food orders. No booze. She was at the same place and time a lot but not partying it up—unless everyone around her was buying her drinks. That's always possible. In fact, Courtney lowered the number of purchases women needed to make to be included on her list to take those kinds of things into account."

I filed that little bit of information in the back of my head. Courtney had said she'd catch both the partiers and the creepers. Maybe Amy's creep radar had been off.

"Do you have an address?" I asked.

CJ tapped her fingers on her tablet. "Courtney put the manifest on both our tablets. She'll show you how to navigate it if you need."

"It's a PDF?"

"Yes."

"I think I can manage that. I'm a modern dinosaur."

That got no reaction from CJ. She was all business, her attention back on her screen. "The address for Linda Mayak is a business one—a tower not too far from here. I'm texting it to your phone now."

"Thanks. I'll visit her tomorrow. I'll take the afternoon to go down to the Keys and visit Walt Rosling."

CJ gave it two seconds' thought before declaring it a good plan.

I raised a finger in a plea for time, got up, and closed the door before turning back to her. "Look, there are a lot of people on that Groupies List. I wasn't expecting sixty-seven. I guess those guys were that popular. Point is, I asked you earlier, but now I'm asking you privately. How much bandwidth do you have, you and Courtney? Business was decent before this. You're doing two or three times the work on every other case."

"Same answer in private. We are good." This time, she was willing to expand, probably to avoid my asking her the same question twice a day, every day. She put her hands on her desk on each side of her keyboard and looked at me, tearing her eyes away from her monitors.

"Look at this morning," she said. "Courtney wrote her query, installed the manifest on our tablets, and she's already helping me on other cases. We're managing the workload well. Though, we owe Courtney a raise. She's been exceptional, even before this."

CJ had a point. Courtney had been more than a pretty smile behind the front desk for a while. "I think you're right."

"What about you?" CJ asked. "A murder case is no joke—professionally or emotionally, and you're close to this one. And don't you bullshit me, Malone! We may not be together anymore, but you're still my partner."

Calling me by my last name was as good as a warning. Anything more, I'd already be in trouble.

"I'm okay," I said. "Somebody died, and we have a chance to do something about it. This is something I need to do. And, yes, I'll tell you if I become not okay."

"You better."

"Just like you'll tell me if your bandwidth narrows. Subcontract some cases if needed, even if it eats into the profit margin. The business will be fine. You don't need to run it by me."

CJ took a second to think about it. She was never one to placate me. She kept her eyes straight on a spot somewhere a hundred miles behind my forehead and eventually nodded, just one short bow of her head. We were on the same page and good to go.

I left the office as quickly as I'd come in. *Key West*, I thought. Three hours down and three back. I hated it already.

CHAPTER 7

I don't know how the Key West Chamber of Commerce ever convinced people that driving on a bunch of two-lane bridges from island to island was some picturesque journey worth the time in its own right, yet all my buddies outside South Florida seemed to think it was some kind of highway to heaven. Bullshit. Driving down two-lane roads with semis and geriatrics is the same test of one's patience no matter where you drive. There was only one difference between this and the Kansas country roads I drove on when stationed at Fort Riley with the First Infantry Division. Here, all there was as far as the eye could see was water. There, it was corn.

I checked my watch for the third time in twenty minutes. I cranked up the radio—we spent enough time in our cars that we splurged on a good sound system for the CR-Vs. Buck Owens was singing "Hello Trouble." It felt like the car was talking to me.

It took two more detestable hours before I reached Key West and stopped for gas. I ate a gas-station egg salad sandwich and drank gas-station coffee. The CR-V got better fuel than I did.

I had an email from Courtney. She'd checked out the address I was going to. It was under an LLC that belonged to another LLC, and another, and it all ended up off-shore. "Typical real estate investor bullshit," her email concluded. I replied with a "Thanks" and thought she was earning the raise CJ had floated by me. I'd never asked her to check into it. She just did.

I pulled up to the house some ten minutes later. It was a squat building, larger than most on the island but not showy. Come to think of it, it lacked any personality at all, just four white walls at right angles with a few windows cut into them and an attached garage on the right side. I got out of the car, walked to the door, and rang the doorbell.

The man who answered was tall—taller than me—a little overweight, with big bushy eyebrows and an unruly mustache that distracted me from the rest of his face. Heather and her friends had said he was older than his two partners, and he looked it. He was graying at the temples and in his facial hair. He was wearing brown pants and a matching vest over a dress shirt.

"You're Walt Rosling?" I asked.

"Who the fuck are you?" he asked. Despite the gruff vocabulary, he was not snarly. It was just the way he spoke, like he wanted you to know he did not need to care about what people thought. At least, he was not trying to turn away, or not yet. I hadn't thought he would. He'd want to know how I found him holed up in the Keys hidden behind a half dozen shell companies.

"Name's Malone," I said, handing him my card.

He took it and frowned at it. "Who sent you?"

I looked past him. He was wedged between the door and the wall. The house looked dark and uninviting. "Can we talk inside?"

"Who sent you?" he asked again, enunciating his words as if I had not heard or understood him the first time around. His bushy eyebrows moved closer together as he stared me down.

"Someone who figured out things aren't quite what they seem."

"I don't give a fuck that someone figured out things are not quite what they seem, whatever the hell that even means. So, I don't see why I should talk to you."

He started closing the door slowly, giving me a chance to answer the question. I took that as an invitation.

"Because I'm a nice guy, compared to the alternative," I said.

"Like what?"

"Like cameras in your front yard, microphones in your face, and a fake blonde with a TV smile asking you what happened to your business partner."

Rosling stared at me, then he grunted and stepped aside, letting me in. He walked slowly with his shoulders stooped. The house smelled musty, like it had not been lived in for a while before he chose the place to wait things out.

Rosling led me into a small study just off the entrance. A large window to the left of the room let in just enough light to make it not spooky, but not much more.

I scanned the rest of the room as I walked in. Rosling had pushed a roll-top writing desk against the far wall. It sat there with the tambour rolled down. An ergonomic office chair, out of place next to the ornate desk, was askew in front of it. To the right, two armchairs faced each other at a 45° angle, antiques in a gaudy pattern of golds and dark reds. I sat down in the one nearer the door without waiting for an invitation. Rosling slumped into the other.

"Why did you answer the door?" I asked.

"What?" His head snapped in my direction.

The question had taken him by surprise. That was the point.

"You're clearly not happy to see me," I said. "I doubt you'd be happy to see anybody else. Why answer the door?"

"You're so smart, you tell me, Mr. Cooper Malone, Private Investigator." He flipped my business card back at me. I didn't bother picking it up.

"Curiosity killed the cat," I said. "You'd rather know who may be making a fuss than not know."

"Say you're right. Why are you making a fuss?"

"It's what I'm paid to do."

"By whom?"

That again. Give the man credit; he didn't give up. I shook my head.

"Mardi Gras is offering to move on, do right by us," Rosling said. He was leaning in, making eye contact. He'd assumed the pose every salesperson does when trying to close a deal. His deal was making me go away.

"Speaking for StarQuest," he continued, "we're interested in working with Mardi Gras. So's William's family. So, I can't help but wonder, who cares? One of the women he had sex with? No one can be that stupid!"

There was an edge to that last comment. I didn't pay too much attention to it. Mostly, the whole comment pissed me off. Someone was dead. Looking into it seemed pretty damn smart to me.

I snapped back at him. "Someone cares, so I care. I care enough to drag those TV cameras in here and let the chips fall where they may. Now, are you going to talk to me, or are we going to throw bullshit at each other all day?"

"I've crushed bigger than you, Malone."

"You're welcome to try."

He looked in my direction for a moment, a blank stare on his face, muscles frozen in place. The way the armchairs were angled, his body looked contorted in his effort to kill me with a look.

"You're not worth it," he said, the volume turned down. "Get it over with."

He'd figured out the odds, tried to decide if I would go through with it. Would I call or fold? In the end, he'd probably tossed a coin in his head and it came down my way.

"Who killed William?" I asked, not expecting an answer. I wanted to make sure I had his full attention.

"How the fuck should I know?" He didn't raise his voice. This was just normal, cantankerous Walt.

"Okay," I said, "you don't know. Who do you think killed him?"

He leaned back in his chair, talking to the empty space in the opposite corner. "William had a talent for pissing people off. He could make people like him at will; that's what he did for StarQuest. But he could piss them off just as quickly, and, sometimes, he enjoyed doing it just for the hell of it. I grant you it's hard to piss someone off enough to get killed, but if anyone could, that'd be William fucking Morrison."

Amy had told me William lived in the fast lane but never crossed the line into mean. She hadn't known him well or long. On the other hand, Walt Rosling knew him well, but he didn't seem to like the man much, so I took him with a grain of salt. I filed the competing versions away and pushed back.

"In a week?" I asked.

Rosling shifted in his seat and went from talking to the wall to talking to me. "I've seen him do it in an hour. I'm in real estate, Malone. It's a world full of thick skins and sharp elbows. And William could still get under those people's skin if he wanted to."

"You started the company that way, right? Real estate?"

"It was called LandQuest then. I started it when the other two were still in little-boy shorts. William wanted something flashier after we partnered up. Land still provides a solid portion of the revenue. It's steady money."

I took that in. It sounded like a prediction that Morrison's star would have faded sooner or later and he, Walt, would still be there counting his money. I poured a little salt on the wound.

"How'd you two work together, earnest land man and flashy stock market speculator?"

Walt dropped into a bored monotone. "We worked in the same company. We did not work together. He ran one side, hobnobbing rich assholes for their money. I ran the other, Cabe did his freaky algorithm shit no one understood, and we all got rich."

"Is that why you partnered up?"

"That's why we stayed in business together even though there was no love lost by now. We partnered up because William can charm as easily as he can piss people off, and because it would diversify both portfolios, so we'd grow faster. That's Business 101. You keep growing or you sink. There are no other options."

"Who did Will piss off last week?" I asked, getting back on topic.

Walt had sat up once he was done talking about the company, starting to push on the armrests to stand up, maybe hoping that had been the end of our conversation. Now, he slouched back into the antique armchair and spat his answer at me.

"Take your pick. Half a dozen guys yelled at him that his shit stank too, and half a dozen more joked he should leave some for the rest of them except they weren't really kidding. Not every woman got the attention they wanted, and some of those who did maybe got more than they bargained for. I thought you had a fair idea of the man."

"Why don't you pick two or three for me?"

He machine gunned his words at me, fast and irritated, without thinking.

"One guy who looked like some skinhead punk seemed too young to know the game. He yelled a lot. I think his posse called him Sonny or something like that. One gal, a tall, skinny brunette, was always hanging around without really partying. Weirdo, if you ask me. I don't know her name. Another loud guy had the biker look, unruly beard, covered in tats, leather getup, all that stuff. Yelled a lot too, flexed his muscles and showed off his ink. Could be the way he always was for all I know. I don't know his name either. Are we about done with this nonsense?"

I didn't think murder was nonsense, any more than I thought those who cared about it were stupid, but I let it go. I cracked my knuckles, stifling my irritation as best I could, which wasn't all too well.

The woman could be Linda. For the others, I'd see if CJ's and Courtney's vetting came up with anything matching the descriptions Rosling had just given me. You never knew. Still, it was all low-rate info. I was tempted to come up with more questions just to annoy him, but I was even more tempted to get the hell out of there.

"We can be," I told him. "I just need your cell number, you know, in case I need to follow up on something."

"Fuck you." He was grimacing, half his face lighter than the other from the sun coming through the room's only window. He reminded me of a Batman villain.

"Or I can stay a while, make sure I'm not forgetting anything," I said, wrapping an arm over the back of my chair, making myself comfortable.

He told me to do something that was anatomically impossible, but he gave me a number. I dialed it to make sure it wasn't bogus. His phone rang in his pocket. I hung up, stood up, and showed myself out. Rosling did not move.

CHAPTER 8

After being cooped up in a musty house's claustrophobic study with Rosling, the afternoon heat felt like a breath of fresh air. I inhaled the hot, muggy vapor and exhaled slowly. I got in the car and turned the A/C full on—hurricane strength.

I stayed parked in the driveway for a while, half to see if anything interesting happened, half to take a minute and check in with the office.

"Anything new?" I asked CJ when she answered my call.

"No," she said. "We're doing our due diligence with Courtney's list, but nothing so far. How was Rosling's interview?"

"The guy's an asshole, which means nothing. I'll write it up, but don't expect anything earth-shattering, just noise and fury. I'll make my way back now."

"Why don't you call Danny while you're down there? A couple of hours won't make a difference in this case, and you can use a break."

Danny was an old friend from my Army days. CJ wasn't wrong. She's a smart woman, and I'm a social Neanderthal.

"Yeah, I'll do that," I said. "Thanks." Then I hung up with my customary grace.

Danny jumped at the chance for an early happy hour together. We met at a bar he liked away from Duval Street. We each ordered a drink, hoisted our glasses, and shouted "Hail to the Big Red One" from the First Infantry's drinking toast. A couple of patrons enjoying some afternoon cheer turned their heads, then went back to their own business. One rose his glass to us.

"How's the best sharpshooter in the Army?" I asked him after slamming my glass down.

"I'm no longer in the Army, remember?" he said.

"Okay, how's retired life, then?"

"Half retired. I have enough clients to keep me busy. And life is good."

"No regrets hanging the combat boots to live a quasi-Caribbean lifestyle, huh?"

Danny ordered another drink as if to make the point that he could. "Not a one."

"Well, you earned it," I said. And he had. He'd put in his twenty, not an easy day in the mix. He'd earned his degree along the way. Now he did the books for a few businesses around Southern Florida, mine included.

Danny and I reminisced some more, telling some old war stories and catching up with each other's lives. The renewed friendship filled up my tank after two days grilling strangers about someone getting his head bashed in—at least, that was my subtle interpretation of Morant saying Morrison was found with his head split open. I was more drained than I'd realized, and happily let the afternoon linger for the sake of banter and to make sure the drink I had toasted our reunion with was out of my system before I got on the road.

The sun was still high and hot, but the afternoon was beginning to stretch into the evening when I eased the CR-V out of the parking lot. Traffic thinned out once I left the Lower Keys behind. Not many people were making their way back to the mainland on a Wednesday night, or vice versa.

I noticed the big black Tahoe when it pulled into the lane behind me. It did not worry me. It was coming from a tourist trap restaurant in one of the empty stretches between Marathon Key and Key Largo, and those behemoths are about as rare on the road as a turkey on a Thanksgiving table. But when a second, identical SUV pulled right in front of me, the hairs on the back of my neck stood up.

They acted quickly, showing no hesitation, and executed a tactically sound ambush. The lead Tahoe slid to a stop sideways across both lanes of traffic next to the ramp for a scenic overlook. Traffic was likely to be at its lightest on this part of the road. They picked a good spot, and it paid off for them. There was no traffic at all.

My tactical brain kicked in. In a split second, I determined that ramming them was not an option. It would damage my car more than theirs. Stopping in the driving lane was no good either. I would have witnesses as cars came along before long, but it would limit my options as much as theirs, and they could still ram me from behind. That left one option. I accepted their invitation, however rudely extended.

I merged onto the overlook at full speed. There were no cars there, no tourists taking in one more expanse of water. I kept the accelerator floored. White stripes marking parking spots on the asphalt looked like zebras in reverse as I sped past.

I slammed on the brake and stopped on a dime at the overlook's far end, blocking the lane between the parking area and the ramp back to the highway. To my left, the lead Tahoe was already repositioning, parking its fat tires at the other end of the ramp. The second one was coming to a stop behind me. It made sense for them. I wasn't dealing with amateurs. It sucked for me. Still, I'd given myself as much room to maneuver as I could.

I leaned over to the passenger side, unbuckled my seatbelt with my left hand, and pulled my .45 and its holster from the glove compartment with my right. Shifting my weight back the other way, I threw my door open and got out of the car, leaving the engine running. I clipped the holster on my belt, pulled the gun, chambered a round, and put it back in its holster. I bunched my shirt on top of the weapon, making sure they could all see I was armed.

I walked to a spot on the overlook's far end, closer to the road, putting myself between them and the setting sun. Let them squint at me. I took my sunglasses off. My eyes adjusted quickly after a moment's discomfort from the sun reflecting off the ocean.

Car doors opened and slammed shut. Three figures started walking toward me. Two no-neck gorillas flanked the leader of the gang. They could have been twins: white, stocky, square-jawed, with bulges under their jackets. They looked left and right, jittery, their entire torsos moving with each glance.

Their erstwhile leader came face to face with me. He looked to be in his forties with a military-style haircut and a bright blue suit too expensive to be honest. He buttoned up his jacket and looked at me through movie-star sunglasses. The three of them had formed a human wall in front of me. With a driver in each car, that was a lot of muscle for little ol' me.

"I'm Alan Dunn," the blue shark in my face said.

"Your driving sucks," I said.

"As do your manners, I'm afraid. You've been sticking your nose where it does not belong."

"All part of the job."

I didn't like how close they were to me. I needed room to move in case our little piece of paradise turned into the OK Corral. I figured I could head butt the shark and shoot one gorilla, but that would leave me in one spot too long. I'd be a sitting duck. That made me the weak link in our impromptu rodeo.

"This is one job from which I strongly suggest you back off," the distinguished Mr. Dunn said.

"Says who?"

"Why . . . I just did. Or are you deaf?"

"I heard you just fine, but you're just the mouthpiece."

"Now, now, Mr. Malone. Our positions here may be adverse, but that does not preclude a modicum of professionalism, does it? I do not expect you to divulge your client's identity. Please do not be so crass toward me."

So the guy was a PI, not in-house security. Interesting.

"You're asking me to drop the case," I said. "Pretty crass if you ask me."

"Unfortunate, to be sure. But we've all had to step off a job now and then. Necessary for survival. Elephants fighting, mice trampled, and all that. Things happen."

I bared my teeth and leaned in until he could smell my breath. "It's very dangerous to threaten me."

"At least we understand each other," he said. He sounded like a proud parent, happy that his kid had learned a hard life lesson. He dropped any hint of a smile and added three clipped words: "Drop it, Malone!"

Dunn turned his head to the meat locker on his right and nodded. The gorilla walked to my car, pulled a telescopic baton from his jacket, extended it with a flick of the wrist, and smashed the driver-side back window.

When the muscle returned to his spot next to his boss, he still had the baton in his hand. I stepped closer still to the three of them. I had no room anyway—I might as well shorten the guy's swing if I was the baton's next target.

Dunn was smiling again. "They're always looking for something to break," he said.

I thought the message had been clear enough without pulling my insurance company into it and didn't feel the need to dignify that with an answer.

Nor did Dunn wait for one. Without another word, he and his goons returned to their black SUV. I guessed they'd delivered their message. The sharp noise of metal on metal rang again as car doors closed, then engines revved as they drove off, crushing landscape as they went around the CR-V.

I exhaled for the first time. I let my eyes linger on the ocean, which had reappeared now that the wall of humanity had receded. The salt air chased the smell of too much testosterone. I wiggled my fingers, forcing them to relax. Then, and only then, did I pull my shirt over my holster.

I walked back to the car and sat down behind the wheel. I gave my pulse time to slow down before pulling the door shut and getting back onto the road. My mind was racing faster than the car. For whom was Dunn working? Did Rosling call him? It was a stretch from being an asshole to me. And if he did, they got damn lucky I spent two hours with Danny. They needed time to get in position.

Mardi Gras was a more likely suspect if they wanted badly enough to keep me from messing up their private settlements, killer-at-large be damned. They could have waited for the inevitable moment when I went to find Rosling in the Keys. Did Morant know about Dunn? And if he did, did he know about the little stunt they just pulled?

And if somehow it was not the company, or even Rosling, then who on earth did I spook and how did they know where I'd be? I had too many damn questions and not enough answers.

CHAPTER 9

I clicked the phone on the car's blue tooth and called CJ, asking her to meet me at the office.

"Why?" she asked. It wasn't like her to demand an explanation. We trusted each other implicitly. Something in my voice must have triggered her.

"I'm okay," I said. "Just meet me there." I hung up before she could go on. I'd apologize for being a jerk later, but I wasn't about to go through what had just happened over the phone.

By the time I walked in, she was already there, leaning against the front desk, arms crossed over her chest.

"What happened?" she asked.

I extended my arms and did a three-sixty in front of her.

"What happened?" she asked again.

CJ can be a tad protective of Courtney and me. I knew it and she knew it. I did another spin.

"I am fine," I said. "Perfectly, one hundred percent fine."

She uncrossed her arms and put her hands on her hips, her body square toward me. Her eyes narrowed. I smiled and arched an eyebrow at her.

She took a deep breath without relaxing her posture. "Yes, you are fine. Now tell me what on earth happened, and maybe I won't go volcanic."

I told her what happened, leaving nothing out. When I was done, we moved around the front desk as one and used Courtney's computer to look up Alan Dunn.

CJ had the mouse and scrolled methodically through each page as we read, standing side by side, bent toward the monitor. Dunn was a PI, sure enough, with offices not far from ours. He clearly had a widely different idea of his profession than CJ or me.

Dunn's website flaunted a big firm, well equipped and well organized. I hadn't needed the computer to tell me that. More sleuthing added "well connected" to the mix. He had received his Florida license despite his role in an ugly extortion case in California that cost him his license there.

We left the computer and sat down in the waiting room chairs. CJ folded one leg under her so she could sit sideways and look at me.

"I think you need some backup," CJ said.

"I thought about that on the drive over after my confrontation with Dunn. In some situations, I will, but I don't think I do on the routine stuff. They probably tailed Cabe and got lucky when I went to the Keys. They've delivered their message. I'd rather keep a low profile. I won't poke the bear for now. Now, if the bear pokes as much as a nose out of the woods again, I'll bring in the big guns."

CJ gave me a long, hard stare. I could tell she did not like the answer. Eventually, she gave me a short nod. Then she chuckled, shoulders shaking.

"Did you just put you and 'low profile' in the same sentence?" she asked,

"Yeah, why?"

"You're about as low profile as a lion on the loose in Central Park, but okay. As far as backup, you may be right, for now. So, what's next?"

I ignored the jab and answered her question. "I'll barge into Morant's office first thing in the morning."

"I thought you were not going to poke the bear."

"I'm not poking the Dunn bear. All other bears are fair game. And while, so far, I trust the guy, Mardi Gras could still be who hired Dunn, so I'll go and ask and see what happens. You know me. Low profile or not, the best defense is a good offense."

I could hear CJ's wheels turning. She had not had the benefit of an hour's drive to mull things over. She was looking for a better idea. I was all ears. Neither of us came up with one, so I'd go shake the Mardi Gras tree tomorrow.

"I'll start there," I said, "then I'll look for that Linda Mayak who keeps popping up."

CJ nodded. We updated each other on the rest of the day. I told her about my meeting with Walt. She and Courtney had not unearthed any gold yet from the Groupies List, but they were working on it, mixing social media and the good ol' telephone.

"One last thing," I said, twisting sideways in the chair to look at CJ face-to-face. "I have to say it because I'm a guy and we do that overprotective thing, even in business, not that you would know anything about that, mama bear."

CJ squinted at me. She looked unsure of where I was going with this.

"This is a different kind of case now. Investigating a murder is bad enough. You've got someone who really doesn't want to be found. But this case just went major league on the danger scale. Someone doesn't want us to solve this, someone with enough money and resources to hire Dunn and his posse. They don't want us there badly enough to run me off the road and break the car. My gut says it was 50/50 whether they'd go after my knees next, but Dunn decided he'd passed the message strongly enough for now."

"But it is our case," CJ said. "It is our job. Sometimes, it can get risky. We investigate crimes. But we still do it." There was a tone of finality in her voice. I wished I had her calm, her certainty.

"It's our case until it's not," I said. "If you or Courtney want to drop this, we will. I can bet the farm that Heather does not want anyone getting hurt to find out what happened to a cruise party buddy. I don't either. If this is getting too hot, there's no shame in that."

"No," CJ said without hesitation. "Especially not now. I will not suffer the likes of Dunn dictating what we do. I will ask Courtney, but I'm pretty sure she'll say the same thing. And she's as good a shot as me, if things got that hot, so I'm okay with her answer either way."

I had to chuckle. CJ and Courtney's idea of a girls' night out was to go to the shooting range, then have cocktails. CJ knew her better than me, and I trusted CJ, so I was happy to leave it at that. Courtney was a bit of a mystery to me, anyway. She was the computer geek who could make big bucks in tech but took a job working my front desk, who liked to shoot guns and knew how, but spent her time at a keyboard. She seemed too smart for her job and was always cheerful doing it. I hadn't quite figured her out. I hadn't pushed, but I didn't like mysteries, even from my own employees—especially from my own employees.

I deferred to CJ on my team. I could have argued, given voice to my misgivings. There was a difference between shooting at the range and getting in a gunfight. But CJ knew that, too. She'd made up her mind and would let Courtney make up hers. I hadn't really expected a different answer.

I gave myself another moment to be honest with myself. I didn't want to keep the case just because I was stubborn or wanted a big case to inflate my ego. All that aside, though, CJ was right, which was a bad habit of hers. What we did always carried risk, even if this one was riskier than most. We weren't going to turn back with our tails between our legs because Dunn said "boo!" Not to mention, I don't drop cases.

"Okay," I said. "We press on."

CJ leaned over and put her hand over mine. "And thank you for asking. It was not overprotective, just protective. And I do know something about that." She stood up and headed to the door, looking at me over her shoulder. "Go home, Coop." There was a tinge of concern escaping from the back of her throat. "I have a feeling it will be a long day tomorrow."

The door closed behind CJ, sounding louder in the empty office than it usually did. I stared at it. A closed door. It felt symbolic. Maybe there had been a way out of this case once. Now, the door had closed. Now, I no longer had a choice.

My eyes fell on my name, blurry and backward behind the frosted glass. My name. I took the case. I stayed on the case even after I realized it was not just another job, after I sobered up enough to realize I shouldn't take the job just because it was there for the taking or because Heather was my friend. Murder was different. I wanted what I did to matter again. Maybe there had never been a choice.

I strolled to my office and opened the gun safe. Next to the short-nosed .38 was a good bottle of rye and a clean glass. I took them back to the waiting room and the closed door and poured myself one. I wondered if finding Morrison's killer really mattered.

I thought about Heather, sweet Heather. Most people would not have lifted their little finger to figure out what happened to Morrison. But she did. That's who she was. I thought about Heather the fashionista, her bouncy hair like a Hollywood starlet, wearing dresses as if she lived her life on the runway, yet she was the most decent and unassuming girl I'd ever met. I thought about her at Nick & Nora that night, all wrapped up into herself, haunted by Morrison's death. And I poured myself another.

She'd looked better in the office the next day. Her ghost was not haunting her anymore. I guess I had my answer. It mattered. But it meant that Morrison's ghost was mine now. And when it wasn't him, it was Alan Dunn and his goons. I poured myself another glass.

There hadn't been many cases that drove me to carry the .45 on my hip every time I left the house. This was turning into one. I couldn't figure Dunn out. I didn't know who had hired him or why. I thought it had to be somebody I talked to, or at least somebody who knew them and knew they'd talked to me.

Mardi Gras' bosses had an interest in keeping me quiet. Cabe and Walt did too. They had a lot of money riding on this, on the absence of scandal, on avoiding an exodus of big money if and when investors learned Morrison croaked. Was I being pushed away to keep the illusion or to keep me from finding out who killed Morrison?

Old Walt was an asshole. Was that all he was, or was there something more sinister to him? Cabe played the innocent-kid card. Was it real, or was he acting? Was there something else happening in that math brain of his, something I couldn't figure out? That was the thing. I couldn't figure anything out in this damn case. I'd ruled out more people than I'd ruled in. That's how cases go early on, but I never liked that part. I don't like not knowing.

And this case felt worse than the others. It felt like I needed another drink. I wouldn't be driving home tonight.

CHAPTER 10

I ended up falling asleep on the chair. I could blame the Army for the habit of taking what sleep I could, wherever and whenever I could, but I was that way before I joined—full speed ahead, then drop. The whiskey didn't hurt, but I wasn't down to sloppy drunk. When I woke up, the bottle and glass were neatly on the front desk, the cap on the bottle.

I'd had the presence of mind to set an alarm early enough for a fresh day. I rinsed the glass and put it and the bottle back in the safe. I left the short-nose .38 in the safe too. I had the .45 that usually lives in the car still on my hip in its custom-made holster. It would stay there. It was turning into that kind of a case.

I stopped home, showered, and changed. Once I had coffee, I felt almost human. It was time to visit Mardi Gras Cruise Lines' offices. I parked in front of their door right at nine.

It was already sultry outside. The car's air conditioning had tried to fend off the heat coming through the broken window and failed. My shirt clung to my skin as I walked to the company's front door in long strides and burst in, flinging the door open ahead of me. I heard it slam shut as I reached the counter. The same bored-looking woman who had been there two days ago was standing behind it. She barely looked at me from beneath heavy eyelids.

"Morant," I barked.

History repeated itself. Once again, she nodded to the security guard to keep an eye on me. Once again, she disappeared behind the recessed door behind her. Once again, she escorted me along the corridor with the dark gray walls and the dark gray carpet tiles. Once again, she motioned me into what may or may not be Morant's office.

I entered the room. It felt just as claustrophobic as before. *Mix in a window or something*, I thought. Morant looked at me without standing up.

"Would it not have been more judicious to call?" he asked.

"I got past 'judicious' when your goons tried to run me off the road."

His eyebrows lowered over his eyes, and he extended a hand to the chair across the desk from him. I sat down.

"Explain yourself, please," he asked.

I gave him the thumbnail version of what happened on the way back from the Keys.

"Mr. Malone," he said when I was done, leaning forward a little and looking at me straight in the eye, "we have many people involved in this matter, as you may imagine, even if they are not the kind of people I wished. I am referring to lawyers, public relations people, and other such people in suits with fancy titles. I can assure you, however, that we have not hired a private investigation agency, Mr. Dunn's or any other."

"Could the company have done so without you knowing? You wanted them to investigate. They may have been hired to make sure no one did."

"It is I who have authority to hire outside vendors in this area. Additionally, please keep in mind there are two reasons I hold the position I do now. One is that I do my job well, at least when I am at liberty to do it. The second is that I play the corporate game just as well. I do not believe anyone would cross me in this manner. Nevertheless, if I should find out otherwise, you will be the first to know whose head will roll. Figuratively speaking, you understand."

Morant folded his hands. That was the only suggestion of impatience or irritation.

"If not Mardi Gras, who?" I asked.

"That is a question to which I do not have an answer."

"You guys ever worked with Dunn, maybe some time ago?"

"We have not. The idea of hiring private investigators in general is one that makes my employer vaguely nauseated. I can assure you, without even looking, that we never did. This is yet another reason I very much doubt anyone at Mardi Gras ordered Mr. Dunn to intimidate you."

"But you knew Walt Rosling was in Key West."

Morant inhaled deeply through his nose before answering in a measured tone.

"I did not personally know that, no, and I do not believe anyone else in the company did. I understand all our communications with StarQuest are going through legal counsel." He raised a finger, asking for a minute's patience, and reached for the mouse. Three clicks later, he turned his attention from the screen back to me. "Her name is Denise Friedmann. Two ens."

I made a mental note of it, even though attorneys rarely gave good interviews. Every third word out of their mouth is "privileged." It comes to them naturally, like people with allergies who can't stop sneezing. They're allergic to questions.

I sighed. Morant had had enough, and I couldn't blame him.

"Well, maybe you reporting how this asshole Malone barged in will shake something loose somehow."

"Regrettably, I doubt that. But again, I will keep you posted." His posture was as stiff as his starched white shirt.

"And turnaround is fair play," I told him. I had promised I'd keep him posted, so I gave him the five-minute version of the last two days.

"I am happy someone is actively investigating." That's the most he could say with a straight face. We still had nothing actionable, not the first clue about who killed Morrison.

"One last thing. Any luck getting us on board on Sunday?"

"Why were you asking about a Linda at breakfast yesterday?"

That had nothing to do with what I asked. Or maybe it did. The real question was whether trust was going both ways, enough trust to put his neck on the line any more than he already had. I went with my gut and told him how Mayak had become a blip on my radar, someone who showed up on both Courtney's list and witness statements.

Morant nodded slowly as I finished talking. Then he told me what I needed to know.

"Come to the Port of Miami at noon on Sunday. You can use the main gate. Drive a pickup truck and dress like a dock worker. The Port Security will have your name as a Mardi Gras contractor. Instead of turning into the parking garage, you will keep driving straight until you pass the last berthed ship. You will reach an area cluttered with containers and warehouses.

"Park by one of the warehouses to your left. Jump the retaining wall at the back and walk through the brush. It's only ten or fifteen feet to the water. A boat will pick you up, people I trust. They will take you and two people with you to the ship. Two others at most, not a single person more."

"Got it. And thank you."

"My men will guide you once on board. Please be careful to follow their instructions."

"Understood."

"It was not an easy feat to pull off," Morant added, "and it remains risky despite my best precautions. Please be extremely careful. I hope it will prove worth our trouble."

"I understand. And that makes two of us. Now, you couldn't get them to go easy on the cleaning for the next few days, could you?"

That finally broke his façade. His lips curled into a smile.

"I am afraid we must live with certain realities in our respective professions," he said. He reached across the desk. I shook his hand and renewed my thanks with a short nod.

I stood up and left the way I came in. My nice, clean theory about Dunn had vanished like a ghost the night after Halloween. *What the fuck were those goons about?* I wondered.

I thought back on the previous day's encounter. I replayed the conversation in my head. Dunn had not given away any hint about his client. The comment about me sticking my nose where it doesn't belong had made me think of Mardi Gras and their obsession with secrecy. Looking back, it was a little thin—logical but thin. I asked myself the question I'd asked Morant. If not Mardi Gras, then who?

CHAPTER 11

All of that swished around my mind on my way back downtown to the office-tower address that had been in Linda Mayak's reservation. The drive also gave me time to call CJ and ask her to get started recruiting a couple of techs, the kind that would not be too squeamish about sneaking into a crime scene, somewhere where they may not be supposed to show up. Between us, we came up with some names to try before I reached my destination.

I parked in the garage and took the elevator up to the twenty-second floor. My stomach lurched as the express elevator came to a stop halfway to the sky. I stepped through the open doors and glanced left and right into a lobby with beige heavy-traffic carpet and light gray walls. There was only one door, a plain but heavy-looking one with no name on it and a camera above the upper right corner, the red light staring at me. That only meant they—whoever they were—wanted me to know it was there. It was a power play.

I walked to the door and tried it, just for kicks. It was locked. I rang the doorbell next to the handle and waited.

"ID please," a disembodied voice demanded.

I pulled my PI license from my wallet and presented it to the camera's lens. I heard a magnetic lock click a few seconds later. The door opened an inch, pivoting on its hinges. I pushed through. The door's weight caused it to swing shut behind me. The sound made my hand move closer to my .45 even though it would do me no good in here. I was in some kind of airlock-looking room with a locked door behind me, one ahead, and a booth with thick glass to my right. A young man with a buzz cut and a stubble beard looked at me through the glass. He wore a corporate-appropriate dark blazer over a corporate-appropriate white shirt.

He moved closer to a microphone. "How may we help you, Mr. Malone?" he asked, his voice distorted by the mic. He was leaning his head to one side as he spoke, like a curious puppy.

"I'm here to see Linda Mayak."

"Does she know what this is regarding?"

"Tell her I'm here about William Morrison. She will want to see me," I said.

He pressed a button on the microphone, and I could no longer hear him when he spoke. He picked up a phone and said a few words. A few moments later, he performed the same pantomime in reverse. The phone came down and the microphone buzzed back to life. Mr. Corporate Appropriate told me someone would be here to see me in shortly. I didn't answer. He cut off the microphone before I could anyway.

I tried not to show my aggravation, standing there like an idiot in a room small enough that I could touch opposite walls by spreading my arms. I kept my gaze at a spot at the edge of the door and waited. Time was mercifully short before a man who could have been a clone of the one in the booth opened the door in front of me.

"This way," he said with a wave of the hand as if there were more than one way out. I followed him along a maze of corridors. There were none of the cubicles that normally pepper corporate offices. Office doors appeared at regular intervals, all of them closed. Metal gray walls gave me the impression of walking through a battleship. The clone stopped in front of the sole open door and extended his hand toward the office. I went in.

Linda Mayak was standing next to her desk, a polished smile on her lips, fingers of one hand resting on the desktop. She looked exactly as Amy had described her. The skirt may have been a little bit longer and the shirt may have had an extra button or two buttoned, but her office uniform did not differ much from her party one. She stood there, unmoving, a queen in her kingdom about to grant an audience.

I looked past her to the floor-to-ceiling windows and the simple wood furniture sparsely occupying the large space. It was luminous and unthreatening. That meant she was the threat.

"Welcome, Mr. Malone," she said.

"Thanks."

"Would you like to sit down?"

She started walking toward a round table just large enough for the four chairs around it. Her heels clicked on the floor. I sat down and she took a chair next to mine. Her posture remained straight, dignified. Even though she lost the advantage of her heels when sitting down, and I had a good four or five inches on her, she seemed to be the one looking down at me. An outfit that would have looked somewhere between sexy and slutty on someone else somehow looked like a power suit on her.

"What is it you wanted to tell me about Mr. Morrison?" she asked. She extended a slender hand over the table to give me the floor. I took a second, observing her. She wanted me to tell her what I knew, not ask what I did not know. That was fine. We could dance a little.

"You were with him on the *Mardi Gras Rio* last week," I said.

"That's something about me, not about him."

"Okay. He was with *you* on the *Mardi Gras Rio* last week."

"And to think I agreed to see you because I thought you might have something interesting to say," she said. She got up, pushing on the table with her fingertips.

"When he was killed," I said.

"I see." She betrayed no emotion. She stepped back to her desk, her heels once again echoing in the big office. She picked up a small purse, the same kind CJ carries for her phone and gun. I half expected to see a muzzle pointed at me. I swiveled on my chair, clearing the hip on which I wore my piece.

Linda Mayak smiled a tight-lipped smile, looked down in my direction, and shook her head the way a disappointed parent might. "You won't need your weapon," she said.

I sheepishly kept both hands on the table in front of me.

She headed to the door. "Let's talk somewhere else."

She was using space to control the flow of conversation. I did not like it, but I respected it. I stood up and followed her. She led me the opposite way from where I'd come, to a private exit and a flight of stairs. One floor down, she opened a door. We walked in, and the noise assaulted my ears after the eerie silence upstairs. This was where the cubicle people lived. All around us phones rang, keyboards clattered, voices were raised, and shoes slapped thin carpet. We walked through the chaos to the elevator bay without having to check in with Mr. Corporate Appropriate in his booth.

Once inside the elevator, Mayak pressed the button for the atrium. The doors opened to more noise and chaos as the elevator let us out into the corporate version of a touristy district in a foreign port. We started walking side by side, anonymous among the horde of well-dressed people, past coffee shops, juice bars, and lunch counters. We stayed silent at first, getting lost with each step among the masses, looking like one more pair of professionals in a downtown Miami courtyard.

"It is important that I learn what you know," Mayak eventually said as we walked. "In return, I will answer your questions. Fair?"

"In principle."

"In principle," she said, echoing my sentiment.

I guessed we had what lawyers call a meeting of the minds. She had spoken without looking at me. She walked in even, measured steps, her eyes scanning the crowd ahead of her, from near to far, eyes lingering on selected individuals.

"You left a bit of an impression on board," I said, offering a crumb to keep us talking.

"Oh?"

"Always around the party guys but not partying yourself."

"I cannot do my job drunk, drugged, and horizontal."

Half an hour earlier, the word "job" would have made me do a double take. After the way she spotted my piece in her office and now kept her eyes moving from one group of people to the next, I nearly expected it. Her high-rise office meant she was in a position of power. Her demeanor meant she wore it well. The gun-spotting and her sober proximity to Wall Street types, that put her somewhere in my world.

She snapped her purse open. I reflexively moved my hand a hair closer to my hip. She pulled out a business card and handed it to me without breaking her stride. It read, "Linda Mayak. Personal Security."

I looked straight at her as we kept walking, and nearly ran into a woman on her cell phone, all high heels and power suit. If Linda Mayak had been protecting StarQuest's golden boys, she'd just lived her worst nightmare.

"Who did you do PS for?" I asked. I was pretty sure I knew the answer, but I needed to hear it from her.

Her jaw clenched, the words barely escaping through her teeth. "William Morrison. Walt Rosling. Cabe Roper."

"What happened?"

"What happened is there was one of me and three of them. I could not be everywhere at once. I could only have eyes on one out of three people at any given time. That's what happened." Her voice was cold as deep space. The staccato rhythm of her heels on the ground sounded like gunfire, shooting her anger out into the world.

She bee lined without warning to an open table on a café's patio and sat down. I took the chair across from her. The noise of the crowd receded into a hum behind me. A waiter came and we ordered espressos. The coffees came a minute later.

Mayak started talking. Her voice seemed to be coming from far away. Her words had no inflection. Her eyes were looking at a spot in the ether no one else could see. "The night William was murdered, I stuck to him most of the night. He partied the hardest, so he had most of my attention. There was nothing out of the ordinary, if you call drunken debauchery, rampant drugs, and damn near orgies ordinary."

Our waiter walked nearby, his eyes on our table, and moved on, seeing our still-full cups.

Mayak went on. "It was about one or two in the morning, I think—the witching hour. I saw Rosling gesticulating in the distance like he was arguing with someone I could not see, so I headed his way, making my way through a crowd of sweaty bodies slurring their words and trying to grab my ass. Whatever had Walt excited, it was all over by the time I got close.

"I turned back around. William was taking someone upstairs who did not look like a threat. I had not seen Roper in a while, though. I figured he'd gone somewhere with that chick he'd met on board but thought I'd better check. It took me a bit. I eventually found them at the back of a bar, all snuggled up, looking like they were into each other."

I figured the chick in question was Jen and nodded at her, careful not to interrupt.

"By the time I circled back to William's cabin," Mayak continued, "the door was jammed open an inch and it was quiet inside. It was the right time for him to pass out, so I kept walking and went to bed."

She paused and put a hand on her coffee cup. She had yet to drink from it. "I've relived those steps past William's door in my nightmares every night since."

I spared her the platitude of how Morrison was probably killed before she walked by his door. She already knew that, and it wouldn't help. I gave her a minute before asking, "Who hired you? StarQuest?"

"No. It was William, personally. And not because he felt the need for it, either."

"Then why?"

She picked up her cup and sipped some espresso, her gaze still lost on the horizon, somewhere beyond the tower's walls, behind people milling about. I leaned in to better hear her over the echoes of the crowd's chatter.

"Two reasons," she said. "One was ego. It made him feel important. He loved being the only one who knew. Rosling and Roper were protectees, but they had no clue who I was or that I existed. The second reason was generosity. I've known Will since childhood. He was throwing some business my way, giving me a push on the partnership track. But he didn't fear an assault or anything like it. He wasn't worried. And so maybe I let my guard down . . . ."

She downed the rest of her espresso in one gulp and slammed her cup down so hard the saucer clattered on the table.

"You still watched them," I said, "every day, closely, with a trained eye. I see how you look at the crowd. You know what you're doing. Do you have a sense of who did it?"

"No one presented an immediate threat, and that's the extent of what I do. What you're asking, that's your wheelhouse. Still, I can give you a few people who did not do it. I tracked down a couple of women Will slept with and a couple more who might have wanted to but didn't, just in case it came down to a jealousy angle. They're in the clear. Give me your card and I'll email you the list."

She took the card without looking, her eyes scanning the crowd behind me, left to right, right to left, like a laser beam. "We've been in one place long enough," she said.

I realized I hadn't touched my coffee. I drank it in one gulp, the bitterness jolting my taste buds alive. I picked up the bill the waiter had slipped under the saucer and left enough cash on the table to cover it. We stood up and resumed our walk. She was back in her element, her footsteps like a metronome on the fake cobblestones, eyes assessing each person as they passed.

My silence exposed me for being at a loss. She had been aboard with Morrison. I didn't think she was lying, which meant I didn't think she'd done it or knew who did. I could have grilled her, given her the third degree. It would have been a shitty thing to do. That did not bother me. I do shitty things when I need to. But my gut told me it would add up to nothing. I'll take making CJ and Courtney's day as a win. Mayak had probably cleared some names off the Groupies List.

She took the hint from my silence and asked her own questions. We had a deal, after all. She started with the one that mattered most to her and her bosses. How did I find her? I told her about a partier hearing her name, the list Courtney had created, and putting two and two together. She shook her head, exhaling a chortle through her nose.

"I don't know about God," she said, "but our business sure works in mysterious ways."

"I guess it does."

She asked about the investigation in general, and I gave her general answers, just not too general in case some detail shook something loose, something she saw or heard but hadn't remembered or thought about. No such luck. Our feet had brought us back toward the elevators as she asked one last question.

"Will you find who did this?" she asked.

"That's the idea."

"Please let me know if I can help."

"I will."

"And who did it—when you find out."

"Yeah. You got it. The problem is, I don't fucking know where this is headed."

Saying the words out loud triggered something in me the moment they left my mouth. I could barely push them out through the pit in my stomach. It came without warning. My head pounded hard enough I could feel my pulse in my temples.

I walked away from Linda Mayak, trying not to let anyone see the vise gripping my brain. I swallowed back the bitter taste of bile at the back of my throat, and I kept moving, keeping my head down.

CHAPTER 12

It felt like I was fleeing Mayak. Maybe she noticed, maybe not. I didn't care. Admitting I had no clue what happened had made my frustrations bubble over. I could feel it inside me, physically, bad enough to make me hurl.

I was tired of getting nowhere, of answers that were not really answers—not to the question I was hired to figure out. Maybe something I'd learned so far would make sense later. Maybe something would turn out to be a piece of the puzzle. It usually happened that way. Right now, I didn't care. It wasn't enough.

So, I ran—figuratively, but I ran. I needed time. I needed space. I needed to calm the fuck down. I went home even though there was plenty of time left in the day, not that there was anything at home to help me figure this case out.

I sat on my couch and brooded. I tried reading and couldn't hold onto the words, so I got up from the couch and paced like an animal in a zoo and talked to myself and got pissed off as the evening dragged on. So much for calming down.

I didn't sleep much, and, when I did, it was in the wee hours of the morning, the first glow of the day tentatively lightening the sky.

Of course, that's when Heather called. The woman had a sixth sense or something, calling at a time like that. If she got tired of fashion, maybe she'd become a PI

"You sound awful," she said. I'd barely croaked a "hello," but she could tell. What is it with women? They can always tell.

"I'm alright."

"No, you're not. I know you, Coop. Is it the case? Because I can still fire you if it is."

"Look," I said, "most clients aren't good enough friends to call me at the crack of dawn, and they certainly don't know me well enough to know when I'm not a hundred percent."

"But I am."

"You are. But even you don't really know what it means. Tough cases, important cases, they always get to me at one point or another. They did back in my Army days, and they do now. It's part of the deal. This is normal. It's just a part of working a case that most people don't see. Or hear."

"But if I fired you, it wouldn't get to you and you'd feel better."

"Doesn't work that way. For one thing, you can fire me, but I'll keep looking. I won't let it go. I can't do that any more than you could. And for another . . . ." I closed my eyes and let the rest of my sentence hang for a moment. I wanted her to hear the truth in my voice.

"For what it's worth," I said, "I am okay. I'm good. This work is what I do. Some days it sucks. Some days it sucks so bad it shows. Most days, I love it. But either way, it's part of who I am."

Heather blew out a long, loud sigh at the other end of the line.

"I don't like it, and I'm not a hundred percent sure I believe you, but okay. Promise me you'll take care of yourself, though."

"I promise."

We both knew it was a stretch, but we let it go. There was an awkward silence while she probably wondered whether to ask for an update. I figured that's why she'd called. In the end, she didn't, and I didn't give her one. There was none to give.

Heather's call had saved me from sleeping into the morning, but it was already later than usual. And I had a pounding headache. *Fuck, at that rate, I should have had a few drinks last night.* I showered at warp speed, foregoing a shave, and went straight to the office.

Courtney raised an eyebrow at my unshaven face, and I hurried past CJ's door. I plopped down heavily on my chair, flipping the computer to life. The first thing I did was make an appointment to replace the CR-V's window. That made one easy, productive task accomplished.

Then I brought up the Morrison file. It looked just like it did the last time I pulled it up. The only difference between last night and this Friday morning was the headache that the first two ibuprofen had not quite extinguished. I had trouble concentrating. My brain played around with an alternate reality where this had all been an elaborate hoax and no one had been killed on the *Mardi Gras Rio*.

When I managed to focus, I read through the reports of calls that CJ and Courtney had made to people in the Groupies File. It looked as I'd expected. Some people had been pleasant and a couple downright nasty. Some tried to help, and some hung up in seconds.

Courtney gave it context with extra intel from social media accounts. I didn't really want to know if she was supposed to see everything she saw. Some of it could have made good gossip, but nothing that seemed relevant to the case. Most of the reports came with a picture pilfered from social media, so I could put a face to the words on the screen. *This was a pretty-people cruise*, I mused.

I played around with the manifest for a while. This was the first chance I'd gotten to take a close look at it. Courtney had made it searchable and sortable. A name popped out, tied to one of the VIP cabins. The name was on the booking for the cruise, along with a passport number, but no other information other than StarQuest's. I fired off an email to Courtney, addressed to "Courtney, cybersleuth," with what info there was and a single question: "Who is Claire?"

I closed the file. My reflection stared back at me on the blank monitor. The reports were thorough. It was quality work. It didn't matter. What CJ and Courtney got mainly confirmed what we already knew. No matter how hard I looked and how badly I wanted it, I saw nothing that moved the needle.

I was just about to get up, stretch my legs, and go in search of food to help settle the buzz behind my eyes when Courtney appeared, framed in my office's doorway.

"Coop?"

"Yeah?"

"There's a detective here," she said.

She walked up to my desk and handed me a business card with the official MDPD logo on it. I looked from Courtney down to the card in my hand.

"Det. Jorge Rodríguez. Homicide Bureau," it read.

"He wants to see you," Courtney said, standing very close to me, nearly whispering.

I smiled up at her. "Then I better see him." I thought for a moment, scratching my stubble. "Give me three minutes, then show him into the conference room."

"Okay."

I crossed the hallway to CJ's office and told her about Detective Rodríguez. Her face betrayed no emotion. It never did. She got up from behind her desk in one smooth movement and followed me to the conference room a minute ahead of our unexpected guest.

The detective that walked in had a round face and thick, black hair. He was probably not as young as his baby face made him look. He extended his hand as he walked in. I shook it and introduced CJ. They shook hands. He presented his badge if only so we knew he was who he said he was. I invited him to sit down and took the seat across from him.

With that little dance behind us, I readied myself to get down to business. My job puts me in contact with the police as often as not, and it is usually friendly. This time, I felt pins and needles travel up and down my legs.

Detective Rodríguez pulled the oversized sunglasses hanging from his shirt's open collar and put them on the table. That done, he reached inside his sports coat and retrieved his notebook and a pen. He opened the notebook, put it on the table, then looked at me.

"Thank you for seeing me," he said.

"Sure," I said. We both knew I had little choice in the matter, but polite words never hurt a relationship, so we both nodded and smiled across the table. The pins in my legs were itching, and I was trying hard not to tap my foot against the conference table. *Why are you here?*

"Do you know an Owen Morant?" Rodríguez asked.

That was not a question I had expected. I knew without looking that CJ was keeping a perfect poker face next to me. I did my best to emulate her as I answered him.

"You know I did, or you wouldn't be here."

"I know you met. People in his office remembered you."

The bored Asian lady at the counter? I wondered. She didn't look interested enough to remember anything.

"Well, that's about the extent of it," I told him. "I met him twice, briefly. I can't say I know him."

"What did you meet with him about?"

"They were professional meetings," I said, weighing each word.

Rodríguez raised his hands, palms up, his pen hanging between two fingers.

"You're gonna have to give me more than that," he said.

"You're gonna have to tell me why," I said. I raised my hand like a stop sign as he jerked his head up, about to speak. "Look, I have a good relationship with most people I've met at MDPD. We complement each other. I like you guys. But I can't shell over confidential information without a good reason."

The line about my fondness for MDPD was overblown. It was closer to pure bullshit than overblown, in fact. I trusted a few individual cops on the force who were good people and good at their job. But I hated bureaucracy, any bureaucracy, and a sprawling police department was no exception. Besides that, anything below a first-degree felony, maybe a second, and Miami's finest won't lift a finger. You have to chew their food for them.

For all that, I must have sold my limited appreciation for the men and women in blue just enough. Rodríguez relaxed his shoulders an inch.

"Mr. Morant was killed yesterday," he said. "Is that reason enough?"

I made a conscious effort to pull my jaw back up. "How?"

Rodríguez's face darkened. This was his interview, and I was hijacking it. I could tell he didn't like my asking questions. He must have decided to give me that much, though.

"His body was found in the water in the Port," he said. "The waves were slamming him against a concrete pylon. By the time someone saw him and fished him out, there was as much ripped flesh as intact skin. Maybe whoever did this counted on the ocean to hide their crime, or the pier tearing through Mr. Morant's body was a bonus. Either way, it didn't make a difference. The M.E. did not need long to determine the lethal wounds came from something like a baseball bat, not the broad surface of the pier. Now, Mr. Malone, if you please."

I stared back at Rodríguez. The table's surface felt cold and hard under my hands—like a corpse. Thoughts swirled in my head. I'd promised Morant I wouldn't come after Mardi Gras seeking headlines. Now Morant was dead. Was it related to Morrison? I had no way to know, and I didn't have time to think. I needed to give Rodríguez an answer. My head was throbbing again.

"I was hired to investigate whether an incident occurred on last week's cruise," I said. "Morant was helping me out."

"Did one occur?" Rodríguez asked, tapping his pen on his notepad. "What kind of incident?"

"I'm guessing one did because a bunch of gorillas in fancy suits cornered me on an empty stretch of highway to get me to back off."

Rodríguez stopped tapping his pen and started using it the way God and Bic intended, jotting notes as I spoke. I gave Rodríguez enough about Dunn's dirty tricks to keep him happy for a while and make him someone else's problem.

"What kind of incident was your client talking about?" Rodríguez asked again.

I had a split second to decide, but it was not really a decision. I didn't know Rodríguez from Adam or Eve, and distrusted big, state organizations by default.

"Assault by roofie," I said.

And just like that, I went from undersharing to outright misdirection.

I could feel CJ's eyes shooting daggers into my skull. She had a point. If the murders were related, I was sending the cops on a wild-goose chase. They might even call it obstruction and make a case of it.

I cared that CJ wouldn't like this, but that's about it. I didn't care about the cops wasting a little bit of time, or trying to jam me. I didn't know if I could still get on board the *Rio* Sunday, but, if I could, I didn't want the cops swarming all over it. This was *my* investigation.

"Did your client know where this may have happened? Who was around? Anything?" Rodríguez asked.

"Just some descriptions, nothing overly specific, I'm afraid." I threw in a couple of mental pictures from the Groupies File I'd stared at all morning.

"No names?" Rodríguez asked.

"Not yet. It's only been a few days."

"Is that what Morant was helping you with?"

"That and trying to talk to other people in the company, yes."

"Anything else?" Rodríguez was back to tapping his pen on his notebook.

"I'll let you know if I learn more. That's all I have right now. It's a young case."

Rodríguez grunted. He clicked off his pen and picked up his notebook and sunglasses. "Anything else you can tell me about Mr. Morant?"

"No. As I told you, they were very short and specific meetings."

"If you remember anything else," he said, not trying to sound like he meant it, "you have my card."

"I do. I won't hesitate to call you."

Rodríguez grunted again, staying one step short of saying out loud he didn't believe me and another step away from saying there'd be hell to pay if I was messing with him.

CJ and I walked him out and shook his hand goodbye. Then, the moment the door closed behind him, CJ's impassive face distorted. Her eyes narrowed. Her teeth clenched. She turned on her heels and power walked to her office.

I glanced at Courtney, who mouthed an "ouch" at me as I followed my partner and closed the door behind me.

CJ turned around to face me.

"You lied to the police!" Her words barely escaped through her clenched teeth. She was mad at me. She could get protective of Courtney or me like a mama bear. And she could also get that mad at me.

Not that I was blameless in our little history of fights. I had the bad habit of not backing down even when I should. This was no exception. I fought back.

"I have a better chance of figuring this out than those fools."

"It's obstruction! You could go to jail. It's a crime, Cooper. You committed a crime."

"Obstruction Schmobstruction. I could have given them the entire file, and they'd call it obstruction if they wanted to because it did not have a bow on it or I didn't say please and thank you or a word was transcribed wrong. If they want to jam me, they will no matter what, and if they don't, they'll let it slide. There's no real crime here. It's not so black and white."

"If I am asked a direct question about what we knew, I will tell the truth."

I felt a heat wave rise from my chest to my scalp. I was pretty sure my cheeks were turning red. Courtney's presence on the other side of the wall was all that kept me from yelling.

"Now why would you do that?" I asked, my sense of betrayal dripping from my mouth like drool from a horror movie zombie.

"Why would I not?" There was no venom, no meanness to her question. It's how calm, how comfortable she was with her position. That pissed me off even more.

"Say that again?" I asked.

"Why wouldn't I? It's not like you don't know me. I come from big business, and it could as well have been the government. I am most comfortable inside big institutions. Joining you in this agency was my big, scary leap of faith, but I still work best with institutional clients and partners. I like to work with the system, not against it.

"And here you go telling the Miami-Dade Police Department a blatant lie, right in my face. I won't sell you out. I won't volunteer anything. But I will stay true to me—a 'me' you know well, I might add."

"Yeah, I know you. You do what you have to, Ms. CJ Do Right. But I'm not going to leave this in the hands of a bunch of cops juggling twenty other cases and tripping all over each other. I'm in this, and I'm going to figure this shit out because that's what I'm paid to do and because someone does not want me to. I'm going to do it because it fucking matters. And I'm going to do it without bending the knee to the badge." I could feel my heart pounding in my chest as my emotions rose, and I worked on not letting my voice rise with them.

"We must work with the police, not against them," CJ replied. Her faith in law, order, and the institutions that represented them was unshaken by my tirade. I knew it wouldn't be. It was part of her upbringing. Grandma Vinh had been like a second mother to her after CJ's parents divorced, and the GI grandma had married died in a training accident. She infused respect for elders and authority into CJ.

My partner was right about one thing. I knew her. And I should have known this argument would get me nowhere. That didn't stop me from mouthing on.

"We work with them when we can," I said. "It so happens this is not one of those times."

"We have obligations to a civilized society," CJ answered, unfazed, not a blush to her cheek or a hair out of place. What might have sounded like a stump speech from anyone else came out like a perfectly natural statement coming from her.

The problem was, I couldn't care less how sincere she was right then. I was a little ball of pent-up energy. Her unnatural calm only fired me up more.

"We have obligations to our client," I said. Even to my own ears, I started to sound more like a growling beast than a human being. "I have obligations to myself."

"These obligations are not incompatible."

"I hate to tell you, but, sometimes, they are fucking incompatible." I shook my head and exhaled deeply. I realized my hands were balled up into fists. I forced them open, turned around, opened the door, and walked to my office.

We'd argued enough over the years that I could tell when it was down to playing ping pong, talking past each other. CJ recognized the impasse too. I heard her sit down behind me. Keys were clicking on her computer before I crossed the hallway.

I sat down behind my desk, took a deep breath, and tried to let the moment pass, staring at the screen for another minute. Then I powered down and walked out of the office.

CHAPTER 13

I dropped off the CR-V at the dealership to have the busted back window replaced. They gave me a base Accord as a loaner, and I drove home to change into shorts and running shoes before heading to the beach. A run beat a binge, and I knew myself well enough to know it was a likely alternative.

I started on my run focused on the sound of the waves, feeling the packed sand under the soles of my shoes. I emptied my head of all other thoughts. Then I let them trickle back in, nice and slow.

I was nowhere on the Morrison murder. I had no suspect and no motive. For all I knew, the perp was long gone, out of the state, maybe out of the country. I didn't know whether Morant's murder was connected. Both had been brutal, savage even. Had Morant pissed off the same people who tried to scare me off? I had too many questions and not enough answers. I'd still try and take a forensic team to the ship on Sunday in case Morant had it all set before he died. It was worth a shot. Other than that, I'd focus on his death.

My feet continued to pound the sand as my mind ran through the cases. Left, right, left, right . . . . The sound of my heartbeat merged with the waves. I ran around groups of people. Some waved. Most just kept talking among themselves. I kept running. Thoughts kept forming in my head.

Rodríguez said Morant had died from blunt force trauma, maybe a baseball bat. Unless he was taken by surprise, it would have taken more than one person. Morant was tall, strong, knew his stuff. So maybe this wasn't related to Morrison. Morrison's murder felt improvised, with his head split open and the door left open.

Fuck. This was all speculation. I needed facts. I needed information. I needed to do a little goddamn police work, and I would need to do it without a badge or a friendly judge with a quick pen on warrants. An idea started building up in my mind, one that would not make CJ happy.

I slowed down my pace before I passed out from the heat, ocean breeze and all. I walked the rest of the way back to the parking lot where I'd left the Accord. I turned the engine on and let it run without getting in while the A/C did its thing.

While I leaned on the car, still panting, still thinking, I pulled out my cell and sent a text to CJ. "Sorry I got mad," it said. I was man enough to admit that much. No point in staying mad either. I wouldn't change her mind, and it only aggravated me. If I said more than that, I'd be full of shit and she'd know it.

My bad idea was taking residence in my head, so I drove home, showered, changed, grabbed one of the cameras I used on surveillance, and got back in the car. I pointed the Accord toward the airport and the nearby Mardi Gras offices. There was just enough rush hour traffic to give me cover and plenty of light for a good look-see at the place.

I drove around the block, grateful for once for the slow pace of traffic. I snapped pictures as I drove, arm extended toward the open passenger window. The professional-grade Nikon and its telephoto lens felt heavy in my hand. I tried not to shake as I took photo after photo, hoping I'd have enough clear ones to cover the perimeter. I would need them to refresh my memory and zoom in on details later.

I crawled down the street, breathing the exhaust from the beater in front of me. The front of the building was as I remembered it. There were two buildings joined together. Both looked like warehouses. The smaller one now housed the offices where I'd barged in twice within a week. The larger one had its own door, which I had not noticed before. It looked heavy, maybe metal, painted the same white as the walls.

I went around the block. The first side street was a working loading dock, with four semis backed up and a squad of workers in sweat-stained T-shirts hustling to load or unload their cargo. The back of the structure was hidden from the street by a line of trees, though not one so thick I couldn't glimpse past it. It looked like a short fence on the other side of the sidewalk, then maybe a courtyard. I focused on the building, catching slices of it through the trees as I drove as slowly as I dared without getting noticed. There was at least one back door—one I could see, anyway. Maybe the camera captured more details.

The second side street fronted the employee parking lot. I drove past more quickly and left the area. I had all I needed and went straight home.

Once there, I even managed to put all the pictures more or less in the right order on all the right devices. Things were looking up, but that had been the easy part. I was about to cross another line. I dialed Courtney's cell.

She picked up on the second ring and knew better than to expect more small talk than "hi" or "what's up" from me.

"I'd like us to meet tonight," I told her once those were out of the way. "It's work, but it's off the books, even from CJ. You do not have to come if that makes your Spidey sense go off. And you won't have to go through what we'll talk about if you come, either. No problem either way. I probably shouldn't even be making this call."

"Well, now I have to come and listen, at least. You made me curious."

I had a feeling that would be the kind of answer I would get.

"Curiosity killed the cat," I said, meaning it as a warning. To Courtney, it probably sounded like a challenge, and I'd never known her to turn those down.

"Satisfaction brought it back," came the cheery response. "It wouldn't be the first time curiosity got me in trouble. I'm still here to talk about it."

I had a feeling that was probably true.

"Alright, then." I named a restaurant with a popular and crowded happy hour and we hung up.

I changed into a nicer shirt and headed into the city's twilight on a Friday night. I love Miami, this illegitimate child of New York and Havana, in all of its glorious, sweaty mess. I love its energy, its rhythm.

Working two murders, I didn't love it tonight. The city was too bright across the windshield. It was too noisy, reaching past the sheet metal into the car, pulsating inside my head. A young kid was walking on the sidewalk, shirt half unbuttoned, high-top sneakers on his feet, and giant headphones on his head. I envied the headphones. I craved quiet. I craved some peace.

I got to the restaurant's bar early, taking my tablet with me. I elbowed my way through a thick crowd of loud people with drinks in their hands. I leaned against a wall, on the lookout for a table. I was lucky, and it did not take long before a hostess in an impeccable business suit called a party of four colorfully dressed people to the dining room. I slid right behind them, claiming their high top and pointedly ignoring the glare from the matronly woman who'd spilled her drink trying to rush to the same corner of real estate only to find me sitting there first.

I ordered a rye, two waters, and a hummus platter from the waitress who appeared out of the mass of humanity surrounding me.

"Coming up," she said, her voice sounding hoarse from straining to be heard by the parade of patrons she'd already served.

I tucked the tablet under my leg and waited for the order and food to arrive.

Courtney came in ten minutes later, dressed the way a young woman should in a place like this—high heels, mini skirt, and a top that made her tits look even better than they usually did. She saw me right away and twisted her hips this way and that, carving a path through throngs of people until she took a seat next to me. She greeted me with a peck on the cheek and ordered a cosmo from the waitress who once again materialized at the right moment.

"I appreciate you not making it look like work," I said as we settled back in our chairs, "but you went above and beyond."

"Me?" she asked, throwing her shoulders back and putting her fingers on her cleavage. "Maybe I thought I might stay a while after we talk shop."

I chuckled, more at myself than anything else. "Hell, if I were your age and had your looks, I'd stay a while after the old man's gone, too."

"Thank you," she said, taking the compliment for what it was. "Now, what is all this mystery about?"

"Mardi Gras' offices," I said. "Can you find out what kind of security system they use?"

Courtney looked at me from the corner of her eye, grinning. "You want me to hack?"

"Since when do I tell you how to do your job?" I asked, reprising our routine. "I'm talking about . . . research."

When she spoke again, all traces of a smile had disappeared from her face. "You're seriously thinking about breaking into their offices."

"I'm not thinking about it. I'm doing it if I can. I need to get into Morant's office."

"When?"

"Tomorrow night. Any later and the cops will have beaten me to it."

She leaned back, her mouth pouting as if to whistle, but no sound came out. "You're right," she said. "CJ would not like this."

"And you don't have to get in the middle of it if you don't want to. I can pretend this conversation never happened."

"I'm a big girl. I can make my own decisions. And in this case, I trust you more than the cops to figure this out, so, basically, I happen to agree with you. *This time.*" She let the weight of those last two words hang for a moment. I nodded my understanding.

"All right, then," she said. "I'm in. Those are secondary offices, right, essentially old warehouses?"

"Yes. I have no idea if security was upgraded, but I did a little recon this afternoon."

I handed her the tablet. She scrolled through the pictures. Her eyebrows had lowered over her eyes, wrinkling her nose. She was fixated on the screen, unblinking. She moved from picture to picture, swiping the screen with her index finger in quick flicks of her wrists. With her other hand, she mindlessly dipped carrots in the hummus.

"It should be doable," she said, as much to herself as to me. "Most of the information we need should be open-source."

"Should?"

She looked up from the screen.

"Should. No guarantees in life but death and taxes."

I slid the tablet closer and found the picture of the warehouse's front door. "This door looks heavy to you?" I asked.

She took the tablet back and flipped between a few pictures, zooming here and pinching there, eating a piece of celery in between, changing the view quicker than my eyes could process.

"Maybe," she said. "All the doors have at least one camera. I see where you're going, though. Maybe this one has less electronic security inside because it has more heft. I just can't tell, at least not yet."

She put herself back in continuous motion over the tablet. I could barely register what she was looking at by the time she was looking at something else. She spoke as much to herself as to me.

"The docks are the most vulnerable physically—built to go in and out. On the flip side, they're covered with cameras. Biggest shrinkage comes from the loading dock in places like that."

Courtney had used the euphemism for employee theft as if she worked in retail. I knew what she said was true. I'd known it since my college days studying criminal justice. Part of me wanted to ask how the fuck she knew that, to start peeling the veil of mystery still hanging over her. But I decided to leave that for another day.

"Can I airdrop those pictures to my phone?" Courtney asked, pulling me out of my reverie.

"Sure."

She did that while I made a scribbling motion in the air, asking our waitress for the check. When I looked back in Courtney's direction, she had an impish smile on her face.

"This will be fun," she said.

I saw the waitress approach from the other direction. The bill came my way, and my credit card went hers.

"Time for you to stay a while?" I asked. I sounded like an indulgent dad—or maybe a dotting uncle.

Courtney must have thought so too.

"Don't tell mom!" she said, batting her eyelashes, elbows to her side, arms squeezing her chest, mouth open to mimic a shrieking teenager.

"My lips are sealed."

I got my card back and signed the receipt. By the time that was done, Courtney had given me a peck goodbye, picked up her cosmo, and, just like that, she was gone, swallowed up by a younger crowd. I smiled to myself and sank back into the seat. I swirled the rye in my glass. Tonight, I could have just one. Tonight, I had a plan.

CHAPTER 14

Zero-Two-Forty, wee hours of Sunday morning. It was raining like it only rains in the tropics, and, that night, Miami qualified. It was raining so hard that "sheets of rain" was no longer just an expression. I couldn't see past the windows.

I sat hunched on a chair in my breakfast nook, staring at the black knapsack still covered with rivulets of water at my feet. My clothes clung to me like a second skin, if one's own skin could feel that unpleasant—clammy and cold.

The knapsack held the contents of my illicit expedition to Mardi Gras. It wasn't much—a busted hard drive from a locked drawer in Morant's desk and two thumb drives I palmed from an unlocked one, but at least I'd gotten there before the boys in blue. I'd also liberated a zip lock full of marijuana. It wasn't for personal consumption. The four-twenty wasn't my jam. I figured it wasn't the cops' business if it had been Morant's.

I pulled the last item from the inside pocket of my rain jacket. I opened the faded credentials wallet, its leather cracked with age. Morant's name stared back at me from a distant past. That Owen Morant had been an Inspector for the Jamaica Constabulary. Morant had kept the keepsake with him. Maybe CJ or Courtney might find a next of kin to pass it on to, and it wouldn't have to spend years in isolation in an evidence locker.

The op had been improvised by most standards, but, if you looked at it from the outside, it had gone smoothly. Courtney had done her part and dived into the security system. It was old and had weaknesses. After a little brainstorming, we'd decided to keep it simple. I short-circuited it—a quick and dirty job that could be blamed on some random hoodlum and would give me ten or fifteen minutes while the home office tried to troubleshoot what showed up as a malfunction.

That had been enough time for me to search Morant's desk and get a general idea of the place from the inside, not that it taught me much. There were a couple of offices, a small cubicle farm, and a large warehouse. In short, it was exactly what it looked like from the outside.

The cold and dampness penetrated my body. My teeth clattered. My fingers shook. I peeled my clothes off. Peeling was just about right. They stuck to me as I pulled them off, coming off with a sucking round, like peeling the back of a sticker.

I was still shaking. I thought about getting in the shower to warm up, then I changed my mind. I wasn't cold, not that cold anyway, not anymore. The shakes came from the adrenaline leaving my body. I recognized the sensation. My brain started flooding with memories. *Don't flash back!*

I focused on the mundane. Four steps to the bedroom, two more to the dresser. Count them. One, two. Open the drawer. Pull out a pair of sweats and a T-shirt. Walk to the foot of the bed. Count the steps. Put the clothes on, one leg, one arm at a time. Sit on the bed, look around the room. Notice the walls, notice the furniture. Breathe. Above all, breathe.

My hands steadied. Little by little, mentally staying in the room no longer required an effort. I stood up and exhaled. I could relax now. I was back. I'd never really left this time.

Whatever happened to me at moments like this wasn't bad compared to what others go through. And it never happened to me in the middle of the action. It came later, in the dark of night. That was enough for me to justify stating I had no mental impediment to owning guns and staying away from the VA's head shrinkers.

Just then, the doorbell rang. I went to the door. It was still raining so hard that I could only see a shape on the security system's screen. My heart was beating a little too fast in my chest. Did something go wrong? Was a cop on my front porch? Or Dunn's thugs? My .45 was still in the gun safe in the other room. I opened the door anyway.

Courtney was standing there in black jeans and a black sweater, so wet from the rain she looked like she was taking a shower with her clothes on.

"What are you doing here?" I asked, blurting the words. I took a step back to let her in.

"Bringing my contribution," she said, holding up a memory card.

"Your what?"

"Don't be mad . . . ."

Mad? I wasn't mad. I was in a state of disbelief, not sure what she was going to say next. My mouth was hanging open. I was staring at her without blinking, and yet I wasn't quite seeing her.

"Courtney, what did you do?" I asked.

Her answer came in something closer to a whisper than I expected.

"So, you see, when you took down the security system, you took down all the cameras, and, when that happened, I got into the warehouse from the loading dock and took pictures of what was there."

"Do you know how fucking dangerous that was?" I still wasn't mad. I was horrified. My heart was beating twice as fast now, like it had to beat for both me and Courtney in case hers stopped or ended up in prison. I could feel each beat in my temples. Words spilled out of my mouth. "I'm trained for this. You're not."

She pouted a bit.

"Well, not trained, but you don't know what I did in my misspent youth."

"Because you're old now?" The incongruity shocked me more than the extra layer of mystery that had just wrapped itself around the kid.

"You know what I mean."

"No, I don't, and it doesn't really matter right this moment. You could have . . . . You could have . . . . If something happened to you . . . ."

She whispered her answer again. "I know. You would have skinned yourself alive with guilt, and that's assuming CJ didn't flay you first. But seriously,

I was careful. I waited until all the red lights on all the cameras went out, and I stayed in dark corners, and, afterward, I drove around in circles and I'm pretty sure I wasn't followed." Her words must have sounded as hollow to her as to me. "Maybe, you know, it wasn't as smart or professional as I thought. I'm sorry."

My ears stopped ringing with the sound of my blood pumping through my veins long enough to realize she was still standing there, sopping wet, dripping water on the tile floor.

"No, I'm sorry," I said. I forced a smile. "I'll get you a towel." I turned on my heels to do just that when Courtney called after me.

"Coop, you think..."

"Yeah?" I asked, looking back at her over my shoulder.

"Maybe I could borrow an old T-shirt or something while this dries a bit?" She was tugging at her sweater.

"Sure. Yeah. I'll get it for you." I double quicked it to the bedroom and pulled out a towel, a T-shirt, and a pair of running shorts that would be way too big on her but might not fall off her if she tied them tight enough. I laid it all on the bed and came back out.

"Take your time," I told her. "I'll make some coffee."

"Thanks."

A couple of minutes later, the smell was already starting to permeate the room, chasing away the wet-dog odors Courtney and I had brought in. Coffee fixed everything. I was even starting to calm down.

I could not help but snicker when Courtney reappeared. My clothes looked like a clown suit on her, except where her chest pushed the shirt farther than it was meant to.

"I look ridiculous," she said, "but I'm dry and mildly warm."

"That's good," I said.

"I used your hairbrush," she said. "Tell your girlfriend it's my fault if she finds strands of blond in there."

"No worries. I'm beating them off with a stick anyway."

She held up her wrung-out clothes in her hand. "Is it okay if I throw those in the wash?"

"Yeah, of course."

"You want me to throw yours in too?" She was pointing at the pile of wet clothes on the floor, where I left them a few moments before.

If I had been given to blushing, I'm sure I would have. I certainly felt embarrassed enough. Courtney smiled and saved me from answering her. She just picked up the pile.

I pointed the way to the mud room. Courtney went in, did all the things I should have done, then her bare feet slapped on the tiles as she made her way back to the kitchen.

"The coffee smells wonderful," she said.

"You want some eggs with it? That's about all I can offer you except beer or whiskey."

"N . . . . Actually, yes. I'm starving. Would you mind?"

"Sure."

I poured some coffee, and Courtney took her mug to the breakfast table. I cracked some eggs, whisked them in a pan with some cheese into a semblance of a scramble, and threw in some bacon for good measure. That marked the limits of my culinary talents away from the grill. Courtney sipped her coffee quietly while I worked. Color was returning to her cheeks as she took in the hot liquid.

I slid the eggs and bacon onto two plates, brought them to the table, topped off our coffees, and finally sat down.

"I have a gift for you," I said.

"Besides the best sober breakfast ever at drunk-breakfast hour?" she asked with a mouth full of eggs.

"Besides that." I leaned over and dragged the knapsack next to my chair. I pulled out the hard drive.

Courtney's face lit up like a kid's at Christmas. She reached for it with both hands, the best sober breakfast ever forgotten on her plate.

"Gimme, gimme!" she said.

She took hold of the drive. She turned the device around in her hands.

The little wrinkle just over her nose she gets when she concentrates on something returned to her face.

"Somebody really did a number on this," she said.

"Can you get something out of it?"

"I don't know." She put the hunk of metal on the table and looked at me, wolfing down some of her eggs at the same time. "But I'll find out. Do you have more?"

"Eggs or tech?" I asked, chuckling.

"Tech!"

I grinned and went to fetch my laptop while she polished her plate. I sat back down, the computer in front of me, then plucked the two thumb drives from the knapsack. I was about to plug one into the laptop when Courtney slapped her hand over mine.

"Are you insane?" she shouted.

"What?"

"Your laptop is on Wi-Fi, connected to a dozen things, not to mention the internet, which is, well, the entire world. And you're going to plug a random thumb drive in there, a stolen thumb drive no less, one you know nothing about and could contain all kinds of malware?"

I did my best to keep a straight face.

"And that's bad, right?"

She held her hands on either side of her face, mouth half open, as if she was wondering how I could be that much of a bumbling idiot when it came to this stuff.

"Just bring them to the office on Monday," she said.

"I will. Can we check your memory card, then?" Coffee and the evening's rush were keeping me awake.

Courtney had grabbed the memory card containing her ill-advised, not to mention illicit work in the Mardi Gras warehouse before I was done asking the question. She plugged it into the laptop. A few moments and clicks of the mouse later, pictures were populating the screen.

"What are we looking for?" Courtney asked, leaning over the table, face straining toward the computer.

"You've cruised, right?"

"Yes, of course."

"Then you know, or at least you can guess, what goes aboard a cruise ship. We're looking for anything that's out of place."

I looked at her, saw how eager she was. I put my hand on the mouse to distract her from the screen. I put my other hand on her shoulder. I needed her attention.

"Look," I said, "there likely won't be anything. You took a big risk on low odds. If you really want to get in the field, I'll train you. CJ will too. You're tough, and you're smart. You'll be good at it. But you've got to promise me not to go rogue like this again."

She looked back at me. Her features had softened, and she looked tired all of a sudden.

"I would like that very much," she said. "And I promise."

"Okay. Let's take a look, then."

We went through the pictures at a leisurely pace marked by the clicks of the mouse. Most of the crates had foodstuff of one sort or another. There were cases after cases of booze and coffee. Further back, we saw supplies spanning more than the ship's restaurants and bars, things like toilet paper, light bulbs, or bed sheets. The stamped labels on the crates boasted the vendors' compliance with the U.S. Public Health Service.

"I know it's a party boat," Courtney said, letting a whistle escape, "but they have washers, don't they? How much linen do they need?"

I gave a courtesy chuckle as we kept clicking through. The pictures captured posters on the wall pledging loyalty to the Stevedores' Union. I was surprised I could make them out.

"How did you get that much light?" I asked, worried at what the answer might be.

"I have a night mode on my camera. It uses long exposures, and there was just enough light to make it work."

"You did a good job." I meant it and felt a little guilty for thinking she might have screwed up.

We scrolled some more. My eyelids were getting heavy. Courtney had to be battling sleep too, no matter the fifteen-year advantage or so she had on me. I didn't want to cut her work short, though, so we kept going. By the time we were done, nothing looked out of place.

"We'll go through them again next week," I said. "Often enough, you see things the second or third time around you missed the first time."

"Okay," she said. Her voice was firm, but her rounded shoulders betrayed her disappointment. She got up, stretching her back and grunting.

"Do you want the guest room for a few hours?" I asked. She looked left and right from one end of the house to the other, trying to decide.

"You're sure?" she asked.

"Yeah. I don't want you falling asleep at the wheel."

"Me neither."

"It's done then. Good night."

"Thanks, Coop. Good night."

We retreated to our respective dreamlands without another word.

CHAPTER 15

I'd never needed much sleep. I was grateful for that on that Sunday morning. I only had a couple of hours before it was time to get my forensic team to the *Rio*.

I woke up feeling uneasy about it. I did not relish the thought of having to sneak in. I was skirting the law again if I wasn't breaking it outright. CJ would say it was no way to solve a case. It shouldn't be. That little voice in the back of my head was nagging me again, telling me this was out of control, that I should let it go. I ignored it just like I'd ignored it every other time it piped up. I was going to do whatever needed doing.

I'd nearly forgotten that Courtney had taken the guest room. In my brooding, I hadn't heard her get up. By the time I was showered and dressed, she was back in her own clothes, standing in the living room, looking ready to go. An indentation in the couch told me she'd just stood up when she heard my bedroom door open. She had her hands together and was looking at me. She opened her mouth a couple of times as if trying to figure out what to say.

"Thanks for not yelling at me too much last night," she finally said. "You know, for acting like the wrong kind of maverick."

"Sit down a minute," I told her. She did, and I sat next to her on the couch. The house was silent for a moment. It wasn't a bad silence. It politely waited to be filled and gave us room to talk.

"You thanked me for not yelling at you too much," I said. "But maybe I did. Fact is, we would have nothing at all without you. I couldn't have gotten in. As for you going rogue, you showed initiative—maybe not in the way I'd have preferred—but initiative. I shouldn't have scolded you for that."

Courtney reached out for my hand. "Thanks, Coop. Truth be told, I didn't really sleep last night thinking about all that. This means a lot. And I know I should have talked to you first. That was dumb."

"It's in the past. I'm curious why you did it, though."

"You ever wonder why I went to work for you instead of some tech company?"

"All the time. I asked you that at your interview, and you gave me some canned answer about figuring out what you wanted to do and a PI agency sounded like fun. I knew it was bullshit, and you knew I knew it. I also didn't care. You were obviously smart, and that was good enough for me. CJ saw the same thing I did."

"It wasn't completely canned." Courtney was talking with that tone people have when they're half talking to themselves. "I *was* trying to figure it out. I've always been kinda bored with life. I'm really good at tech, but it's not a passion. I wouldn't want to do that and nothing but that for the rest of my life."

"Okay, I hear you."

"Boredom is how I ended up doing stupid shit in my . . . even younger days," she added with a chuckle. "Anyway, you're right that working a front desk sounding like fun was bullshit. I just needed a job. But then, CJ and you started giving me more and more to do, things that actually helped you investigate. I loved that—finding answers. Long story short, I do want to do more, and not all of it from behind a computer."

She looked at me from the corner of her eye, gauging my reaction.

"If you want to get in the field, CJ and I will get you properly trained. You don't need to go rogue again."

"Just like that?"

"The way I look at it, it's to our benefit, too. So, yeah, that's the deal if you want it."

"I do," she said. "It is. Deal. Absolutely."

"Good. Then I'll talk to CJ about it tomorrow."

She stood up and made a fist with one hand. She looked like Tiger Woods sinking a birdie at Augusta. "Thanks," she said.

"Consider it done."

She walked out with a determined gait and a grin on her face. She looked back at me from the front door. "Good luck with the *Rio*!"

"I may need it."

I didn't have much to do to get ready after she was gone. I had already put on my most stained T-shirt, ragged pair of jeans, and dug out my work boots from the recesses of my closet. I just had one call to make. Courtney had been part of planning today's little excursion, but not all of it. CJ and I had stayed behind, wargaming worst-case scenarios, just the two of us.

We'd accepted there was nothing we could do if we were ambushed on board. If someone tried something stupid at the Port or on the water, on the other hand, maybe we could increase our chances. We rented a motorboat and bought a sat phone that would work offshore. Neither was cheap, but we had cleared it with Heather, who was all too happy to approve the expense. CJ would be positioned some distance from the port with a pair of strong binoculars, ready to take action. She was probably at the dock now with the rest of the gang.

The gang in question included my old friend Danny. The motorboat would be too far for his sniper rifle, no matter how good he was with it. But once I'd called him to bounce a couple of ideas off him, there was no keeping him away. He'd driven up from Key West at dawn.

The last member of our motley crew had a more helpful weapon: a radio. A friend of CJ's dad, a recently retired Coast Guard officer, would be ready to cut in on the right frequency and could speak the right lingo. The Coast Guard provided security for the berthed cruise ships with Rigid Hull Inflatable Boats—basically big bad Zodiacs. Those RHIBs and their .50-caliber machine guns could mean the difference between living and dying if things went wrong on the water.

I called the number CJ had texted me for the sat phone she'd purchased for the occasion. It rang, and my partner answered. Her voice provided some reassurance.

"Everything good on your end?" I asked.

"Yes, we're loading the coolers now."

I smiled at the picture of those three straddling dock and ship, passing coolers along like they were going fishing. No one would know those coolers held a military-grade radio and the disassembled rifle Danny insisted on bringing, "just in case." Nobody said coolers could only carry beer, sandwiches, or bait inside.

"Good," I said. "I'm sure we won't need what's in them, but I'm glad you're there."

"We'll be in position."

"Thanks, CJ."

"You got it."

I instantly regretted not letting her know about breaking into Morant's office the night before. The theory that what she didn't know wouldn't hurt her sounded weaker the longer I used it as an excuse. I pushed the thought out of my head over another cup of coffee. I sat down, and spent the time I had focusing on the task at hand. I would deal with my decision later.

CHAPTER 16

I drove up to see a buddy of mine first. The beat-up pickup truck I'd asked to borrow was sitting in the driveway as I pulled up. Jim must have seen me coming. He walked out the door just as I extricated myself from the Accord.

"What the hell is that?" he asked, looking at the Accord with horror.

"What the hell kind of a greeting is this?" We clasped hands, smiling at each other. "The CR-V's getting some work done. They gave me this to drive."

He shrugged and jerked his thumb toward the pickup.

"You really want *that* for a stakeout?"

"Yeah. It's just a few hours' surveillance down by the docks." It didn't feel like a lie. I would be doing some kind of surveilling and I would technically be close to the docks. There was no point telling Jim too much. It would only get him in trouble if I was caught somewhere I shouldn't be.

"Suit yourself. But work done or not, that CR-V is mine if anything happens to the truck."

"The CR-V is worth four times this rust bucket," I said, pointing at the faded, rust-ridden tailgate behind Jim. "How 'bout I don't let anything happen to this fine example of American engineering, and then we won't have to debate the issue?"

"Even better. That and a beer," Jim said.

"You drive a hard bargain, man. I guess I owe you one for making you drive a sedan, even for a few hours."

"You damn right you do. With a little luck, it will never leave the driveway. But just to be seen with it on my property . . . . You owe me big time right there."

We were both laying it thick and loving it. A beer with Jim never sounded bad. We shook on it and swapped keys. He went inside to escape the hot sun. I hopped into the truck. It had no air conditioning. The steering wheel burnt my hands, and the dash radiated heat. I puffed my cheeks and exhaled. This would be a long drive.

I headed to a parking lot behind a bunch of big-box stores to pick up the rest of my team. They looked the dock-worker part like I'd asked. They'd even repacked their equipment in a collection of lunch boxes and canvas bags.

Finding two techs willing to go in covertly had taken some doing, but we got two good ones to commit, and I'd sent the names to Morant. Keeping them on board had been even harder after Morant died, but we'd all agreed at the office that the techs should know about it, so they did. We'd pleaded and begged and thrown in a fair amount of bribery to make it work. In the end, Hank Tao and Liam Saban's skinny frames were there, on time, looking the part and waiting for me on a mostly deserted parking lot. They were some of the best around, and I'd take these two, no questions, outrageous "weekend" rate and all.

Even with the windows open on the ride over, the truck still felt like an oven when the two techs climbed in.

"Thanks for coming, guys," I said.

The heat swallowed whatever they were about to say, reducing words to grunts. Hank wore denim shorts and was shifting from one leg to another on the leather seats. I put the truck back in gear and rolled on toward the port. Before long, my team acclimated to the heat and sat back for the ride.

Traffic was light at this hour. Later, the thousands of tourists who thronged to the cruise ships would clog the approach to the port. For now, they were only trickling in, like water dripping from the end of a hose before it flows fully through.

Even so, we were backed up by a few cars approaching the gate. When only two vehicles were left in front of us, I could see the skinny white kid manning the booth. He looked like a college student barely out of puberty, making a show out of carefully inspecting every last driver's license. I rolled my eyes and drummed my fingers against the door, hanging my arm through the open window.

We reached the booth and I handed all three licenses to the kid. He laid them up in front of him and started typing on his keyboard. It took him a moment before he looked back up. "Uhhh . . . I don't find you on any passengers list," he said. "You're sure you're at the right port?" He looked behind us, a quick, side-glance look, probably worried we'd hold up the line even more than he already was.

"We're sure we have work to do out back," I said. "You're looking at the wrong list."

"Oh, right. Shit. I mean, sorry."

"'Doesn't fucking matter. You got another list, don't you?"

He answered with a vigorous nod and a thin smile, pulling a clipboard from a nail on the wall. Working stiffs didn't rank a place on his computer. It only took him a few seconds after that. His shoulders relaxed, and he fumbled for a pen to put three check marks in front of three names. He was probably supposed to ask us what cruise line hired us or which contractor we worked for. He was too flustered for protocol by then. He just handed back our licenses and waved us through.

We rolled along a broken line of early travelers, their cars and SUVs loaded with luggage. When they turned one way into the parking garage or the other way to the drop-off zone, I kept going straight. Soon, the cruise ships were behind us and squat buildings appeared in front. There was nothing but pavement between us and the warehouses. I drove slowly, cautiously, my foot barely touching the accelerator. I didn't figure a bunch of day laborers would be in a hurry.

Liam looked a little pale against the passenger door. "Perk up, guys," I said for his benefit. "We'll either find our friends or turn around. That's the worst that can happen."

Hank gave me a tight-lipped smile and Liam nodded. I doubted either one meant it or believed me. Maybe they shouldn't have. My heart was pounding in my chest too. It wasn't a complete lie, though. Those were the most likely outcomes. Just not the only ones.

I found the warehouse Morant had described the last time I saw him. The last time I would ever see him. I parked backward for a quick exit should we need it, and we all got out of the truck. I kept reminding myself not to hurry even though we'd passed through the gate late. I looked toward the ocean, past ten or fifteen feet of overgrowth. I couldn't see anything, but there could be a small boat bobbing against the sea wall.

"This way," I called out to my team as I headed across the vegetation. The guys followed me at a distance, a little slower, weighed down by their gear.

I was about halfway through when I saw it—a Zodiac waiting for us. Its engine hummed along, louder than the waves. I focused my eyes on the two men in the boat and raised a closed-fisted hand in the international signal for "stop and drop." I was hoping the techs had watched enough war movies to get it. Their footsteps stopped.

I took the last few steps toward the ocean alone—three more steps toward the outboard and the men in it. Three more steps toward the two guns pointed straight at me.

CHAPTER 17

The man at the front of the boat had a military posture. He stood straight-backed, legs apart for balance, eyes like a laser cut in a hard face, hair high and tight. He held his gun like he'd done it before, steady despite the boat's movements, displaying a textbook grip with his index finger on the trigger guard, both eyes open.

The tall, thin black man with sunken eyes behind him made me think I was seeing a ghost for a second, but he was half Morant's age. He held his gun properly, but he was a little unsteady. His aim wavered—barely, but you could tell. I'd seen it before. Nearly everyone shook like that the first time they pointed a weapon at another human being. He'd been taught to shoot, but he'd only shot at paper targets.

I took one last step toward the water's edge. I was already too close for them to miss, so I might as well look them in the eye. I pointed at the front man's gun. "Owen said he trusted you. He said you were the good guys. If he's right, I'd hate to see the bad dudes."

"Say your name!" came the response. The gun barrel was still pointed at my chest.

"Cooper Malone. But you knew that already."

"You're the one here for Morrison."

"I am. For him and for Owen, too."

Before the man in front could answer, the one at the back screamed at me, arms outstretched, finger on the trigger, visibly shaking now. "Did you kill my dad?" His voice pierced through the waves and chilled the soul.

You're Morant's kid? No wonder I'm seeing ghosts.

A direct answer would have to wait.

"Do me a favor, son," I said. "Put that finger back on the trigger guard. Your dad wouldn't want you to have blood on your hands by being careless."

The kid took his eyes off me and stared at his hand and the pistol in it. He jerked his finger away and lowered the gun. A tear started forming at the corner of his eye.

"I did not kill your dad," I told him. "We were working together. We wanted the same thing. I think you and I still want the same thing—to find out who killed him."

"But you're here for Morrison," he said. Tears were flowing freely now.

"Like I said, I'm here for both of them. Morrison, someone's paying me for. Your dad, that's personal."

The man in front had holstered his gun while Junior and I were talking. He spoke up now. "I'm Marco Ruiz. I was one of Owen's Deputy VPs, supervising at-sea security. You and your team may come aboard. And I'll hold you to that promise, Mr. Malone. Owen was a friend."

I signaled the techs to come forward, and we transferred their gear into the Zodiac. The younger Morant moved to the back and sat down. Gently twisting the outboard's throttle, he maneuvered the boat to keep it against the jetty while we stepped aboard. The techs weren't exactly grace personified, but they made it, and that's all that mattered. I was the last one to leave dry land behind.

I shook Ruiz's hand, the kind of firm handshake I'd expected from him, then worked my way back to Owen's son. I put a hand on his shoulder. His gaze was unflinching, looking ahead, clearing the boat's course with his eyes.

"I'm sorry about your dad," I said. "I didn't know him well, but I knew him well enough to like him."

The kid nodded, eyes still on the horizon. "Most people did. That's just the way he was. I'm Ollie, by the way."

"Nice to meet you."

Ollie slowed the boat a minute later as a Coast Guard RHIB approached us. The machine gunner was aiming safely away, but not so far away he couldn't traverse quickly and let loose a metric shit ton of lead on us if we proved to be a threat—or if he thought we were. If *she* thought we were, I corrected myself, taking a second look at the sailor behind the .50-cal.

Ruiz presented some kind of credentials and exchanged a few words with the RHIB's crew chief. I couldn't hear what they said over the engine noise, but it must have been the right words. The crew chief motioned behind him with his thumb, toward cruise ship row. Ollie twisted the throttle on the outboard. The Zodiac raised its nose and accelerated with a roar and a vortex of white water churning behind. A minute later, we were speeding along gleaming white hulls.

Ruiz put his gun in a lockbox as we pulled alongside the *Rio*'s loading bay, just past the aft tugboat marker. My team and I filed out behind him. Ollie waved and pulled the boat a distance away. I took one last look behind me. I could see the Zodiac bobbing in the waves. The small craft looked oddly reassuring in the big blue sea.

"This is a restricted area," a voice warned ahead of me. It belonged to a uniformed guard with a beer belly. Both his hands rested on a utility belt loaded with equipment he'd probably never used.

Ruiz flashed what looked like a credit card—probably some corporate ID, and the guard's attitude changed from self-important to dejected in one heartbeat.

"Oh . . . I . . . Ummm . . . So sorry, Mr. Ruiz," he stammered. "I didn't recognize you."

"It's okay," Ruiz said. "They're with me," he added, walking us and our bags around the metal detector.

"Sure thing, Mr. Ruiz."

The loading bay occupied the width of the ship. Across it, I could catch a glimpse of the pier through openings in the hull. A small army of forklifts was delivering pallets into the cavernous hangar. I smiled, wondering how many of those had been photographed by Courtney the night before. Once the loot was inside, an even bigger army of people armed with motorized hand carts was taking it all down unseen corridors into the ship's bowels.

Ruiz walked quickly through the loading bay, down a small corridor, then left into a wider passageway. I followed through two more turns, trying not to lose him or my techs in the chaos that was a cruise ship mid-replenishment. I dodged the electric carts loaded with supplies as best I could. The whir of their engines was the only warning before they'd take your ankles out. I caught up with Ruiz next to a service elevator. He was moving a hand back and forth toward us.

"Come on," he said, "The quicker we go, the fewer people see you."

The rest of the team joined up, a little out of breath, hauling their equipment. We crowded the little elevator, and Ruiz pushed the top button.

"This will take us straight to the VIP deck," he said.

When the doors opened again, I let out an appreciative whistle. I'd never seen a corridor that wide or carpet that thick on a cruise ship. Ruiz allowed no time for sightseeing and marched us down to the end of the passageway.

"The forwardmost suite is called the Grand Marshall Suite," he said as he walked. "There is only one of its kind on board. It was Morrison's."

Once we reached the door, Liam reached into his canvas bag and pulled out sterile booties and jumpsuits for everyone. The scene may have been tampered with a dozen ways from Sunday, but there was no point making it worse, and it gave me time to take one more look around. Nautical-themed art on the wall looked a notch above the poster-style quality we'd seen on the other decks. Except for a spot in the upper corner of the passageway that had just been patched up, with two wires left coming out of it, walls and floors were immaculate, not a smudge on the paint, all clean and airy.

We were done donning the moon suits, and Ruiz produced a key card and opened the wood-paneled double doors before I could ask him about the patch. He all but pushed us in, always an eye down the passageway. The cabin took my breath away. It covered two stories—two decks—with 20-foot windows from floor to ceiling overlooking the front half of the ship from on high. I could only imagine the view at sea.

Immediately to my right, there was a full-size bar with high-end liquor on the shelves and every shape of glass on the counter. I smirked; it was all so neat and clean now. I could imagine the way it looked during Morrison's wild nights, bottles all over the place, a broken glass in the sink, the bar top sticky with spills, the stir sticks, now politely in their container, upended, half of them on the floor. From the mental picture I had of Morrison, the bar would not have looked the way it did now for very long.

I turned around and realized the door had closed behind me. I mentally slapped my forehead. It's not like I hadn't been on cruise ships before. Cabin doors always close automatically.

"I thought the door was ajar the morning of the murder?" I asked Ruiz.

"Morrison and his friends always jammed something in the door to keep it open so partiers could come and go at will. It seems the killer forgot about it or didn't know, or didn't notice or care."

"Huh . . . ." Something about that was bothering me. I just couldn't put my finger on what.

I walked deeper into the cabin, intent on taking in the lay of the land, on seeing it the way it might have looked that night. I vaguely heard Ruiz suggest to the techs that they split the work by level, one upstairs and one downstairs, then the sound of hurried footsteps going up.

I looked around the suite, seeing it half as it was and half as it could have been the night of the murder. *This isn't a cabin*, I thought, *it's the fucking Taj Mahal at sea*. Even with the oversized leather couches and trendy furniture, the room was airy, bathed in sunlight. To the left, carpeted stairs led to the second level. Lots of people could easily mingle here, but there weren't many places to hide, not too many nooks and crannies.

"Where was the body found?" I asked.

"Under the stairs," Ruiz said

"The room would have had to be empty when it happened. There's no way that no one notices a body peeking out from beneath the stairs."

"Maybe they thought he'd passed out if you could not see the blood."

"Anything's possible."

I kept walking around, thinking. My gut was telling me the murder took place at the later part of the doc's estimate, after the room had cleared. One person stayed behind. Presumably one, anyway. A random drunk? A jealous guy? Someone Morrison knew? I mumbled my questions out loud but didn't expect Ruiz to pull out a magic wand or spew ready-made answers.

As I mulled, a flash of light caught my eye. The sun was shining brighter through one window.

"Was that pane of glass replaced?" I asked, directing the question at Ruiz.

He reached for his phone, which required some contortion with the moon suit on, opened an app, and started tapping and scrolling, talking as he found what he was looking for.

"Yes. And a centerpiece was missing from the room, a solid-metal abstract sculpture of some kind. The security staff speculated it was the murder weapon, and that the perp threw it through the window."

I nodded. Something still did not feel right. I headed upstairs on autopilot, Ruiz on my heels. Even expecting a new level of luxury, I couldn't help letting another slow whistle escape my lips. Besides a marbled bedroom and bathroom, the upper level had its own outdoor deck, complete with a hot tub overlooking the ocean.

"I'm in the wrong business," I said out loud.

"You're telling me," came a voice from behind the jacuzzi.

I walked around the tub and found Liam, folded over like a human origami, digging into plumbing below the floor in search of trace evidence. I put a hand on his shoulder.

"You already know."

I took a few steps and leaned against the railing, facing the ocean. On the horizon, container ships toiled in the shipping lanes. Closer in, fishermen and weekend sailors dotted the oceans. CJ would be on one of those, not that I could tell which.

Ruiz settled next to me. His gaze, too, locked on the ocean's vastness. We talked without looking away from the wild blue beneath.

"Something's weird with this scene," I said. "I don't get this perp. He could have chucked the murder weapon from up here, but instead, he breaks a window and risks someone hearing the glass shatter, even at that hour. And he leaves the door open. The body could have been discovered earlier. Fuck, *he* could have been discovered. That screams improvised crime, probably a crime of passion. And yet that same perp takes the time to clean up the blood. With bleach. All of it. Methodically."

I was inhaling the salt air between sentences, listening to the waves crash against the *Rio*'s hull. Ruiz nodded next to me, his gaze out toward the sea—or inward, deep inside his own mind. There was no way to tell.

"So, the perp is smart," he said, "or at least he thinks he is—I'll use 'he' for now even though we don't know. He knows he should erase traces of himself. He gets bleach, cleans the blood, and splashes more of it around the cabin. We found traces of it all over the place."

"Smart, but not a born killer," I said, keeping up with Ruiz's train of thought. "His brain does not fully engage. He panics right after the blow and chucks the murder weapon through the window like it's burning his hands. And he's not all there, not quite. He forgets about the door."

"For the window, he may not have known about the upper deck. This is the only two-deck cabin on the ship. But overall, I think that's a fair picture of our man—or woman."

We stayed silent for a while, contemplating our murderer, letting the ocean clear our minds.

"You think Owen's murder is related?" I eventually asked.

Ruiz groaned. "No way to know. It seems to be too close in time to Morrison's to be a coincidence. On the other hand, insisting we find Morrison's killer was not the only thing Owen was doing that ruffled a few feathers in the company."

"Like what?"

"Everything from calling out assholes who didn't like a black man for a boss, or a Latino for that matter," he added, poking a thumb at his chest, "to trying to slow down the flow of drugs onto our ships."

"Racism enough of a problem it could play into this?"

"Let me put it this way. Have you noticed how people from Southeast Asia fill most of the thankless jobs on the cruise ships?"

"Yeah. Not my favorite part of the experience."

"At the top, it's all about labor costs, not race. But some people on the ships seem to think it creates a human hierarchy like they're on a damn civil war plantation. So, yes, it's a problem."

"Fuck that."

We had fallen back into silence. I was taking in everything Ruiz had said—personal conflicts, the drugs, Morrison's death, the odd crime scene. I didn't have long to think it over, though. A booming voice in a southern drawl interrupted my thoughts, coming from downstairs yet easily heard from our perch.

"Will you look at that?" the deep voice blared. "We have regular astronauts on board gracing us with their heroic presence."

CHAPTER 18

Ruiz raced downstairs amid a flurry of mumbled curse words in Spanglish. I followed at a distance. This was his turf, and I didn't want to get in his way. By the time I reached the lower deck, he had squared off in front of the owner of the too-loud, southern voice. To say that was a big guy wouldn't do the man justice. He was plain fat. The tailored linen suit and starched white shirt he wore couldn't contain the massive belly hanging over his belt or the way skin and fat wiggled under his chin when he talked.

I made a beeline toward Hank, pretending to work while keeping an eye on our visitor from the corner of my eye. He was flanked by two uniformed guards, one of them the pot-bellied man who'd given us such a warm welcome back in the loading bay. The other was a skinny guy with bad teeth and a scraggly goatee who kept grinning at nothing.

"Barging in like a bull in a China shop again, Dagheretti?" Ruiz asked the intruder.

"See," the man drawled, "when the company's esteemed deputy *VeePee* comes aboard this here ship, and seeing how I'm the *Rio*'s Chief Security Officer, I can't help but think it's my duty to welcome you." The way he said the word *deputy* left no doubt he thought it should stay that way—if Ruiz had to be there at all.

"Consider me welcomed," Ruiz said.

If that was meant to end the conversation, it didn't work. Dagheretti went on.

"I also can't help but think it's my duty to inquire what people are doing poking around on my ship. It could well be a security risk."

The skinny man grinned even wider at that, showing off holes in his mouth where he was missing teeth.

"I assure you it isn't," Ruiz said.

"That's fine," Dagheretti answered. "It's just that I have trouble taking your word for it, notwithstanding all that jazz about rank and all, given the lack of courtesy you've shown me boarding my ship the way you did. Some might even think you were concealing your presence."

"This may come as a shock to you, Dagheretti, but this isn't your ship." Ruiz took half a step forward. Even in the moon suit, he exerted more authority than the man with the two flunkies by his side. "You serve on this ship. That's all. But you are right about rank. All security matters on all ships are within my purview. This one too."

I adjusted my stance in case this verbal joust became physical and Ruiz needed backup. I didn't make it obvious, and I doubted Ruiz would need much help, but I wanted to be ready if he did.

"Does this have anything to do with that Morrison business?" Dagheretti shuffled his feet back and forth. "The Board said, 'no investigation.' The company's policy is crystal clear. I must inquire about your business here." He probably wanted to take another step, match Ruiz's aggression, but he couldn't bring himself to do it. He resorted to squaring his shoulders as much as his belly allowed, and the uniforms closed rank.

"My business is above your pay grade," Ruiz said. He did not elaborate. He said his piece and stared back. His arm muscles flexed under the moon suit. He was ready to pounce if he needed to, I had no doubt about that.

Dagheretti got red in the face. He brushed back the side of his jacket. A small revolver flashed into view. If he meant to get my attention, he succeeded. Ship security wasn't supposed to be armed, as best I knew, and certainly not in the course of day-to-day business. Pot-belly put his hand on his baton. I got up and moved next to him.

"Why don't we let your boss and Mr. Ruiz have a civilized conversation here," I said, "and you keep your hands to yourself."

"Back off," the man said.

"If I back off, your fingers will be broken."

The guard had more bravado than common sense. Or maybe he thought the uniform protected him. Whatever went through his mind, he started pulling his baton out of his utility belt.

He moved awkwardly, not used to action. I'm sure it all looked a whole lot better in his mind. In the real world, he fumbled trying to get the billy club out. It got caught between the belt and his belly. By the time he had it out, I had both hands on it, twisted it, and disarmed him. I flipped it around in one hand, holding it by the long side, and jerked it up until I made contact with the underside of the guard's jaw.

Then I kept pushing. He grunted. I pushed some more. I was hurting him. There's nothing that didn't hurt where I was hitting him. He was not in a position anyone would enjoy.

Dagheretti looked back and forth between Ruiz and me. He had one guard out of action. He pulled his jacket back again. His fingers twitched an inch away from the gun on his hip. The man had some kind of high-noon cowboy fantasy, but that's all it was, a sad little fantasy. He deflated quickly. His shoulders slumped, he shoved his hands in his pockets, and his lower lip quivered.

He tried without success to straighten his mouth into a sneer.

"Don't break anything," he grunted, then he turned on his heels and departed. I tossed the guard's baton into the corridor, and the two uniforms scurried after their boss like two obedient dogs. At least dogs follow you out of love. These two losers were a waste of DNA.

I kept my eyes on the big man as he left, red in the face and weak-jawed, beads of sweat on his forehead. There was both rage and humiliation behind that, the kind of things that can make someone dangerous. I didn't like what I was seeing. I didn't feel like waiting for more guns to show up.

"Wrap it up, boys," I called out to my team. "Pronto."

We all started moving with purpose. Hank was already packing up. Liam had come halfway down the stairs during the confrontation and was now on his way back up, taking the steps two at a time. Ruiz and I started peeling our moon suits off. I turned to him.

"Is that guy going to try something crazy? You're his boss, after all. You can bring anyone you want on board."

"There's no way to know with people like him. You are right to hurry your men along. And do not forget that I have bosses too, bosses who do not want Morrison's death investigated. At all. This makes things a bit complicated. Bigger fish than me would not want you here."

I nodded. Big business and big governments were the same—too much politics. And I was well placed to know that politics killed. I wasn't about to argue with Ruiz anyway. My gut said to beat it, and his gut said to beat it. We were out of here.

"We go back the same way we came?" I asked. I did not know the ship. I did not have a clear tactical picture.

"Yes, let's be quick, not cute," Ruiz said, looking up the stairs to where Liam was already coming back, holding his untied canvas bag against his chest. Both techs were ready. I gave Ruiz a nod, and we hurried back.

We crowded the service elevator again. Liam floundered about, taking three tries to tie his canvas bag. The tension in the cramped space was palpable. I could feel Hank's breath on the back of my neck.

We held our collective breaths as the doors opened and sighed in unison when no one with guns waited for us. Ruiz marched us down the passageway. We stayed in a tight group and paid no mind to the electric carts or to our toes. We just kept going, eyes up front, moving quickly but not running, striking the best compromise we could between speed and not attracting any more attention.

Any hope we had to succeed in that evaporated around the last corner before we reached the loading bay. Four goons in uniform, batons in hand, marched like they were on parade at the County Fair.

Ruiz pivoted, nearly rolling his ankle, and turned around, reversing course, back up the passageway we just came down. He grabbed Hank by the collar and started leading us in the other direction, quickening to a jog, discretion be damned. I couldn't argue with him. Those guards didn't look like they gave his rank and position their due.

I took Liam's bag from him and gave him a good shove, my hand flat on his back.

"Hit it," I said. "I've got the bag."

Liam nodded—whether in thanks or agreement, I couldn't tell. He was getting red in the face, but he picked up the pace.

Ruiz slid to a stop before Dagheretti's men saw us, swiped his key card, yanked a side door open, and ducked through.

"This way," he said. "Quickly."

I pushed the techs across behind him like a drill sergeant pushing an Airborne trainee out of an airplane for the first time. I brought up the rear and slammed the door closed behind me.

"These are the crew quarters," Ruiz said. "They will not look for us here."

We ran past microscopic cabins. We were in a part of the ship passengers never see. Ruiz turned this way and that, up and down incomprehensible passageways.

"They better not," I said. "This is pretty damn narrow." I may have been stating the obvious, but I didn't like our chances if we were ambushed in a place where we were limited to moving in a single file.

"They won't," Ruiz answered without breaking his stride or looking back. "Dagheretti thinks I'm just some corporate puke. He forgets I was here when they built this *maldita nave*.

I gave a mental shrug. I was grateful for the reassurance, even as I realized it made no difference. We were committed. And it seemed Ruiz was right, anyway. We were the lucky beneficiaries of how well he knew the *Rio*. There were no uniformed guards in sight, not even the distant sounds of heavy boots on the metal floor. Hell, we were pretty much alone. The crew was hard at work, and security was looking for us in all the wrong places.

"This is all fine," I said, "but where are we going?"

"The forward port gangway."

Port was left, and to the left was the ocean. The gangway on which passengers board and disembark from the ship won't be extended, not on this side. It will also be locked tight.

"I'm guessing your key card is coded to it?" I asked.

"Full access. And Ollie can pick us up there."

It was music to my ears, and we kept moving. Moving and panting. The air was getting hotter. It started to smell like steam and chemicals. We ran past a sign pointing to the laundry, and I couldn't help but smile, remembering Courtney's remark the night before.

Breathing became easier again as we left the damp heat of the laundry behind. Ruiz slowed down and found the door he was looking for. He unlocked it and ushered us into a disembarkation area. Empty, it looked twice as big as I pictured it. It was dark, too, with only minimal lighting. The ramp was folded up and stowed at one end. At the other end was the door to freedom.

We crowded behind him as he grabbed his cell phone, unlocked it, and tapped his most recent call.

"Pick us up at the forward gangway. Now."

He hung up without waiting for a response, focusing on the hull door instead. He entered a code on a keypad, swiped his card, and turned the watertight lock.

I kept an uneasy eye on the door from which we came, wondering when Dagheretti's men would wise up to where we'd gone, and a gang armed with batons or guns would rush through and overwhelm us.

Just as I started thinking this was taking too long, bright sunlight bathed the room as Ruiz pulled the gangway door open. The ocean's salty scent and the swish of the waves were welcome sensations. The hum of the Zodiac's engine sounded even better. Ollie had not wasted any time—or been gentle on the throttle.

"Hand me your gear!" Ruiz said.

We did, and he threw the bags the other way, into the waiting Zodiac.

"It's a two-foot jump down," Ruiz said, turning to the rest of us. "Just drop in and move to the middle of the boat to make room for the next man. I'll go first to help receive you, then you go. Move quickly."

Ruiz stepped through the door and quickly disappeared. Hank moved up to the doorway next. He was grinning like a fool, like this was some kind of adventure, a SEAL team ride-along. He dropped like a pro, and soon he was out of sight too as he moved toward the back of the Zodiac.

Liam was nervous, hesitant, holding to the gangway door for dear life, refusing to jump. Two feet might as well be twenty to him, the vastness of the ocean overwhelming the tiny outboard.

"Get in that inflatable, or I'll make you swim," I said, not feeling particularly compassionate right at the moment.

Liam took one hesitant step and another, and, finally, he jumped. When I stepped to the edge, he was crawling on all fours, trying to get out of the way.

I dropped into the boat. Ollie yanked the Zodiac away from the *Rio* before I had my second foot down. I flailed for a second, arms like a windmill, but managed to stay upright.

I looked back toward the ship. Ollie's sudden move had attracted plenty of attention. A gaggle of security guards had gathered at the edge of the loading bay, pointing at us. One of them carried something—the sunlight reflected off it. I squinted, focused my attention there. It could be the lenses from a pair of binoculars. It could be a rifle's scope.

CHAPTER 19

Ollie started jerking the Zodiac around, and I held on for dear life to the rope lining the side. I had my phone in my other hand, thumb poised over the screen, one tap away from dialing CJ's sat phone to tell her to send the Coast Guard and their .50-cals our way.

But the shot never came, and Ollie straightened the boat and slowed us down, back on a leisurely straight line to the warehouses. I sat down next to Ruiz, adrenaline pumping.

"This guy does not like you very much," I said.

I locked the phone and stuffed it back in my pocket. My eyes trailed our course, keeping an eye on the receding *Rio* behind us. At my side, Ruiz was clearing a path ahead with his own gaze, alert to any kind of trouble.

"You could say that," he said. "And he hated Morant. Remember the civil war plantation problem we were talking about?"

"I take it he's part of the problem."

Tension still ran through Ruiz's arms and shoulders, bulging his muscles as surely as if he was lifting a barbell. He talked without looking at me, gazing firmly ahead of the Zodiac's course while I continued to clear our rear.

"He is," Ruiz said. "His name is Brett Dagheretti. He's a former sheriff in some backwater county who somehow weaseled his way to be the *Rio*'s Chief Security Officer. See, some linguists in suits and ties told corporate that a southern drawl sounds friendly to foreigners. So, they started looking to the Old South to recruit security officers who interact with customs and law enforcement in ports of call. Altogether, it's not a problem. Most of them are great. The top officers in our New York ships are men I'd serve with or drink with any time. Dagheretti's rotten."

"In other ways besides his bigotry?"

"I don't understand how he was ever law enforcement. He's much happier turning a blind eye to drugs and petty crime than keeping a semblance of order. The *Rio*'s a mess. And Dagheretti and his people think they have more power on board than the captain, so it's not likely to get better. In practice, they may even be right.

"Owen had started the long work of cleaning things up. He and Dagheretti clashed early and often. For a while, we all managed to fake civility. Now, the kind of confrontation you witnessed is par for the course. Except for the gun. That's new—and unauthorized."

"Unauthorized enough to get him canned?" I asked.

"He has friends too, but possibly. I have not yet decided whether to play that card."

I digested all that as we sailed past the Coast Guard RHIB. Ruiz waved, and the crew chief waved back. He'd seen us come in, and we were moving away from the ships. I let out a sigh of relief. I wanted those machine guns on our side in case the shit hit the fan. Short of that, I had no desire to explain why I entered a U.S. port facility under false pretenses. With the security cordon to our back, I turned to Ruiz.

"Dagheretti will bitch to corporate?" I asked.

"Maybe, maybe not. He'd have to explain away carrying that firearm. I can handle it either way. I always knew this was a possibility, and I have a cover story ready for them. I will make a few adjustments, push one button, and Corporate will have to sort out two competing narratives. It will take Dagheretti longer to act, too. He didn't expect us, so he needs to craft his story. And as lazy and incompetent as he is, he'll have to be on deck with his hands full for boarding this afternoon."

I looked over my shoulders. As if to make Ruiz's point, the line of cars streaming into port was now an unbroken ribbon on the shoreline. I turned back around and nodded to him.

"Hey, and if corporate doesn't buy it," he said, "I'll just knock on your door for a job."

I smiled. Running your own business is a different animal, but CJ did great coming from the corporate world. You never knew. I extended my hand to him, and he shook it.

"Thanks . . . Marco, right?" I asked.

"Yes, pleasure doing business with you, Cooper."

"My friends call me Coop."

"Coop."

"And you don't have to need a job to knock on my door," I said.

"I'll remember that."

I wobbled about to the back of the boat and shook Ollie's hand. "Thanks for the ride," I said. "And I'll do all I can to find out what happened."

He nodded. He started saying something back but swallowed his words.

"When are you going back to New Jersey?"

He shook his head. "Dad lived in Jersey, most of the year anyway. I live here." Half his mouth twitched in a grin. "I work for the competition. We used to sass each other over it."

"I'll see you again, then. And Marco's got my numbers. Reach out any time you want, doesn't matter why."

He nodded as he gently pushed the Zodiac toward the sea wall by our truck—well, Jim's truck, which hopefully was not any more damaged now than when I borrowed it.

The techs climbed out. I joined Marco at the front of the Zodiac, and we handed them their gear. When that was done, I squeezed Marco's shoulders; he wished me good luck. I did the same and climbed out without looking back. The outboard engine grew louder as the Zodiac accelerated behind us, then it faded as the boat sped away.

We high stepped through the brush back the way we'd come and scrambled into the truck. We'd been gone long enough for the heat in the cab to be overwhelming. The trusty old rust bucket started at the first crank of the key. That didn't mean any air, though, besides slightly less hot air coming through the windows once we started off.

I gently pressed the accelerator and we crawled toward the gate to the sound of gravel under the wheels. I drove slowly, the way three weary dock workers might after a shift. It felt even slower than our actual pace—two heartbeats per turn of the wheels. I could feel every single one of them in my chest.

Hank sat quietly next to me, but Liam was fidgeting like a rat on speed, pulling at his fingers and tapping his foot.

"Cool it, Liam," I said. "Act like you belong here. You do belong here. You had a job to do, and you did it, like everyone else. End of story."

He nodded twice and put his hands flat on his knees. The slap of his foot on the floor kept going, loud and off-beat with the music.

"The foot, too," I said, smiling sideways at him.

Hank chuckled and fist bumped my knee. Liam stopped moving and managed a weak smile. He no longer looked like he'd just smoked crack. Hell, I was so convincing that even my own heart slowed down.

There wasn't too much security leaving the port. After all, we were exiting the high-security area. The gate opened automatically; a guard turned his head toward us and gave us a disinterested look; we rolled out. By the time I turned into heavy traffic on Biscayne Boulevard, the techs' uneasy smiles had turned into giddy grins. Smile lines reached my eyes too.

I pulled out my cell and tapped the number to CJ's sat phone.

"Go," she said at the other end of the line, all business. The waves splashed against their boat, a background to our conversation.

"We're done, and we're safe. You can bug out."

"Copy."

The connection ended with a click. I shook my head. There was nothing more business-like than CJ in business mode.

I dropped the guys at their cars, back behind the big-box stores.

"Did you have enough time to get some samples?" I asked. Fine time to ask, but it's not like we could have lingered.

"Some, yes," Hank answered.

"Rush the prelim." I didn't need to tell them that. I just felt the need to say something.

"We will."

They both slid out of the truck into the Florida sunlight.

My next stop was Jim's house, to return his truck and pick up the Accord. I took a rain check on the beer. I needed some time alone. I drove home to change into clean clothes, then to the beach. I walked along the ocean, lost in the Sunday crowd, tourists and locals, beach bunnies and families. Did I also look like I didn't have a care in the world?

I stopped at a beach-side café for a turkey sandwich and a beer. I shook my head as I washed the food down with the bitter ale, chasing thoughts away. There were too many pieces of the puzzle missing. Maybe what I got at Mardi Gras' office would help. Patience was never my strong suit. I was tempted to bug Courtney but thought better of it. I finished my beer while it was still cold and went home for the night—twelve more hours of inaction that went against every fiber in my body.

CHAPTER 20

My computer whirred to life, greeting me on a new Monday in the office. CJ and Courtney were here too—they'd called out their hellos. I got up from behind my desk to call them into the conference room. I'd decided to tell CJ about my little escapade. I'd be asking for forgiveness, not permission, and she'd be pissed, but I owed her the truth. Anything else was pure bullshit.

I was too late. I barely reached the lobby when the door opened, and Detective Jorge Rodríguez walked in.

"Detective," I said, pasting a smile on my face. "You have news for us?"

"Maybe I should ask you that," he said. He was aiming his best cop stare at me. I'd been him. I'd practiced that stare in the mirror. It wouldn't throw me off the way he was used to.

"How's that?" I asked.

"There was a break-in at Mardi Gras' offices this weekend. You wouldn't know anything about that, would you?"

"It can't be a coincidence so close after Morant's death," I said, dodging the question.

"Answer the question," Rodríguez said, unimpressed by my effort not to, just as CJ's footsteps resonated behind me. She was joining our lobby powwow.

"No, I wouldn't know anything about it," I said.

"Maybe, maybe not, Mr. Malone. Look at it my way. You are investigating an 'incident' on the *Rio*, one that no one sees fit to tell me anything credible about. Then Mardi Gras' VP for Security gets murdered. Then their offices are broken into. You look more and more interesting every day."

"Did the robbers take anything?" I asked, ignoring the jab. I was leaning against Courtney's desk, arms crossed in front of me, trying to look a lot more relaxed than I felt. Rodríguez was still staring me down, and I was staring right back.

He ignored my question as flagrantly as I'd ignored his dig at me. "What really happened on the *Rio*?" he asked.

I took a second. Courtney was pretending to shuffle papers behind me. CJ stood perfectly still in my peripheral vision.

"Look, Detective," I said. "If I have any reason to think that what I'm working on could be related to Morant's death, I'll inform my client and brief you. I'll come straight to you. Until then, my hands are tied."

I was getting pretty good at convincing myself of those half-lies. A random murder could, after all, be unconnected to the company VP's death. Maybe it even was. Maybe there was no reason I should work with MDPD.

Rodríguez was having none of it.

"Not good enough. You let me be the judge of what's related."

"We're on the same side, detective," CJ said, stepping into our circle. I'd catch hell from her later, in private. But right now, Rodríguez was taking a confrontational stance with us, with the agency. He'd just awakened Tiger Mom. I'd seen Grandma Vinh mad only once in my life and never wanted to again. I'd seen CJ mad a few more times. Grandma was about to be proud of her.

Rodríguez didn't know any of this. He moved his head just enough to shift his glare from me to CJ.

"Is that right?" he asked.

"Yes, it is. On the same side, but, as Cooper said, we may not be working the same case. I hope you will let us know if you come across something relevant to ours, and, I assure you, you will get a call if we find anything relevant to yours."

"With all due respect," Rodríguez said, "my case takes precedence. It's murder, and yours, I understand, is not. And it's a police investigation, and yours, again with all due respect, is definitely not."

CJ didn't budge. She did not shake. She did not shout. She laid it all out for him in her maddeningly calm voice.

"You say 'all due respect' but you do not mean it. This is unfortunate. I have the greatest respect for law enforcement, and it saddens me that it is rarely returned. We are not some bumbling fools, you know. Cooper spent twelve years in the Army, in the Military Police force and in intelligence. I spent nearly ten years in corporate security before joining this agency. We know what we're doing."

"I still need to know what happened aboard that ship." Rodríguez's set jaw betrayed his steady tone. And even that was not as calm as CJ's. No one ever spoke as calmly as CJ, no matter how angry she was—especially when she was angry.

I re-entered the fray, not because CJ needed help knocking Rodríguez on his heels, but because a good one-two punch always worked best.

"You can always subpoena us if that's the tack you want to take. We'll fight it, of course. We have a duty to." I turned partway in Courtney's direction. "I'll alert our attorney it may be coming."

Courtney nodded and reached for her computer. We didn't have anyone on retainer, but she wasn't going to let a little detail like this get in the way of my story. Not only that, but we knew enough lawyers to change that if needed. Courtney was soaking it up, playing it like a champ.

"Or better yet," I said, turning back to Rodríguez, "we can work together, if it looks like our cases could be related, showing each other a little more respect." That last line was as much a *mea culpa* as a demand. It was also as far as I was willing to go.

Rodríguez took three steps toward me, his nose inches from mine, his teeth bared.

"You fuck with me, Malone, and I'll drop you in a shit hole so deep you'll never see daylight again."

I had trouble not laughing. Back in the day, I'd had trouble not laughing at drill sergeants yelling at us in Basic. But at least I knew they had a purpose. They were pulling us together as a team, and that could save our lives one day. It was harder not to laugh at Rodríguez's tough-cop routine. It was harder yet because I could just about read CJ's mind as Rodríguez and I stood face to face, staring at each other like two rough riders in a cowboy movie. *You're both pretty*, she'd be saying, *and you can both piss just as far as the other.*

I kept the hilarity on the inside, careful not to do or say anything to make the situation worse, though I had to say something. Rodríguez wasn't going to back down.

"Noted," I said. "Now, as CJ said, we're on the same side, so why don't you and I back off and take it from here like civilized people?"

He pivoted so he could look at both CJ and me. That moved him out of my face.

"Why don't you tell me about Mardi Gras' offices?" he asked. "You've been there to see Morant, and surely that's not confidential."

He was gruff, but at least he was talking—in a manner of speaking. I shook my head on the inside at the disguised interrogation and kept my poker face on. Sure, it sounded like an olive branch. But it was meant as a trap. If I revealed anything I could not know from my walk from the front desk to Morant's office, things I could only know from breaking in, it would be as good as a confession. I wasn't going to fall for it, but I had newfound respect for the man for trying. I nearly hated to disappoint him.

I told him everything I knew from visiting Morant. I talked about the lobby, the ever present guard at the back of it, the carpet-tiled corridor, and the office where I'd met Morant. I reported everything I knew from these two visits in clear, concise, police-report talk—and nothing else. I also made a point of saying how small the offices were and the tiny portion of the building they occupied. I was willing my story to him. The warehouse is much larger and full of riches. The break-in had to be about the warehouse. *Take the hint, Jorge!*

"What's at the back of the building?" he asked. He was like honey now, showing his appreciation for my cooperation. He was also opening the door to another trap, maybe a smaller one, begging for an admission I'd cased the place.

"I don't know," I answered. "I left the same way I came."

Rodríguez shook his head, either because I was doing him no good or because he didn't believe me. Maybe both. He managed a smile through his tough-guy routine.

"I have a feeling we'll see each other again soon," he said. Then he turned around and left.

None of us moved as his footsteps receded down the hallway. We listened for the faint noise of the elevator opening and closing. I turned around to look at Courtney, who was looking at the screen showing the feed from our hallway camera.

"He's gone," she said.

Then I turned around to face CJ's dagger-shooting stare. Except . . . it wasn't there. It was much worse. She was looking down at the carpet. She spoke softly.

"Oh, Cooper. What have you done?"

CHAPTER 21

was on my way to your office to brief you when Rodríguez walked in," I said. The words sounded weak and guilty in my head.

"So, you did break in."

"Yes. I wanted to get in ahead of the cops."

"And you did not tell me."

I wondered if that's how Catholics felt at confession. Maybe . . . if they had a strict yet loving *padre*. I did the only thing I could and told her the truth.

"We'd just fought about stuff like that. I knew you'd disagree and we'd have another fight about it, and it felt useless, so I did it without consulting you. Looking back, it was bullshit. It lacked respect for you as my partner and as my friend. That's why I wanted to talk to you today, to bring you up to speed and to tell you I was an ass and I'm sorry."

CJ was quiet, her gaze down. It hurt like hell, way more than if she'd yelled at me, but CJ didn't yell. She tortured you with kindness. She mulled my words for what felt like an eternity before looking up at me.

"Did you at least find something useful?" she asked. Her tone betrayed nothing of her emotions, leaving me twisting in the wind.

I stuck to the facts.

"I don't know yet. I have a couple of thumb drives and a damaged hard drive. I don't know what's on them."

"You might as well have Courtney take a look at them if she agrees to do that knowing where they came from."

I opened my mouth to speak, but Courtney cut me off.

"I already have them."

CJ's head snapped in Courtney's direction. The two women looked at each other in silence until Courtney spoke again.

"I helped Coop with the break-in," she said. "I happened to agree with him this time—that we should stay ahead of MDPD. I'm sorry, CJ."

CJ looked back and forth from Courtney to me. Then she nodded slowly.

"Coop, I respect your opinion. I respect you, or I wouldn't be here."

I nearly doubled over from the shot of guilt as CJ turned to Courtney again, her hair fanning along her back. She smiled for the first time since Rodríguez had walked in.

"And Courtney," CJ continued, "I've come to trust your judgment too. So, if you both agree it was best, I accept it. But next time, and I know there will be a next time, please convince me before—not after—you do something stupid."

"I will," I said.

"Promise," Courtney said over me. "Still friends?"

Courtney opened her arms and started off her chair. CJ recoiled in horror, wagging a finger in front of her.

"Oh no, oh no you don't!"

Courtney was a hugger. CJ was not. Courtney won.

When she let go and sat back down, I extended my hand to CJ, not from one friend to another, though we were, or from one former lover to another, though we were that too, but from one professional to another. "I'm sorry," I said.

She shook my hand. That was the end of it. It was time to get back to work.

"Do you have what we need to look at the thumb drives?" I asked Courtney.

"Yes," she said as she reached down by her feet and pulled up a laptop. "I air-gapped one of my old machines."

"Air what?"

Courtney sat a bit straighter, pleased to have something to teach the old man.

"An air-gapped computer," she said, "is one that is completely disconnected from the internet. I yanked the Wi-Fi card from this one, pulled out
the ethernet card too, and I disabled the drivers for them. I even removed
the browser and any software that might so much as look for an internet
connection. I only left readers to open most formats we're likely to find on
the drives. If there's malware, it will only affect this old husk and nothing else."

"Let's go to the conference room," CJ said.

Courtney sat at the head of the table, looking back and forth at CJ and
me on either side of her as the laptop booted up. It wasn't her usual seat. She
had taken the two thumb drives I had given her this morning and put them
on the table. Once the computer was done booting up, she picked one up
and plugged it in. When the familiar menu appeared, she selected "Open
folder to view files."

There were no files. The thumb drive was empty. Courtney's shoulders
slumped.

"One more," I said as I handed it to her.

Courtney ejected the first drive and plugged the new one in. This time,
two icons appeared when she opened the folder. One directed to a PDF file
named "S Lo" and the other to a folder that had never been renamed. It still
said "New folder."

"PDF first?" Courtney asked.

"Sure," I said.

"PDFs are safe, right?" CJ asked.

"Yes," Courtney answered. "At least, best I know they always are. I can't
swear some hacker who's way better than me can't disguise an executable as
a .pdf—not just called that, but a file that the computer will identify as such.
But I've not heard of anything like that."

She double clicked on the file.

"Here goes nothing."

The world did not end or even try to. An eight-page document opened.
The first page had a name and a picture of a round-faced Asian woman with

heavy eyelids.

"I know this woman," I whispered to no one in particular, leaning toward the screen. "She was sitting behind the front desk at Mardi Gras each time I went there."

The name on the screen said Stephanie Lo. The rest of the PDF contained her personnel file. There was not much to it. Her job application and résumé showed she had only been at the company for a few months. They pegged her as a late-blooming college student who had enough of odd jobs and got serious about studying logistics. A well-written cover letter expressing a particular interest in how her chosen field applied to cruise ships reinforced that point. Beyond that, she hadn't been there long enough for her file to have more than her college transcripts, an offer letter, and tax paperwork.

"Why would Morant have her file?" I mused, again to no one in particular. CJ and Courtney both shook their heads.

Courtney closed the file and double clicked the next folder. It contained several PDF files with random names. I frowned.

"Scans?" CJ asked.

"Probably," Courtney asked.

"Looks like the kind of names a printer/scanner assigns—before Courtney or I rename them for you," CJ added for my benefit.

Courtney opened the files one by one. They all looked like spreadsheets. As they opened, they started to look familiar.

"I've seen that before too," I said, "or something like it." I angled the screen to get a better look.

"Where?" CJ asked. Her eyes narrowed. She could guess where, and she already didn't like the answer.

"Michael Nixon's office. He runs Mardi Gras' warehouse. I only walked by his office last night when I broke in, and he had documents like that all over his desk. I didn't pay much attention. That's the kind of papers someone in his position would look at all day."

"Looks like records of bills of lading, invoices, inventories . . . ." CJ provided specifics as she scrolled through the file, leaning in and reaching for the mouse in front of Courtney.

"Yeah, that," I said, as if I knew one from the other. "I can't figure out what Morant would want with them, though."

"Ruiz said Morant was pushing back against drugs aboard the *Rio*, right?" CJ asked. I wasn't surprised she'd already read the preliminary report I'd hammered out the night before, or that she remembered every little detail in it.

"That's right," I said. "You're thinking he was trying to figure out if some of it came in from their own warehouse?"

"Exactly," CJ said. "They have one day to load supplies for thousands of people. Even with all the port security around, it may be a soft point of entry."

Courtney was beaming with excitement, nearly jumping out of her chair between CJ and me.

"Then we can compare those files to the . . . ." And she deflated, hands in her lap, her excitement reduced to the lowest whisper. " . . . the pictures I took," she finished.

"What pictures?" CJ asked. She was trying to ask with a smile, but it was the kind of smile that did not reach the eyes.

I held a hand up before Courtney could answer.

"Courtney did something reckless," I said. "I already had a talk with her."

"With your usual charm?" CJ asked, turning to me.

Great, now she's madder at me than Courtney!

"Yeah, exactly. So she probably doesn't need any extra bluster from either of us—just so you know when she explains everything to you later. Bottom line for now, she's itching to get in the field. I think she'll be good at it, and we could train her, but I wanted to talk to you first. I was going to do that after this meeting. My timing is just not going as planned today." I chuckled, thinking about the best laid plans of mice and men. "We can still do that later if you prefer."

"No need," CJ said, "unless we still need to discuss the other thing we talked about."

"The other thing for Courtney? No, we're good. Go ahead."

Courtney was looking from CJ to me and back, mouth slightly parted, hands on the table, waiting patiently. I felt bad talking about her with her here. She wasn't a child, and, even then, it's not okay with me. I would have screamed in frustration in her place.

CJ turned to face her.

"You're already doing a lot more than we had hired you for," she said. "We were going to give you a raise to recognize that. We are going to do that, effective . . . ." CJ looked at me for a moment.

"The coming pay period?" I offered.

"This coming pay period," CJ said. "And I agree with Coop that you have qualities that would do well in the field. I have no problem including field training in your promotion if you want to learn that kind of work. Coop and I will discuss the details, the whats, hows, and whens, and start you up as time permits, but as soon as possible."

If excited tears or another hug had been Courtney's first instinct, she reigned that in. She sat a little straighter in her chair, looked at us both, and said a firm, "Thank you."

I liked that. I also liked that we were ready to get back to working the case. I let a couple of seconds go by and steered the conversation that way, turning to Courtney first.

"Have you taken a look at the hard drive I found in Morant's office?"

"Yes, and I have it here to keep working on it. It's pretty far gone. I have not been able to recover any files yet. But I can tell you every one of them is in a video format."

"Surveillance?" I asked.

"Could be. I'll keep working on it."

"Okay," I said. I sat back and gathered my thoughts. "You and CJ, work the inventory angle—as time allows. I know this isn't our only case. I'll go back to Mardi Gras and have a chat with the suddenly mysterious Miss Lo."

I tapped the thumb drive sticking out of the laptop.

"Now that this thing is no longer a threat to world peace, you think I can get hard copies and a copy of the files on a spare drive, too?"

"Sure," Courtney said. She was getting as good as CJ at ignoring my sarcasm. That did not bode well for my future.

"What about the Morrison case?" CJ asked. "You know, the case we were actually hired to investigate?"

CJ was right, but I did not have anything new to work from. I tapped the table, looking for an idea to pop out of my brain like a rabbit from a magician's hat. I was not having much luck.

"If we don't get a prelim from Hank and Liam by the end of today," I said, "bug them for an ETA. We're paying them enough. Besides that, fuck, I'm open to ideas."

I turned to Courtney first. I knew CJ would have something to say. I wanted Courtney to be free to contribute.

"I found Claire on social media, well, probably. I found someone with her name in Miami. Her profile is as private as can be, but the birthday matches her passport info. Do you want me to direct message her? I wasn't sure how obvious you wanted us to be."

"Valid concerns last week," I said, "not this week. Not anymore. Message her, breach her privacy wall, whatever you need to do. She may have nothing to do with this, but I want answers."

Courtney nodded and CJ took over.

"I can back up your interviews," she said, "see if I can elicit different memories by asking questions my way. People will have had time to think about it, too, and they may react differently to a woman."

"That sounds good. Start with Morrison's friends. They were closest to him and their partying."

"Walt Rosling, old real estate asshole, and Cabe Roper, math boy genius, check," CJ said to herself. "What about Linda Mayak? She's a professional, but she was under the shock of being in the limelight, not to mention verbalizing for the first time that her protectee got killed."

"Good point," I said. "Make her a priority too."

"I'll start with them then," CJ said. She grinned from one side of her mouth. "Hopefully, I won't break a car window if I have to go to Key West."

"You just be careful," I grumbled.

CHAPTER 22

I parked in front of the Mardi Gras Miami offices for the third time in less than two weeks. It seemed impossible so little time had passed since Heather fought back tears at Nick & Nora to tell me she thought someone died and there was something shady about it.

I put a smile on my face and walked in. Smiles are good. Smiles help. I just had a hard time keeping mine up as I crossed from the hot pavement outside to the carpet tiles inside.

A woman stood up behind the counter as I entered. She was white, about my age, and barely bothered to force the corners of her mouth upward. She stood there picking at the ends of her dry, brown hair. The only thing she had in common with Stephanie Lo was the tired eyes that wished they did not have to look at me. *Of course, Lo's not here. That would have been too damn easy.*

I approached the familiar counter and the unfamiliar woman behind it. I glanced left. The security guard sat on a stool in a darkened corner, ready to make his presence known if called upon. I couldn't tell from here if he was the same guy who'd been here before, let alone if he would recognize me.

"What happened to Stephanie?" I asked, trying to sound cheerful even though cheerful wasn't my strong suit.

"Who?" the woman asked, bored.

"The lady who used to be here," I said, rapping my knuckles on the counter. "I felt like she and I were starting to get to know each other."

"No clue. Is there something I can help you with?"

"I hope she's okay," I said. "I thought she came with the building." I was turning not answering questions into an art form.

"Again, I couldn't say."

Movement in my peripheral vision told me the guard had stood up. I could picture him, at the edge of the room, a hand on his belt.

"Now, what can I help you with, Mr. . . . . ."

I scratched my chin, opened my mouth as if to speak before closing it again.

"You know when Stephanie will be back?"

"Unless you have business here . . ." the woman behind the counter said, extending her arm toward the front door. I heard the guard take two steps, getting just a little bit closer to me.

"Never mind, never mind," I said, raising a hand and shaking it back and forth in the air. "Maybe I'll come back later, see if she's here."

It was pretty clear I wouldn't get an answer, so I beat a hasty retreat before the guard decided to get frisky.

It was a bit early for lunch, but I drove to my new favorite Mexican lunch counter anyway, the one with the warm corn tortillas, Key West Pinks, and the guy behind the counter who didn't mind my broken Spanish as much as he enjoyed me trying. I tucked a folder under my arm with the printouts Courtney had given me from the thumb drive and entered the joint for a bite to eat.

I got a friendly hello, my shrimp tacos and my Coke, and sat down on a wobbly chair to look at Stephanie Lo's personnel file. There was precious little information in there. Even her résumé was bareboned, with her college work and a collection of odd jobs. I'd go with what I had.

I grabbed my cell phone out of my pocket and spoofed my number. I didn't even need Courtney for that. I'd learned how to do it in my Army Intelligence days. Once done, I called the college listed on Lo's job application.

"Hi. This is Alan, with Dunn Resources," I said, grinning at my own cleverness. "Who do I speak to about a student transcript we just received? We only have a copy."

I was transferred twice and was left arguing with a self-important woman who insisted the student needed only ask her to send an *official* transcript. After ten long minutes, she sighed audibly at the other end of the phone. I imagined the cubicle walls closing in on her and the pain in her ankle from the chain holding her there. I felt a little bad, but I needed information and she had it.

"What's the student's name?" she asked in a whine.

"Stephanie Lo. L as in Lima, O as in Oscar."

"Sir, there's no student by that name in my records."

"That's odd," I said. "Maybe I have a bad copy. Could it be L-E? Or maybe I'm missing part of the name? Any Stephanie with a last name starting with L-O or L-E?" I had a printout of a very good copy, if not an original, and her name on half a dozen other pieces of paper. At that point, I was staying in character, selling the call.

"The student really needs to stop by here and ask us to send an original," the voice answered, exasperation mounting.

"I suppose. Oh, well. Thanks anyway."

I hung up without waiting for a response. I put my phone next to my empty plate. I picked up my cup and mindlessly swirled the crushed ice and Coke in it. I took another look at the picture in front of me. *Who are you?*

Morant had her file. No one else's. Just hers. Then the Monday after he gets killed, she's no longer at Mardi Gras. And I just found out she's never studied at the college listed on her résumé, the one she supposedly had a transcript from. I flipped back through her file. I had one more shot. She had listed an address in her job application in a modest but up-and-coming part of town.

I called the office, gave Courtney a quick report of my visit to Mardi Gras, and told her where I was going. I could hear her keyboard clicking as I talked. When I was done, I got back in the loaner and headed east to NW Twenty-Sixth. I wondered how traffic could be that bad everywhere, all the time, and cursed under my breath. It's not like I was going that far, but what should have taken me fifteen minutes took me thirty, and the loaner lacked a decent sound system. I had no fucking patience for this.

I drove past the house listed on the job application. It was an unmemorable house on an unmemorable street, with a narrow driveway, a covered car park, and a small patch of lawn in front of the porch. I parked a few doors down and walked back. As tradecraft went, it was basic to the point of pathetic, but I'd seen nothing to give me concern or justify more.

I walked slowly down the street, and even slower from the sidewalk to the front door. I was taking it all in. At first glance, the house did not look any different from its neighbors. Still, something felt off. Maybe it was the potted plants that looked a little too good, not a dead leaf among them, spaced exactly the way they would on some home decoration magazine. Or maybe it was the paint without a single flaky patch or the lawn without a browning blade of grass.

When I looked up and down the porch, I saw the telltale sensors of a security system on the window frames. I rang the doorbell, not expecting an answer. I was playing the part in case the neighborhood busybody was watching me from a gap between their curtains. No answer.

I turned my back to the house and made my way to the sidewalk. I started toward the car but stopped at the last moment. I went to the house next door and knocked. A young Latina answered. She had a broad smile and was wiping her hands on an apron. Mouthwatering smells wafted from inside.

"*Si?*" she asked without breaking her smile.

"*Hola,*" I answer. "*¿Habla inglés?*"

She shrugged a slow, lazy shrug with one shoulder.

"*No.*"

I did not *hablo español* near as well as I should, especially working in Miami. All the same, I managed to make myself understood with a mix of broken Spanish and hand gestures. I gave her my card and I explained best I could that a Miguel Ramírez had family back home that was worried about him, and they'd ask me to try and find him. Someone had given me the address next door for him. Did she know if he lived there? I'd made up the name and the story on the fly. It must have sounded good enough.

"*No sé,*" she answered. "*Esa casa, inquilinos.*" She was pointing at the house I had just come from.

"*Inquilinos*?" I asked. I did not know that word.

She looked up, searching for words. "People come and go," she said, moving her hand from side to side. "*No . . . uh, no son los proprietaros.*"

Not the owners. Renters then. That's what she was saying. She did not know who lived there because renters came and went, probably on short-term leases. It was possible, I thought. Maybe the owners took extra care of the house to make up for the disruption. I just wasn't as sure as she was that's what was going on.

I put my hands together in thanks then tapped the tip of my nose with my finger.

"*Gracias*," I said. "Smells *delicioso*."

Her smile brightened even more.

"*Muchos gracias, señor. Adios*," she said before she closed the door, no doubt returning to her oven.

That's me, I grinned, *the Spanglish Charmer in the flesh*.

I sat in the car for a bit after that to see if my visit prompted any action. I divided my attention between my mirrors and my phone, writing a typo-filled report to CJ. I copied Courtney, who would pretty it up and put it in the file. I closed the email with another call for ideas. I was no closer to Stephanie Lo and out of places to look.

Nothing moved on NW Twenty-Sixth, so I started my way back. I was halfway to the office when the dealership called to remind me that the CR-V was ready. I'd been so consumed by the case I'd forgotten it was. I turned around before I forgot again and picked it up. By the time the paperwork was done and I fought another losing battle with traffic, CJ and Courtney were closing up shop. Not that it made a difference. They both had a laptop bag on their shoulder to keep working from home.

"Where have you been?" CJ asked.

I shook the keys in front of my face.

"You got the car back," Courtney said. "Maybe I should take it—for safekeeping, you know." Sure. It had nothing to do with her driving a beater with six digits on the odometer.

"Somebody should," CJ said, piling on. "Somebody who does not get windows shattered." They looked at each other, nodding firmly at their shared wisdom. I was glad Courtney's indiscretion, helping me break into Mardi Gras, had not affected the ladies' relationship—or their sass. I flipped them off, put the keys in my pocket, and headed into my office to the sound of their laughter and the door closing behind them.

I powered down, stuffed the laptop in my own carry bag, and headed home to leftovers. The day replayed itself in my mind as I navigated the streets until I pulled into the driveway. My two-car garage was really two one-car garages side by side, each with its own door. I lined up on the right-hand side but did not open it. Like a good Floridian, my garage was there to store my shit, not park my car.

I killed the engine and lazily slid out. The car door was still open when I jerked around to the sound of a car burning rubber. I was suddenly alert, my hand hovering by my hip, head on a swivel. Then I saw it—a large black SUV rounding the corner. It took it so fast it looked like it might tip over. I retreated behind the CR-V just as the Suburban screeched to a halt, blocking my driveway. I drew my weapon, leaned over the hood of my car, and pointed the gun at the black behemoth's tinted windows.

CHAPTER 23

An odd thought ran through my mind as I looked at the world through my gun sight. *CJ's going to kill me if I break the car again.* Then the thought dissipated, and my mind emptied. Only the black hole at the end of the driveway and the sound of the SUV's engine remained.

The passenger side was facing me. The front window whirred and opened an inch. A female voice came out of the car, echoing faintly.

"Please holster your weapon, Mr. Malone. You will not be needing it."

There was a tone of finality to the way the woman had talked, a calm certainty in her voice. It wasn't lost on me that I'd had my hand on my .45 more often in the past week than the year before, but I took a chance and stood up. I slid my gun back into its holster. I let my palm rest on the handle, the gun's heft a reassuring presence.

The window opened all the way, and I walked slowly toward the truck. My head was on a swivel, moving back and forth, scanning for any more surprises. There were none. My residential neighborhood had returned to its natural calm and quiet. Birds would have fucking chirped if it hadn't been too hot even for birds to be out in the sun.

I didn't know what to expect when I reached the Suburban and leaned into the passenger-side window. I might not have been surprised by a gunned-up bimbo behind the wheel and Dunn in the back seat behind slick sunglasses. I was not expecting what I saw.

"Stephanie Lo," I said out loud. I gave my eyes a moment to adjust, but it was definitely her, even if she was barely recognizable. Her hair was pulled back in a ponytail. Her eyes did not hide behind half-closed eyelids. They were sharp, constantly moving. She was wearing a tank top and jeans and had a large caliber sidearm on her belt.

"You've made a nuisance of yourself, Mr. Malone," she said.

"I've heard that before."

"You probably have." She pushed the door-lock button and the Suburban unlocked with synchronized clicks. "Climb in. We're due for a talk."

I hesitated, so she leaned toward me, elbow resting on the center console.

"I wouldn't need to have a talk with you if you had not been such a pain in the ass. But you have, so we do. Now climb in, please."

I opened the door, sat my ass down, and off we went.

She unclipped a credentials wallet from her belt, on the opposite side from her gun, and handed it to me. I took it and snapped it open. It held a DEA badge and credentials for Special Agent Sally Locke with her picture on it. I handed it back and sank into my seat.

"Sally Locke, then," I said.

"That's me."

We were moving at a good clip now, heading out of the neighborhood. The car smelled new, a mix of leather and polish. It even drove straight, unlike the swaying Crown Vics with the loose transmission I was used to from my MP days, those that smelled of old sweat, molding food, and stale coffee. I looked down to a spot in front of the center console. It held a police radio and the controls for lights and sirens. I guess the DEA rode in style.

Locke headed straight to the interstate and settled into a slow pace in the right lane. Stressed-out drivers in a hurry to make it home for dinner sped to our left, jockeying for position. They got no judgment from me. Locke kept one hand on the steering wheel and laid her other arm on the center console. She glanced in my direction briefly before returning her attention to the asphalt. It was time to talk, but she was waiting me out.

"Thanks for not bullshitting me," I said, tapping the police radio with a fingernail.

"You didn't seem the type."

"I'm not."

She still did not offer anything substantive, and I was okay starting us off. It would show some of what I knew, but we had to start somewhere, and chances were it would only confirm her suspicions. That didn't mean I couldn't start with questions.

"You were undercover?" I asked.

"Yes."

"Morant knew?"

She nodded as I spoke Morant's name. We were on the same page.

"I was there at his invitation," she said. "He contacted us, suspecting there was a sizeable narcotics pipeline upstream from the *Rio*. He wanted it stopped, and so did we. We agreed to work together."

"And they yanked you when he was killed."

"Yanked me, yes. But it did not stop the investigation, which is why I'm here."

"Okay."

"To make sure you don't mess things up for us without having to put you in a jail cell."

She'd taken her eyes off the road long enough to lock her eyes on me, a look that said we were still in the no-bullshit zone. That was fine with me. Now I knew what she wanted—me out of the way. Good thing for her, I wanted something too.

"Then I guess you'll need to help me out," I said. "That way I won't need to make a nuisance out of myself, and I will even help you back if I can."

"What kind of help are you looking for?"

"I want to know everything you know about William Morrison, for one."

"The guy who got killed on the *Rio*?"

"You're investigating it?"

"Not at the moment. We only will if it turns out to be drug related."

"But you haven't told MDPD."

She grinned while keeping her eyes on the road. "Or the FBI. They'd have jurisdiction, maritime law being federal. But they'd make a nuisance of themselves too."

She fell silent after that.

"Do we have a deal?" I asked.

She glanced at me again. Her fingers were barely touching the steering wheel, keeping the Suburban on the straight and narrow in the slow lane.

"I looked you up before ambushing you. Made a couple of calls, too. I think you're a straight shooter overall, but you're cagey."

"Cagey?" I turned to look at her.

"Yes, cagey. Shrewd. Sly like a fox."

"Nobody called me cagey before." *But I'll make sure to brag about it, now.*

She gave me the side eye. She wasn't here to discuss vocabulary.

That was my cue to shoot straight.

"I do what I have to, sometimes. But I keep my word. If I tell you I won't harass you in the middle of your case, then I won't harass you. And if I tell you I'll give you what I have, I'll give you what I have."

We sat in silence for a while. It was not exactly what she'd asked, and we both knew it, but it was enough. Special Agent Locke took the next exit and turned around, back the way we'd come. She didn't say we had a deal. Federal agents did not make deals. They told you what to do. But we had a deal. We merged back onto the interstate.

I laid my head back on the headrest, closing my eyes, feeling the car's smooth ride. CJ hated it when I did that. She said it made her feel like a chauffeur. It calmed my mind, let the brain's wheels turn more easily, without distraction.

"How did I pop up on your radar so quickly?" I asked Locke.

"You blipped the moment you called the college. We have a deal with them for undercovers, but I was already out of their system after I went back above ground following Morant's death. The lady you talked to loves working with us. It's more exciting than her day job. She looked up Dunn Resources, and, when she saw that didn't exist, she called us. Then you triggered the security system at the safe house—don't act like you didn't know you'd stumbled on one—and I decided we needed to talk."

"You have a good system."

"Glad you approve," she said, snickering. "But the better question is, why your sudden interest in me?"

I'd been preparing for that question from behind my eyelids. I opened my eyes and looked at her.

"Accidentally, or just about. I went to talk to the receptionist who guarded the gate every time I talked to Morant. When you disappeared and everyone was being elusive, I started digging. You'd become a loose thread. I don't like loose threads." There was a kernel of truth in there—maybe more than one. But I guess Locke would still be calling me cagey right about now if she knew everything.

"You have a good nose," she said.

"Glad you approve," I said. "Now, what do you have for me on the Morrison case?"

"I'll send you our file on him. I doubt there's much in it. We don't think it was drug related, so we're hands-off for now. I guess if that changes, you and I will need another talk. Anything on Morant popped up in your investigation of Morrison?"

"Nothing about Morant, but I'll give you a name on Morrison. Dunn."

"Your phony company?"

"Alan Dunn's a PI. He's involved in the Morrison mess somehow, or has a client who is, and neither of them is afraid of roughing things up a bit. Dunn cornered me a few days back and tried to get me to drop the case. He wasn't exactly subtle."

I gave her the two-minute version of the encounter. When I was done, she unclipped a small dictation machine from the visor and dictated field notes into it.

"I thought you weren't investigating Morrison," I said. "I was giving you background."

"I said we weren't investigating Morrison for now. That could change.

And if it does, Dunn's name will be in the file."

I nodded as we slowed down to take the off ramp.

"One more thing," I said. "First time I went to see Morant, he was putting away what looked like spreadsheets. I couldn't see what they were about, but it's bugged me since. It's the kind of documents that are more relevant to operations than security, most of the time anyway. Do you know what it was about?"

She pointed at me with her free hand.

"It's about you staying away from it. He was auditing the warehouse for us, to see if anything raised a red flag, something to point to drugs coming in that way. Now you know, and it's my turf, so you forget you ever saw it."

"I won't get in the way." I didn't say in the way of what. Locke's silent glare under the red glow of a traffic light was laden with suspicion, but she didn't say anything. She didn't need to. She had the badge and the gun on her hip, not to mention the weight of the federal government behind her. Rodríguez had hissed at me not to fuck with him. Locke didn't do that, but the warning was just as clear.

We were two minutes away from my house when Locke spoke again, angling her head toward me.

"When I drop you off, I'll get out and we'll hug like we're two old buddies."

"In case your tire-screeching act attracted attention in the neighborhood?"

Her smile brightened her face. She had a friendly smile when she bothered. She raised her hand between us, her thumb half an inch below her index finger.

"I might have had a little bit of a heavy foot getting to your driveway. A little bit." The thumb and index came closer together.

"Yeah, a little bit."

She parked at an angle behind the CR-V, which didn't have a scratch on it. We both climbed out and hugged. When we did, she whispered in my ear. "No nuisance, Malone." Then she got back behind the wheel and left.

Once she was out of sight, I grabbed my cell phone and texted CJ and Courtney. "Keep working the warehouse angle."

I don't always listen too well.

CHAPTER 24

I went into the house long enough to eat a couple of bites I barely tasted and realize I was feeling like a lion in a cage. I was pacing one moment and leaning with my elbows on my kitchen counter the next. I contemplated a cup of coffee I did not really want. I went as far as opening the cupboard before closing it again. I suddenly knew where I wanted to be—and how I wanted to get there.

Moving about the bedroom with purpose, I put on a fresh pair of jeans and a clean shirt, changed my boots, and pulled a leather jacket from the closet. I walked into the garage and opened the far door, the one not blocked by the CR-V outside. I picked up my helmet from its place on a wall peg and straddled the Chief. With one kick, the classic Indian motorcycle roared to life.

I headed west, more or less, taking the bike this way and that through the emptiest streets I found. The farther I went, the easier it got. The solitude while riding was liberating in a way few other things were. I felt as free riding as I had felt trapped in my house. I made a quick stop at a liquor store and found what I was looking for. I put it in the saddle bag and rode on, just me, the Indian Chief, and the empty road.

I had a half hour's daylight left when I parked next to the purple Jeep under the upper cube of the otherworldly house. I took the bottle from the saddle bag and rang the doorbell next to the red door. Amy opened it nearly right away. She was wearing loose shorts and a T-shirt that read "Get Your

Cray On" in bright colors on a black background and a crayfish in the middle.

She flashed that Colgate smile of hers when she saw me, and my heart skipped a beat like a damn teenager in heat. *What the fuck is wrong with you, Malone?* She extended an arm sideways and leaned into the door frame. She looked me over, up and down, with exaggerated movements of her head.

"You're looking rather delicious, Mr. PI," she said.

"Thanks. I need to put some work into it. You always look great."

"Why, thank you. You have more questions for me? I thought I'd answered them all," she said, pouting her mouth a little.

"I'm sure I could come up with some, but I just wanted to see you," I said. I presented the wine I'd picked up on my way. "And I come bearing gifts."

She took the bottle and looked down at it, orienting the label for a good look.

"Sancerre," she commented. She looked up at me over her nose, head still down on the bottle. "Your pick or the salesperson's?"

I tapped my chest. I had trouble keeping my grin on the inside.

"It is what you were drinking the other day, isn't it?"

She lifted her head toward me, inches away from mine, beautiful and tempting. She kept a teasing distance between us.

"Well played, sir, well played," she said. "But don't they say to beware of Greeks bearing gifts?"

"Doesn't matter what they say. For one, you're not the cautious type. For another, I come from long ago Irish stock."

"I guess it's okay, then." She wrapped her arms around my neck, bottle still in her hand, and we melted into each other, lost in a kiss. It was a longing kiss, the kind of kiss lovers share. I let myself enjoy it, enjoy the way her body was pressing against mine. I let myself be with her in that moment—mind, body, and soul. This was crazy, so crazy it nagged at me a little. This was the second time I met this woman. I didn't know her. And yet it felt right, like we were meant to be kissing like that.

"Come in," she said softly after she pulled back.

I followed her into the kitchen, with its bright red walls and immaculate white cabinets. She put the wine down, handed me a corkscrew, and pointed at the walls.

"The color red makes you hungry," she said.

"Really?" I picked up the wine from the counter and got to work on the cork, watching Amy as she moved about her kitchen and took two glasses down from a cabinet. She put them down long enough to lean over the counter and reach for the chiller. She looked at me over her shoulder.

"Yes," she said. "It's a passionate color. It makes your heart beat faster. And that makes you hungry . . ." she paused. "For all kinds of things."

I put the cork I'd extracted on the kitchen island without taking my eyes off her.

"I'm pretty sure the wall color has nothing to do with my heart rate."

"Oh?" she asked, fluttering past me.

I followed her to the deck. She walked past the two chairs where we sat the week before to the sofa around the corner.

"Have a seat," she said, and put the glasses down on a small side table.

I did, and proceeded to pour the Sancerre.

She rearranged a couple of pillows and lounged sideways, knees over my thighs, shoulders propped up against the armrest. She sank into the sofa with a satisfied "hmmm" and took the glass I handed her.

We clinked. I held my wine in one hand and put the other on her thigh, nothing indecent, just enough that she knew I was interested, brushing my fingers back and forth. We sipped in silence for a while.

I waved my glass at the view in front of us, the last of the sun's red glow peeking through the trees.

"I'd have wanted to see you no matter where you lived, but this doesn't hurt."

"Peaceful, isn't it?" Her eyes never left the trees and the setting sun.

"An oasis amid urban chaos," I said.

She turned to me and smiled. "I love that you love it," she said.

"How long have you lived here?" I suck at small talk, but this did not feel like small talk. I actually wanted to know.

"Nearly ten years." She lifted her head for a second. "Heather told you I graduated with a degree in creative writing?" she asked.

I nodded. She leaned back and continued talking.

"After college, I found this great job that—no joke—paid me to write, so long as I wrote advertising. It felt like selling my soul, but I wasn't naïve—money matters. I just knew I needed somewhere to get my soul back. So, I saved every dime I could and still enjoy life a little until I could buy enough land to never see my neighbors, hire an architect and a builder, and create this. These days, I mostly edit what others write, make more money, and I get to spend it how I want because I already have my oasis, as you called it. Life is good."

"You still write for yourself?"

She brought a hand to her face, half hiding behind her fingers.

"I'm not sure I'm ready to tell you this!"

"Spill the beans," I said. She would have just said no if she didn't want to share. We were playing a little game.

"Sometimes," she said, "sitting here, I jot a chapter or two of a young adult fantasy novel, with fairies and pixies and dryads. They come out and recruit two teenage sisters to help them save their world. The two sisters, being as mischievous as me and awfully bored on their big farm, are more than happy to get into all kinds of trouble."

"Sounds like a happy book."

"Thank you. That's probably the nicest thing you could have said to me about it. I hope it will be. A happy book."

"Maybe you'll write a whole series of them and be a best-seller and never have to walk into an office again."

"From your lips to the Universe's ears. But if I don't, that's okay too. I'm at a good place in my life."

She put her hand on top of mine, brushing against it as I was still letting my fingertips play on her thigh. I wanted to believe I could be part of that life.

"May I get the elephant out of the room?" I asked with my patented subtlety.

"Please, chase it right off my patio!" she said with a flourish of the hand, nearly spilling wine. It was a good thing her glass was nearly empty.

"We obviously have a thing for each other. I've known Heather longer than anyone else in Miami. You've known her longer. She'd be cool with us being a thing, right?"

"Are you kidding?" Amy raised her glass in victory (and for a refill). "So long as we don't end up hurting each other, she'll be the one popping the champagne. She often talks about you. She adores you, and she and I—and Jen—have been best friends since college. She'll dance a happy dance."

"I thought so. I'm glad you do too."

"How'd you meet her anyway?" Amy asked.

I leaned my head back, looking at the few stars starting to show, taking a trip in the Way Back machine.

"I was just starting as a PI. She'd had a big promotion. She was managing now, and she wanted to make her mark. That's when she was still on the retail side, before her big break in buying. Anyway, she had the crazy idea of hiring an outside PI to reduce shrinkage. I don't know why she hired me. Maybe because I was new and cheap back then, and the budget they gave her for her crazy idea was ridiculously low. Whatever the reason, the project was a success, and she and I hit it off. Not like you and I are hitting it off. We never dated or had crazy times or anything, but we became fast friends and stayed that way."

"It's kind of easy to become friends with Heather."

"Yeah, it is."

"What did you do before you hung your shingle?"

"More way back talk, eh?"

"I'm curious."

The stars above seemed to be writing the story, short as I made it.

"I paid for my criminal justice degree with an ROTC scholarship. I always knew I'd make a go of the Army, more than my minimum commitment. After graduating, I was assigned command of an MP platoon in the Big Red One—that's what those of us on the inside call the First Infantry Division. I did a few things right and got into Army Intelligence after that, doing things

I can't talk about even now."

Without thinking about it, I let her see a little of the dark side. My mouth just kept moving.

"Some of it was crazy shit. Chances are, if you see me looking like I'm lost in space, or I'm moving a little slow, a little tense for no apparent reason, something pulled me back there."

Amy squeezed my hand, and I was back on the deck, feeling the weight of her legs on mine, the touch of her skin against my fingers, seeing the shape of her chest defining her silhouette as she breathed, her face turned toward the sky. She kept holding my hand, and it seemed okay that my mouth kept moving, forming words I hadn't meant to speak.

"Anyway," I started again. "Do you know the difference between the peacetime Army and the wartime Army?"

"Tell me."

"The Army is built for war, to defend the country when war is the only option. In wartime, leadership rises. It's a powerful, honorable, proud organization. In peacetime, bureaucrats and accountants rise. It's big, slow, obsessed with rules and regulations, and rudderless. Back then, we were a little in between the two, but I still couldn't hack the bureaucracy."

That wasn't the half of it. I couldn't tell her the half of it, how idiot bureaucrats got people killed, how one paper pusher bragging to a girl at a bar could turn into a hole in a good soldier's head two days later, how no one really cared.

My mind drifted, stuck somewhere in the past. I stopped talking—not long, and Amy waited for me to come back.

"To make a long story short," I said after I shook off the ghosts, "I took my promotion to major, got out of the regular Army but stayed in the Reserves. Then I moved to Miami on a whim, got my PI license, and the rest, as they say, is history."

Her hand was still tight on mine.

"All that brought you here now, so all of it is good."

We sat for a while after that, basking in the glow of a Florida summer night with our glasses of wine. Then, eyes lost on the horizon again, she asked, "Is it okay if I ask about the case? I don't want to pull you into work after hours."

"Yeah, of course."

"I'm just curious. It's a thing with me. Is there anything new?"

"Well, you were right about the Linda woman for starters. She was watching you guys."

"And yet by your tone, I'm thinking you're about to say something surprising."

"She was watching you because she was paid to."

"What?" Amy lifted her head with an "are you shitting me" look on her face.

I told her Linda was working personal security, how Morrison had hired her as a favor, and how she'd just been at the wrong place at the wrong time. Then Amy leaned back into the couch, and I kept talking. I told her everything else, everything I knew. I shared it all, even my bad night drinking alone in the office after visiting Linda. The only thing I did not talk about was Locke, just in case she went back under. I couldn't risk exposing an undercover, no matter the circumstances, no matter my own trust in Amy. It felt good to have someone to talk to, someone who listened not because they were working the case but because they cared.

Amy cocked her head and looked at me with one eye at the end of my rambling speech.

"Were you supposed to tell me all this?"

"Our regulations prevent us from babbling, but there's no privilege like there is for lawyers or doctors," I told her. "I claim there is something close to it to keep the cops at bay when I need to. And I do promise my clients confidentiality where it matters, but I'm judge of when it matters and when the case is best served by me saying something. I usually err on the side of silence, but, in your case, I just don't see Heather minding."

"I don't either," she said. "Do you think William's and—what was his name—Morant's deaths are related?"

"Morant, yes. Owen Morant. I can't prove it, so it felt okay telling MDPD they might not be, but my gut says they are. Coincidences happen all the time, events are linked in time but not otherwise related. I just don't think this is one. I'll bet there's a link. I just can't see it yet."

"Can I ask a stupid girl question?"

"No such thing." I meant it, and I loved talking with her, so I was not about to say no to another question.

"You got cornered on a deserted stretch of highway. Morant was beaten to death. Not to be paranoid, but I was aboard that ship. I partied with William. Am I safe? Fuck, forget that. Are you safe?"

"I wouldn't be here if I thought it would put you in danger. I'm not a patient man, but I could have waited to see you. I'd have hated it, but I could have. There's something going on here, but it's something below the surface, something that's not obvious. I don't think the people who partied with the StarQuest trio are at risk." I gave her a wink and half air quotes with my wine-glass hand. "Even those who 'partied' with William."

She slapped my hand and stuck her tongue out at me before holding it again.

"Okay. I trust you."

"And as for me, you don't need to worry, I can handle myself." I leaned over her just enough to be able to look her in the eyes. "This isn't bravado. And I'm not placating you. I know you only got the five-minute version of my life, but you can trust me on that too. I can handle myself. I won't let myself get hurt. Okay?"

She looked back at me for a long moment. Then she closed her eyes and held my hand just a little harder against her leg.

"Okay," she said.

"Do you mind if I ask you a couple of questions since we're talking about this? I don't want to ruin the evening. I can call tomorrow about work."

Her chest shook a little as a giggle escaped her lips.

"I think I can take a few questions and we'll still be good."

"Yeah. I know you can. This is a good evening."

"It is," she said.

"What did William's cabin look like when the party stormed its shores? When I saw it yesterday, it was empty. I tried to picture it at party time, but you were there. You don't have to use your imagination."

"I bet the picture inside your head is pretty close. It was a zoo. There were people everywhere—downstairs anyway. People could go upstairs. William didn't care, and I don't think it was just for the benefit of one Linda Mayak, bodyguard. He just loved attention, any kind of attention, so long as he had people around him. Most people stayed downstairs, though, because that's where the bar was. Some used glasses, some drank from the bottle. More bottles kept being brought up. It kept everyone in a good mood, which is why the three of us went.

"Sex, besides William going all out?"

"It wasn't an orgy or anything, but it could get touchy-feely around the sofas. Sometimes people came and went in twos."

"Drugs?"

"Lots. It's not my kind of wild. A little buzz is all I need to get my freak on. But I don't judge those who indulge."

I shrugged my own indifference.

"Pot? Hard stuff?"

"Coke like a blizzard on Mount Kilimanjaro in the middle of winter. I don't know if William brought a suitcase full or if concierge service on the *Rio* included the illegal stuff, but it was insane."

"How late did the parties go?"

"They weren't all-nighters. I guess that's the thing with drugs and booze—people crash. The room tended to empty quickly. When I 'partied' with William," she added, along with her own half air quotes, "the suite went from deafening to silent in what felt like minutes, which was a great cue for me to get back to Heather and Jen in our own cabin. I guess once a few people crash and leave, the exodus begins."

My silence marked the end of work for the night. Amy straightened up, swinging her legs down, and laid her head on my shoulder. I put my arm around her, and it was her turn to rest a hand on my thigh, just high enough that I knew she was interested too and not shy about it.

The warm night was cloaking us. Her body felt good against mine, and I could have stayed on that sofa all night. But if I stayed any longer, I wouldn't leave. I squeezed her fingers.

"I should probably go," I said.

That's when she kissed me again, freely, passionately, unguarded. She laid a hand on my chest, and I ran mine down her back. There is no telling how long we kissed like that before we walked to the front door.

She opened the door, and we kissed again. She pulled my shirt into her fist and pushed me against the wall, her body against mine. Her passion was infectious. It made my heart race, took my breath away. I wanted her. I wanted to show her how bad. I pushed her right back against the opposite wall, kissing her harder, sliding my hand under her shirt, feeling her chest, her bare flesh responsive to my touch.

"I want you, Coop," she said, slightly out of breath. "You need to get out of here before I can't let you go."

I was breathing too hard to form an answer, even if I could figure one out. What she said didn't make sense to me.

She looked into my eyes, our bodies still glued together, my hand caressing her breast. She spoke haltingly.

"I warned you. I'm the wild one of the group. I goddamn specialize in one-night stands. I know I'll fuck it up, whatever 'it' is, if I fuck you right now, no matter how much I want to. And for some reason, there's something about you that makes me really, really like you, you son of a bitch. So, get the hell out of here so we can have a chance at more later."

I held her face with both hands and touched my forehead to hers.

"I got you. And I'll see you later. I promise you." I gave her one last kiss after that, all soft and totally not me, most of the time anyway. Not the "me" I knew. Then I headed outside, pulling the door closed behind me.

I was certain Amy's heart was beating as loudly as mine on the other side of the red door. But I had the bike. I kicked the old Indian to life and headed west into the countryside. It was just me and the night, and it suited me just fine. Patches of trees made room for farmland and marshes. They all whizzed past in blurry shades of gray. I didn't pay them any mind. I just rode. I'd turn around for home eventually—when the time was right.

CHAPTER 25

For **not having slept much,** I felt pretty good the following day. I poked my head through CJ's open door as soon as we'd all settled in. "Let's have a case meeting if you have a moment," I said.

"Sure," she said.

"You too, Courtney," I called out. I walked around the conference table without waiting and took a seat on the far side. CJ and Courtney came in and sat across from me.

"Things got interesting after I left the office," I told them after my favorite amount of small talk—zero. My captive audience waited while I paused for effect. I didn't make them wait too long.

"Turns out," I said, "that even though I didn't find Stephanie Lo, she found me. And it also turns out she's not really Stephanie Lo, but Special Agent Sally Locke, DEA."

"Oh, dear God," CJ said. She buried her head in her hands, then looked up at me again, her fingers still half in front of her mouth. "Now we have two law enforcement agencies poking around this case. And you probably played games with her too."

"She called me cagey," I said with a grin.

CJ shook her head.

"Great. Just great."

"It wasn't that bad," I said. I gave her and Courtney the details of the encounter. CJ recovered her inscrutable demeanor. She listened to my report with perfect stillness. Courtney was focused, hands flying over her tablet.

"She was right," CJ said. "You were cagey. What will you do now?"

I hadn't spent the entire bike ride daydreaming last night. I'd mulled over how to make the best out of Sally Locke's appearance on the scene.

"I'm going to make a friend," I said. I dragged the speakerphone from the end of the table to a spot between the three of us, looked up a number in my contacts, and dialed.

"Detective Rodríguez," the familiar voice answered on speaker.

"Malone," I announced.

There was a brief pause, long enough to indicate he hadn't expected to hear from me.

"You have something for me, Mr. Malone?"

"Yeah. I told you I'd call if I came across anything relevant to the Morant case. I did, and I'm a man of my word."

"Go ahead," he said.

"Morant was getting serious about stopping the flow of drugs on the *Rio*. He was working the case hand in hand with the DEA. They're still investigating the *Rio* now."

"How do you know that?"

"Never mind how. I'll tell you the story of my genius another time. I'm guessing the DEA did not reach out to you in an outpouring of professional courtesy toward a fellow law enforcement agency?"

"They did not. Fucking Feds." Rodríguez was pissed off. I could nearly hear his teeth grinding over the phone.

"Now you know. Do me a favor, though. You didn't hear it from me. Pull some anonymous tip crap or something."

"Alright. And here's a tip from one of the good guys, since you can recognize us after all. Watch your back."

"How's that?"

"I just heard back from a friend of mine in California. Dunn is bad news. He was all but run out of the state after some shady stuff. I don't know the details, but no one in law enforcement over there would look his way, and he burnt all his bridges with local politicians. It sounded serious . . . serious enough for people to keep their mouths shut even now."

"Understood. Thanks, Detective."

"No problem. Thank you, Malone." He hung up.

"That's how you make friends?" CJ asked. "Playing both sides against the middle?" She wasn't upset. She wouldn't have expected anything different. This did not rise to a case of doing something stupid before talking to her.

"Call it greasing the wheels a little," I said, "trying to make things go our way." CJ shook her head once more. I raised my hands like the shrug emoji. We knew the score. We worked differently. Maybe it was because I came from a long line of hot-blooded Irishmen and she was raised in part by Grandma Vinh and her disciplined Asian ways. But we worked well together in spite of it, or maybe because of it.

I looked from her to Courtney and back and moved the meeting along. "What do we have?"

"No response from my direct message to Claire," Courtney offered. "I'm working on getting more info."

"And I met with Cabe Roper yesterday," CJ said, referring to StarQuest's youngest and geekiest partner.

"What did you think of our math genius?"

"I read him as earnest. I saw no sign of deception. He's high-IQ, low-EQ. He was very close to Morrison, who took him under his wing, but he is processing death differently. Mathematical modeling becomes a coping mechanism."

"Could he have killed William without feeling the weight of murder on his shoulders?" Courtney asked.

"I don't think so," CJ said. "He has emotions. He just lives them differently than most of us. If he's a high-functioning psychopath and faking it, then he faked me too. I do not believe he is."

"Did you get anything more than how he likes his scotch and how sweet he is on Jen?" I asked.

"He mostly talked about Morrison. And he talked about him a lot. I think I caught him at the right time for an emotional brain dump of some sort. I do not deny he is hard to figure out in some ways. But I did not catch anything earth-shattering in all that talk. It's in the report for extra pairs of eyes to double check."

"I'll read it this morning," I said.

"I have a meeting with Linda Mayak tomorrow morning," CJ said, picking up where she left off. Her presentation had all the hallmarks of formal professionalism. There was no middle ground with CJ. Professional meant *professional*. She was sitting straight, hands in front of her, looking back and forth between Courtney and me, making sure she was engaging us both. "And I'm trying to corner Walt Rosling. If we're still fishing after that, I'll reach out to Heather and her friends for follow-up interviews with them too."

"Jen still does not know Morrison died with a piece of his skull missing," I reminded CJ. "At least she didn't last I checked."

CJ nodded. She remembered. She would have an easier time than me being gentle with her anyway.

"And you can cross Amy off your list. I followed up with her last night," I added.

"Why?" CJ asked. "She seemed to have given a complete interview."

"I just did."

By then, Courtney was cocking her head at me with a sly grin on her face.

"Because he likes her," she said.

She pointed a finger at me. "You like her."

"Doesn't fucking matter if I like her or don't like her. I followed up with her."

Courtney was leaning in closer across the table, grinning wider.

"You do," she said. "You really do."

Now CJ was looking up at the ceiling, arms raised to the heavens.

"Thank God." She dropped her arms back onto the table. "If you get laid, maybe you won't be as grumpy."

"If you two are about done," I said a little too loud, "maybe I can give you my report."

"Yep, yep," Courtney said, hands hovering above her tablet, head down, eyes on the screen, looking away from me. She wasn't embarrassed by what CJ had said. Courtney did not embarrass that easy. No, she was trying not to laugh too loud at the boss. She made an admirable effort, but her shoulders kept shaking. *Try harder.*

"No new information per se," I said to a spot on the wall between CJ's and Courtney's heads. I went on to give the new details I had learned about the parties in William's suite-slash-Versailles Palace, including the lively drug trade, which looked more and more like it justified the DEA's interest.

"Just one more question," CJ said when I was done. She was looking at me but leaning toward Courtney. I glared at her. *Et tu, Brute?*

"Did you take the bike or the CR-V to your follow-up?" she asked.

"What the fuck does it matter?"

CJ leaned closer to Courtney and raised a hand to her mouth as if she were about to whisper a secret.

"He took the bike," she said out loud. "He likes her. If she's ever on the Indian's bitch seat, they're a serious couple."

Courtney nodded her understanding with a stupid grin on her face. I liked it better when she was conspiring with me to break into Mardi Gras than conspiring with CJ to probe my personal life.

"You can both . . ." I started.

I was saved by the bell, or, as it were, by the phone. The speakerphone had no display screen, but Courtney looked down at her tablet, which was linked to our caller ID.

"DEA," she said.

I pushed the green button on the speakerphone.

"Malone."

"This is Special Agent Locke."

"Good morning," I said. "You're on speaker with my partner, CJ Beck."

"I'd expect that," she said after a moment of silence. "Please keep my name between the two of you, though."

"You go it." I looked at Courtney, holding a finger in front of my lips even though it was entirely unnecessary.

"Understood," CJ said. "And good to meet you."

"Same here," Locke said. "I'm sending you our Morrison file. I doubt there's much you don't already know in there. He comes through as a rich finance guy who thinks he can do whatever he wants—that he's untouchable. We investigated him for a while because there always seemed to be narcotics around him. He's a user and a sharer, not a dealer, though he shared enough we could have made it stick. We kept the file open for potential leverage later but did not take enforcement action. Anyway, I didn't see anything screaming that he was about to be murdered. It should all be in your email now."

I saw Courtney swipe at her tablet. Three taps and a second later, she was nodding at me.

"It is," I said.

"I expedited the release authorization. You know what federal paperwork can be like. I expect you to hold your end of the bargain."

"I'll play ball. No need to worry about me."

"One more thing," she said. "The name you gave me."

"Dunn?"

"Yes. It made a lot of lights flash red when I put it in the computer. Our pals in the FBI tried to make a RICO charge against him stick back in Cali. They couldn't quite get there. It had something to do with corruption, but there were bodies, plural, in that mess. I know better than to suggest you should back off. You don't seem the type. But watch your back."

"Thank you, Special Agent." *What is it with everyone wanting me to watch my back?*

"You can call me Sally. I have a feeling we'll talk again."

"Thank you, Sally. And call me Coop."

"'Talk soon, Coop."

I was staring right at CJ before the line went dead.

"And I know better than to suggest you should stay away from Rosling, but be fucking careful, okay? I don't want Dunn to have a second go at hurting one of us on the way from Key West."

"I will," CJ said.

That was exactly what I needed to hear from her. When things got serious, the fewer words CJ used, the stronger her commitment.

The meeting broke up, and I went back to my office to read CJ's report on her talk with Cabe Roper. Reading between the lines, it seemed the kid wanted to be helpful. He kept trying to come up with more to say. He just didn't have much.

I spent my time alternating between staring at the file and carving a trail in the carpet. The techs were still working on their stuff, as was Courtney with the hard drive. There was no point bugging them. My irritation was not a good enough reason, even if I wished it were. I hated waiting nearly as much as I hated being out of leads.

I gave some serious thoughts about storming Dunn's office, all those words of caution be damned. I wasn't thinking I could sweet talk him into doing the right thing, like sharing info or even hinting at his client. I was thinking a little shock treatment might shake something loose, and I didn't particularly give a damn whether or not that involved guns going off. Dunn thought of himself as powerful. One prick to his ego and things might fly off like a county-fair balloon with a hole in it. Or like bullets, CJ would say. She would fight me on this, and she would probably be right, but I had to do something.

For the second time that day, I was saved by the phone. I picked up my cell from the desk and looked at the caller ID. It read Det. Jorge Rodríguez, MDPD.

"Twice in a day," I said as I picked up.

"Are you at your office?" he asked.

"Yeah."

"Be downstairs in five minutes. I'll pick you up. Unmarked dark red Taurus."

He hung up without waiting for an answer. I was downstairs two minutes later.

CHAPTER 26

Since I had not waited five minutes to go down, I ended up waiting on the sidewalk outside the building, like a hooker waiting for a john to pull over, hoping he wouldn't be too much of a creep. Before I could dwell on that image too long, the unmarked Taurus flashed its lights in the distance, barely long enough for me to notice it. A minute later, Detective Rodríguez pulled over in the right lane, and I scrambled into the passenger seat. Rodríguez sped up even as I was putting my seat belt on.

"What's going on?" I asked.

"You kept your word, so I'm keeping mine. We got a break in the Morant case."

"What kind of a break?"

"One that started with your DEA tip. And since you're credentialed and I do believe our cases are related, you may attend and observe. Observe only." He punctuated the last words with a raised finger in my general direction.

"Thanks," I said.

"Sure. Anyway, after your call, I contacted some friends in Narcotics and in the Special Investigation Division."

I knew enough about MDPD to know that SID was like a major case squad, including drug ones, so their portfolio overlapped with the Narcotics Bureau and just about everybody else.

"One of the narcs," Rodríguez continued, "has a CI who had reported earlier overhearing three Latino street gang members brag that they had, and I quote, 'war hammered some *mayate*.'" I recognized the Latino gang slang for black people. Rodríguez kept going. "They had no clue if it was true or who the victim might be until I called them. We put our heads together and talked to the CI again. We realized it could well be about Morant. The CI had a bead on the gang when we called, so we got a rush warrant, and we're putting together an arrest operation right now."

Making friends worked. And to think CJ doubted me.

Rodríguez turned on the light and sirens to get us out of downtown. The afternoon traffic parted like the Red Sea.

"How often do you turn those on when you're late for beers with the guys?" I asked.

He glanced at me and winked.

"Never."

Once out of the business district, Rodríguez switched the lights and sirens off. He kept a heavy foot on the accelerator. We were heading north of the airport into some of the less friendly parts of town.

We soon parked at the periphery of organized chaos centered around two armored trucks with SRT painted on the side. That stood for Special Response Team because MDPD refused to call its door kickers "SWAT" like everyone else. Cowboys from the Warrants Bureau with guns on their hips hung around the helmeted SRT crew and their automatic rifles like wolves hungry for a kill.

Rodríguez and I got out of the car. He handed me a clear plastic pouch on an MDPD lanyard. I put my PI credentials in it, hung it around my neck, and stuck close to Rodríguez and his badge. I took in all the gunpowder walking around us.

"You want him alive, right?" I asked.

"Them. And, yes, I want them alive. We also know they're carrying and won't hesitate to let bullets fly, so going in with a dozen guns in their faces isn't a bad plan."

"Are you lead on this?" I asked him.

"On the investigation, yes. SRT is lead on the arrest."

We climbed into one of the armored trucks, the one serving as the command post. A Hollywood-cast officer in an SRT jacket turned to the door—crew cut, square-jawed, blue-eyed, barrel-chested.

"Welcome aboard, Rodríguez," he said.

The two men shook hands, then Rodríguez pointed to each of us in turn.

"Malone, this is Lieutenant Tommy Wood, the officer in command of the arrest. Tommy, Cooper Malone."

We shook hands and Rodríguez briefed Woods in more depth about me and my role in the case, then the three of us joined other officers already gathered before a bank of monitors.

Wood addressed the troops.

"We have a confidential informant with eyes recently on the targets, three bona fide gang members. They are reportedly at this establishment, pounding a few beers." He shone a laser pointer at some aerial and street-view still shots on one of the screens.

He moved the pointer to a screen with a black and white floor plan.

"The space is long and narrow with only two entrances, front and back, in line with each other. No corners to worry about, but there is a side door to a small bathroom, and there are a half dozen booths on the other side from the bar. The plan is for a dynamic entry from both entrances simultaneously. The targets are armed and suspected killers. Get them down on the ground with a boot on their mugs before they grab their piece. Hopefully, they're drinking enough to slow them down, but watch out for liquid courage."

"Any chance of talking them out?" one of the other officers in the room asked.

"Based on who we are dealing with and our objective at this time, no." Wood was firm and on point. He listened then he decided. I decided I liked him, even if I didn't like his plan.

"Anybody else in the bar?" the same officer asked.

"Likely," Wood said. "Position and number unknown. This is not ideal, but we can work with it. Speed is key here, people. We need the targets neutralized before this goes to shit."

Nods around the table sealed the deal.

"Remember," Rodríguez broke in. "They are suspects, not convicts. We need them alive, and we need to take them with a minimum of damage."

There were fewer nods to that, even after Wood stared down the room with a pointed "Got it?" The most emphatic agreement came from the officer who'd spoken up, an oversized tattooed Latino, all muscles from armored floor to armored ceiling. He had the least to prove or the most brains. Or both.

The reasonable thing would have been for me to keep my mouth shut and let the pros do their job. I crushed the reasonable guy inside me. I looked directly at Wood.

"Look, I know I'm a guest, but, if it's okay with you, I'd like to float something."

The SRT commander cut any sneering down before it started.

"All ideas welcome."

"I've got some experience with things like this from my days in the field with Army Intelligence." They weren't exactly things like this, but I could not care less right at the moment. There is a certain camaraderie among people in that world, and I needed them to listen. I wanted the marks alive to answer my questions. I wanted things done my way.

"Get on with it," Wood said. He had no more patience for me than for the itchy triggers.

"Any of you go in there, the shooting starts," I said. "I get that. But I look more like a retired cop than a cop these days. Why don't you mic me up and let me go in there? Just maybe I can talk them out. If it doesn't work, you execute the breach as planned, nothing lost."

Wood's eyes narrowed. He knew just enough about me not to dismiss what I said out of hand. All the same, there he was, scratching his cheek, the corners of his mouth inching up.

"You don't exactly fit in there, man," he said.

"I could go in with him. We can make it work." That had come from the giant tattooed officer who'd spoken up in favor of keeping the temperature down earlier.

Wood shook his head. "Odds are too low. Not worth it."

I took one more shot.

"Depends. Maybe it is. Look at it this way. What's the worst that could happen? If things go sideways, the two of us hit the deck and you breach like you were always going to. The only damage is our ears ringing from the flashbangs. We'll deal. But best-case scenario, we walk them out and the risk of collateral damage drops to a cool zero."

"Concur," the officer who would be going with me said.

I'll give Wood credit. He was in command for a reason. He didn't get pissed at another argument. He was thinking it over. I could see the wheels turning, the way he was playing out tactical scenarios in his head.

He looked around the room. "Any non-obvious objection?"

Nobody spoke. Wood took a long, hard look at me and a shorter one at his officer. "You two dumb shits are sure about this?" he asked.

"Yes," the officer said.

I simply nodded.

"Okay then, we'll give it a try," Wood decided. "Move fast. The window's closing."

My new best friend hurried out of the truck, and I followed on his heels. He walked to a car in gigantic strides and opened the trunk. He took off his vest and SRT T-shirt. His chest and back were covered in tats too. He pulled a wife beater from the trunk, put it on, and slid his Glock in his waistband, gangster style.

"You keep undercover clothes in your trunk?" I asked.

"You don't?"

I spread my arms. My jeans and oversized black tee would have to do. I took the cash out of my wallet and put it in my pocket. Then I dropped wallet, keys, and credentials in the trunk—anything that could identify me. The big man was going through the same motions next to me. As soon as we were done, he slammed the trunk shut.

He extended a meaty hand to me. "I'm . . . ."

"Later," I said, interrupting him. I nodded toward the bar we were headed to. "Just tell me what to call you in there. I only want one name to remember you by right now."

"You can call me José," he said.

"Does that make me Steve?" I asked, blurting out the most common Anglo first name that went through my head.

He threw his head back and laughed. "Yeah. You're Steve. I like it."

I flashed back to some of the shadier off-the-books ops I did when serving in the Army meant not being in uniform. I thought about the bunch of guys (and a couple of tough bitches) I did them with, about the bond that formed from facing danger, laughing at stuff that was not really funny. I missed that part. José's big laugh brought me back.

Tommy Wood came out, flanked by a tech in a golf shirt on one side and Rodríguez on the other. He gave us each a small piece of plastic with metallic mesh on one side. "This is your mic—high-quality shit. You're walking into a pub, so this shouldn't be a pat-down situation. Just put it in your pocket. If that turns out to be incorrect, or if anything else goes south, your distress code is 'hands off.' You say it, we breach. Period. Got it?"

"Yes," José said.

"Hands off," I repeated. "Got it."

Wood went back to the command post.

Rodríguez lingered a minute. "So much for observing," he said. "You're one giant pain in the ass."

"I'd say sorry, but we both know that'd be bullshit."

"I'd say I expected better, but that would be bullshit too. Be careful in there. I'd rather you didn't get shot on my watch. Paperwork and all that."

"Sure. Just for you."

He fist-bumped my shoulder and went to join Wood. I started to feel bad for bullshitting him over Morrison. The guy was all right. I shook my head. There'd be time to think about that later. I had bigger fish to fry.

José and I walked to the dive bar where the three punks we suspected of killing Morant were drinking without a care in the world. I let the anger fill me. Anger was good at times like this. Anger kept you sharp. José looked impressive next to me. I'm over six feet, and I looked like a dwarf. That kind of backup felt good too.

"Let's do this," José said.

CHAPTER 27

We rounded the corner, leaving the staging area out
of sight behind us, and walked the two blocks to the bar. You'd have to
know it was there. There was nothing but a nondescript door cut in one of a
row of stucco buildings. The name painted above was too faded to make out.

Inside, the bar was dark. My eyes took a minute to adjust, and even then
it was hard to see. Dirty windows filtered out the sunlight. The lighting was
dim and haphazard. There was a blurry feel to the place, as if the haze from
long ago cigarette smoke had never entirely left. The floor was sticky underfoot.

The layout was as advertised. I could make out the outline of the back
door on the other side, a thin rectangle of light at the end of the tunnel. A long
bar covered the length to our left, across the aisle from half a dozen booths.

The three thugs we were here to see sat at the end of the bar. A man in
his fifties, all in black with a cowboy hat, was doing his best Johnny Cash
impersonation on a stool closer to the entrance. Two young women in baby
doll tops and jean shorts were engrossed in conversation in one of the booths.
The place was otherwise empty except for the bartender who eyed us as we
walked in. He was hard to miss. He stood nearly as tall as José.

One of the bangers pointed at me within seconds of us walking in.

"What's the white boy doing here?" he said in accented English.

"What?" José asked, mixing in a Latino accent that came naturally but
hadn't been there ten minutes earlier. "You don't like my bitch?"

All three burst out in drunken laughter, loud and boisterous. José grinned as he made his way toward them with me in tow. José sat down, leaving an empty barstool between them and us. I sat down on the other side of him. The smartass at the farthest end of the bar leaned over for a better look at me.

"He's kinda big for a bitch."

José stood up and held his hand next to his head as if he was measuring his height. "Seriously?" he asked. He got another round of doubled-over laughter for his effort.

José sat back down and introduced himself by his undercover name. He and the thugs fell into rapid Spanish, a little too fast and too heavy with slang for me to follow. There was more laughter, and José bought them a round. The bartender's hulking presence slowly moved away. We strangers were not making any trouble.

The guy closest to José kept squirming on his seat, squinting, giving me the once over around José's massive body.

"White boy looks like a cop," he said. It wasn't a compliment.

"Used to be," I said. "In the Army. That shit's behind me."

"Oh yeah? Behind you, uh? You don't say."

"The Army fucked me over, man. Kicked me out for the pretty blue eyes of some pussy officer who didn't like my choices."

"Your choice in men?" the hooligan in the middle asked. He affected a high pitch and was laughing at how clever he was. He was the only one laughing. Even his buddies ignored him.

"My choices of when I drank and whose ass I kicked," I shot back.

"Then what do you do now, 'former' Army cop?" My accuser sniffled, nose in the air. "Still smells like pig in here. I think you still work for the man."

"I work for money," I said. He was playing right into my hands.

Doubting Thomas cocked his head at José. "José doesn't look loaded," he said.

"I don't work for José. The people I work for, they're loaded—serious green. Sometimes, we do favors for José. So, once in a while, José does us a favor too."

"Like what?"

The rubber was about to meet the road. Either they'd bite, or we'd call for the breach, trusting in our microphones. "Like making sure I get to talk to you three assholes before you put a hole in my gut."

"Is this a joke?"

"No joke."

He had not made a move to stand up or reached for his piece. We were still talking. For now. Our interlocutor seemed to be the leader of this band of worthless shitheads. He was still considering what I'd just said, looking down and grinding his boot against the floor like he was crushing a spider.

"And why would you want to do that?" he asked under his breath.

"Rumor on the street is you take good aim with your wood."

"You like wood?" the crew's funny man asked, grabbing his crotch. "I got wood for you."

"*¡Cállate!*" the leader barked and shot the other man a dirty look. *Shut up.* I knew just enough Spanish to catch this one.

"What do you mean?" he asked, returning his attention to me.

I shrugged and took a swig of my beer. I didn't bother looking at him to answer.

"If you don't know, I must have the wrong guys. No sweat."

"And if I knew what you meant?"

"Then maybe you could make some money."

"How much?"

The mighty dollar . . . . How I loved it. It greased every squeaky wheel. I shrugged again, still focused on my beer. "You'd have to talk to the boss."

"To José?"

José laughed. "Hell, no," he said.

"Black escalade around the corner," I said. I looked at my watch. "It will still be there for, oh, just about ten minutes. You want to discuss the job and what it pays, you talk to the man inside."

"I don't like being told what to do."

I raised a hand and swiveled to face him. "No disrespect, hombre. It's

189

an offer, that's all. No one's telling you what to do. My boss wants to see if you three are up for a little exercise that pays well. You decide. You talk to him, or you don't."

"Who is he? Your boss."

I lasered on him, leaning over the bar so José wouldn't block half my face. "You're not that dumb. I'm not telling you personal shit. You can ask him yourself if you make a deal. Otherwise, we'll just have a beer among friends."

He turned around to the other two hoodlums in his crew. "Stay here," he said.

"You didn't hear me," I said. "Boss wants to lay eyes on all three of you."

"I don't work that way."

"Then, we just finish our beers. No hard feelings."

I could sense José tensing up. I was hoping my heartbeat couldn't be heard outside my chest. I ran my fingers along my mug. The cold beer and hot air were making it sweat.

This op was about to go dynamic, one way or the other. We'd either walk out with them into a SWAT storm, or the storm would come to us. All it would take was another mention of beer, José calling out, "keep your hands off my glass," and flash bangs would burst like we were too close to the grand finale at the fucking Fourth of July fireworks. It all depended on how much pull money had. *How badly do you want it, asshole?*

"Okay," he finally said. "Fine. Let's go see what your big boss man has to say." He got up and started heading toward the back. "*¡Vamanos!*" he called to his crew as he passed by them. They scurried behind him like rats. José and I strode along.

Everything happened in seconds. It was a blur even for José and me—the thugs had no chance. The leader opened the door and disappeared sideways, yanked by unseen SRT hands. José and I were ready for it, both of us already reaching for our guns. The other two gangbangers hesitated half a second. That was half a second too long.

I grabbed the shirt of the one closest to me and mashed my gun against his ear.

"Bad idea," I growled.

Next to me, José had his man flat against the wall, a massive forearm across the man's throat, a gun jammed in his ribs.

"Show me hands!" he yelled. "Hands!"

Then before we could take a second breath, shouting men in flak jackets swarmed around us like a wave over a surfer who just wiped out. I felt José back up more than I saw him, and I did the same, pointing my gun at the ceiling. SRT pushed the two skunks we'd just slammed against the wall to their knees, pulled out zip ties, and jammed their M4 barrels into the lowlifes' ribs.

Something caught my eye—something I was not consciously aware of that tugged at a corner of my subconscious brain. I'm not even sure it's something I saw, though it seemed like it at that moment. Maybe it was. I was jostled all around by the SRT tsunami, my eyes catching a little bit of this and a little bit of that in all directions.

Whatever it was, it triggered something in my brain, something honed by training and experience, something that was now indelibly embedded in the deepest recesses of my mind. I acted on instinct.

I crouched low and extended my arms in a shooting stance, keeping my barrel pointed down. I swiveled and peeked toward the entrance, cocking my head to try and see through the curtain of bodies in flak jackets that had surrounded me.

I saw him a fraction of a second before the man next to me did too. There was movement all the way down by the bar. It was like a jigsaw puzzle, part of a man in black flashing in between officers' limbs or through an opening between an elbow and a hip. It was enough. The Johnny Cash look-alike was standing up, a ridiculously large revolver in his hand. He pointed it at us one-handed—no discipline, no training, just rage and blustering.

I called "Gun! Gun! Gun!" My military training had not gone to shit in the past few years. I yelled the words three times in quick succession, the way you're supposed to. Say it once, and you might not be heard, or it might sound like chatter. No. You shout one word three times. That's the proper warning. The one from the officer next to me overlapped with mine.

Even as I yelled, I twisted around so I could aim around the man in front of me. That cost me a fraction of a second, enough to give the man in black time to fire. And fire he did. He barely aimed. He had a group of us massed at the end of the hallway, all conveniently in his line of fire. He didn't really care which one of us he hit so long as he hit someone.

There is a sound a bullet makes when it enters a body, a sound no one ever forgets once they hear it. It's a sickening, squooshy sound all mixed up with a gasp. I didn't hear that sound when the officer next to me fell on his back. If I'd had time, I'd have let out a sigh of relief. He'd taken it in the vest.

I double tapped two shots, center mass, just like I'd trained for. Just like I'd done before. Time slowed down. I could have sworn I saw the slugs hit, rip through my target's shirt. That's all he was now, a target. He was no longer human. Then I saw blood spatter outward as he lost his balance from the force of the bullets' impact.

The SRT men registered the threat and acted on reflex. By the time they registered that I'd hit the target, their brains had already sent the signal to their fingers to pull the trigger. A hail of automatic fire flew at the shooter like a swarm of determined, deadly bees. Wood splintered on the side of the bar, sunshine beamed through new holes in the walls, fake leather ripped on the farthest bar stool. And the shooter's torso was shredded by bullets piercing his body at supersonic speed.

Then, nothing. Nothing but the echoes of gunfire and the smell of cordite. It was the calm before the storm. Chaos came next. Brothers rushed to make sure the officer who'd been shot was okay. Others went to inspect the damage. It was protocol—they had to inspect the body, establish he was dead so they could swear to it later. It was also useless busy work. He'd taken too many rounds to the chest to be anything but dead.

Somehow, my body moved. I was on autopilot. I clicked the safety back on and holstered my gun. I moved out of the way as I no longer had a role to play. I shuffled into the back alley in a daze. I took deep breaths despite the putrid smell from the garbage tossed out back to rot in the Florida heat.

My heartbeat pounded in my ears. I tried to slow it down. I felt José's enormous hand on my shoulder. His voice came through muffled in my ears.

"Thanks, partner," he said. "You did good in there."

There was yelling further down the street, too. That came from the gangster in chief. "Fuck you!" he yelled, "I knew you were a cop!"

I found my way back to the staging area. José joined me a few minutes later and opened the trunk. My mouth felt so dry I thought I was chewing dirt. José had a couple of bottles of water with his gear in the trunk. I grabbed one, twisted it open, and drained it in one go.

The big officer handed me my wallet and keys with a shit-eating grin. I took the mic from my pocket and gave him the precious MDPD property back in exchange. We turned around to find Wood and Rodríguez.

"It's a fucking mess, but you did a good job, both of you," Wood said. He was somber. Someone got killed on this op. That was no joke. But at least the only blood shed was the shooter's. That qualified as a job well done.

Wood punched José in the arm, then took time to shake my hand. "I was running long range recon around the time you were doing shit with M.I.C.," he said. Like a good Marine, he used Army Intelligence's official acronym, the Military Intelligence Corps. No one but the Army put "Army" and "intelligence" in the same sentence.

"Let's grab a drink and tell each other lies sometimes," I told him.

"Consider it done," he said before heading back to the command post.

José shook my hand next. It'd be more accurate to say he crushed my fingers. "I'm Alberto Villadeste," he said.

"Cooper Malone. Call me Coop. Good working with you, Alberto. Really good."

"Yeah. We kicked ass in there. Not quite the way we hoped, but we still kicked ass."

"Exactly as you said, brother." I slapped his back to avoid having my fingers crushed in the vise that passed for his handshake, then he, too, rejoined the troops.

Only Detective Rodríguez was left standing there.

I couldn't make out his mood. He just stood there, hands shoved in his pockets, looking at me like a poker player daring me to figure out if he was bluffing or held the nuts.

"When I told you not to get shot on my watch, I should have been more specific," he said.

"How's that?"

"I should have added not to shoot anyone else, either. It creates just as much paperwork. You don't even know how much paperwork, goddamn civilian shooting a suspect in the middle of an official police operation. And I need your gun."

"You're right. You should have been more specific," I said as I ejected the magazine, cleared the chamber, and handed him my weapon.

Rodríguez sighed. "The SRT guys seem to think you behaved like you belonged in there."

"What do you think?"

The Detective took a few seconds to think that through. I was surprised he wasn't blowing a gasket after what happened. Maybe he could see the big picture after all.

"I think you're probably as good a liar as you're a shooter," he said, "but you're probably on the side of the good guys. Come on, I'll give you a ride to the station."

CHAPTER 28

I didn't see him for some hours after we got to the station. We were both flooded with different versions of paperwork. Hell, it was dark outside by the time I'd given my official statement in triplicate.

The detainees were booked and processed, and the gang leader's butt was on a metal chair on the other side of the interrogation room's one-way mirror. I wouldn't have known it was dark were it not for the clock on the wall. The nearest window was two rooms away.

As I looked on, the clanky metallic furniture seemed to scream "you're screwed" to people in handcuffs and "cheap government furniture" to the rest of us. It'd been a long time since I looked at a room like this. The last time, the man on the other side had a Middle Eastern accent instead of a Spanish one. There'd been plenty with no accent at all. The basics were always the same: us, good guys; them, bad guys. And the good guys had to be smarter.

Rodríguez had decided I'd earned a seat in the interrogation room, so long as I stayed on my side of the glass. And so here we were, watching the unofficial homicidal leader gesticulate to a man in a frumpy, ill-fitting suit who'd been dispatched from the Public Defender's office. At least he'd answered his phone after hours. That was good news for the man in cuffs, whose name was Denny Mina. I knew him as Scum and always would.

I tried to get a clue from his body language and couldn't make much of it. The sound was off to protect the sacrosanct right to tell the truth just once and never have it repeated on account of privilege. Next to me, Rodríguez kept clicking his pen, much like he'd done the first time we met, when he'd come to ask me about Morant's death.

"Do we know anything about the shooter at the bar, yet?" I asked him, half curious and half killing time.

"No ID, but he had gang tattoos. He was affiliated with the other three, though we do not know his status in the organization yet. It's possible gang loyalty is all it took for him to spray lead."

"It's all it took to get himself killed, you mean. It doesn't pay to fire into half a dozen SRT officers with their fingers on the triggers of their assault rifles."

"Gang members are not known for long-term thinking," Rodríguez said.

"Could be. He may have been that stupid. Or we're missing something."

"We're looking into it."

I nodded and didn't press my luck, even if I was tired and in a bad mood.

Fifteen minutes later, the lawyer got up and knocked on the glass. Rodríguez flipped the sound on and walked in. The lawyer sat back down. Rodríguez stayed standing up. The lawyer cleared his throat.

"My client would like to know why he's been so violently arrested," he said. "He's been thrown to the ground, manhandled, zip tied, hit with the barrels of assault rifles. This is unacceptable."

Rodríguez leaned over them and put his hands on the cold metallic table bolted to the floor. "Maybe," he said, "that's what happens when someone 'war hammers a *mayate*.' You wonder if cops could be next if they came in all polite and shit. Damn, counsel, come to think of it, they were shot at."

Denny Mina, aka "Scum," winced just a little at having his own words thrown back at him. The lawyer saw it. He whispered in his client's ear. The client nodded yes and no at intervals. This went on for a minute or two. I was clenching and unclenching my fists behind the glass.

"Let's assume, hypothetically," the lawyer eventually said, "that my client had information on the assault and death of a certain African-American gentleman at the port. What kind of deal could we be talking about?"

Rodríguez looked at his suspect with a sneer.

"Looking at Denny here, I'm thinking his information is about how much he enjoyed it. No deal."

Scum opened his mouth to speak in protest, but his lawyer silenced him with a raised hand. *Why did we have to draw a smart PD?*

"How about hypothetical information about someone possibly paying for that to happen?" the lawyer asked.

Rodríguez did not answer. He walked to a phone on the wall and picked it up.

"Who's the ASA on duty?" he asked, referring to the Assistant State Attorney on call that night. He nodded at the answer and spoke a few words in return. "Okay, good. Ask her over, will you?" There was just enough time for an answer like "sure" before Rodríguez hung up the phone and joined me on our side of the glass without so much as a look back at Scum or his mouthpiece.

It took about a half hour for the ASA to appear. A sharply dressed black woman with purpose in her step and a leather folio tucked under her arm walked in. She went from courtroom stern to an easy smile when she saw Rodríguez.

"Hi, Jorge," she greeted him. "I'm glad it's you. At least I know I'm not wasting my time."

"I think this will be worth your time," Rodríguez said, pointing to the interrogation room with a snap of his head.

"Who's this?" the ASA asked, looking at me.

"Sorry," Rodríguez said. "This is Cooper Malone, a PI and former Army cop."

"A civilian?" she asked.

"Credentialed, and he helped out with the case," Rodríguez said. He turned to me. "Malone, this is ASA Kathryn Tippins. She's one of the good ones. Don't hold her law degree against her."

Rodríguez went on to fill her in about the investigation, the arrest, my role in it, and his short interrogation.

"Short and sweet," Tippins said.

"You know how it is with gangs—they know the score," Rodríguez said. "They'll try for a quick deal if they think we have them, clam up if they think we don't. Never much movement. We have a live one tonight."

"I know the Public Defender," Tippins said. "One of the smart ones. He won't give away the house, but he'll deal fairly based on what we have. I'll try and make it sound like more than one CI's say-so."

Her eyes had never left the interrogation room. She was taking the measure of her suspect even as she and Rodríguez were talking. Then she went in and started the plea-deal dance, sometimes speaking with the lawyer, sometimes with Scum. It took nearly an hour, but she got him to sign on the dotted line, and one Denny Mina narrated his crimes to the one-way mirror behind Tippins's head. Rodríguez and I were glued to it, unblinking, side by side.

"My crew and I," he said, "we have a good reputation in certain quarters."

"He's fucking bragging," I whispered to Rodríguez.

"Kathryn's good," Rodríguez said. "She gave him a deal on very narrow crimes. I'm certain she'll start digging on what other shit he did to earn his 'reputation' so she can fully prosecute him on that."

I nodded. She had not given up much to start with, just took the death penalty off the table. I listened on.

"One day," Scum was saying, leaning over the table and damn near grinning, "this big black SUV drives up on our street, way too shiny for our little corner. This guy gets out like he fucking belongs there, looking like a linebacker on those performance drugs. At first, I thought he wanted product, so I played nice and I didn't cap him. We talked a little bit, and it turns out he wanted our bats on some *mayate's* face, wanted us swinging hard enough to make the guy stop breathing. He gave us ten grand each up front, promised ten more when the job was done. I figured I'd never see the other ten, but I'd have done the job for free, so I said sure, why not?"

Rodríguez and I both winced. This was not the talk of a psychopath. This was hatred, pure hatred, for anyone beyond his neighborhood or street corner. This was hatred no violence would ever quench, yet we all knew he'd try as long as he breathed.

"Describe how you performed the job," ASA Tippins instructed.

Scum did, in vivid detail. He explained how they were told where to find Morant, and he described him in enough detail there was no doubt it was Morant they killed. He took great pleasure in describing many of the nastier blows. Rodríguez pulled up the autopsy report on the computer in the room. I looked at him as Scum went on. He nodded. It matched.

I fought the urge to barge into the room and do to him with my fists what he did to Morant with baseball bats. My nails were digging into the palms of my hand. My biceps and shoulder muscles were so tense they hurt.

"Did you see anyone else in the SUV?" Tippins asked on the other side of the glass.

"Oh, yeah, that's right," Scum said. He was smiling, as if this was amusing, like it was all a game. "I didn't see the driver. The windows were too dark. But I saw the guy in the back when the muscle got back in. He was a white dude, tall, nice threads, fancy sunglasses. He was as fucking shiny as his car."

"Alan Dunn," Rodríguez and I said at the same time.

The Detective looked at me, his demeanor a lot less friendly than it had been a minute earlier. "You still want to pretend our cases are not related?" he asked.

I kept looking at the scumbag across the glass. I barely heard Rodríguez, but I heard him enough.

"No, Detective." I sighed. "But this may take a while. Let me buy you a drink."

"Fine," he said.

We walked to a cop bar down the block. It was the kind of bar that would do honor to law enforcement or military types across America. Its altar was a large three-sided bar where regulars congregated. There were pictures on the walls, so many you could barely see the walls beneath—pictures of legends and old timers, a history of the city through the men and women in blue. There were a few booths at the back for serious conversation and a lot of high tops to save space or to move around, quick and easy, as people gathered. It was quiet that time of night, but I doubted the place ever closed, no matter what city regulations said.

Rodríguez and I took a high top. He signaled the barman, and we each ordered a bourbon. It took two of those before I was done filling him in. I didn't tell him everything. I did not talk about the break-in, though he asked. He was a straight arrow and would probably book me if I fessed up. And I didn't tell him about Locke or a couple of other things. But he got the big story straight up.

When I was done, Rodríguez was playing with his coaster. He was flipping it from side to side, slapping it on the table. His jaw was working back and forth like he was checking whether it still worked.

"I don't know whether to thank you or toss you in a cell and throw away the keys," he said. "I warned you not to fuck with me."

"Nothing personal, Detective. I had a job to do, and I couldn't be sure we wouldn't be in each other's way. I get you, but I vote against the cell."

"No shit."

"No shit. For one thing, it would be a shame to ruin the beginning of a beautiful friendship." I let a smile pass through my mind as I thought Amy would appreciate the *Casablanca* reference. She was an artsy one, after all.

"It would, huh?" Rodríguez said. He seemed unconvinced.

"Yes. And the other reason, I have a favor to ask."

Rodríguez leaned back in his chair, and the coaster took another beating. "You've got some *cojones* on you, Malone."

"I trust you," I said, ignoring the compliment. "We've done good work together. But I don't want the whole damn MDPD bureaucracy with their big mouths and dirty handprints all over this. We work the cases together, but please keep Morrison in your pocket. You get an extra collar and tag it to the Morant case."

Rodríguez was staring at me. His jaw was getting another workout, jutting up and down, back and forth, hardening the features of his round face.

"Okay, Malone. You convinced me you know your stuff, and, believe it or not, I care more about getting the bad guy than the collar. So long as we work hand in hand as we did today, I'll play along. But you have until

Thursday night. That's all. On Friday, I pick up the bullhorn so the boys will be on the *Rio* like flies on shit when it's back in port on Sunday."

This was exactly what I'd promised Morant I'd avoid, but I couldn't exactly argue with Rodríguez. It was a fair deal for him to make. We shook on it. I signaled the bartender for another round. I looked at my watch. It was past midnight. Wednesday had started.

I had two days.

CHAPTER 29

Rodríguez dropped me off in front my office building a little before one in the morning. It seemed like an eternity had gone by since he'd called me to say there was a development in the Morant case, and I could be an observer. It had only been a few hours, not even half a day.

It seemed surreal that, in those few hours, I'd killed a man. Yet I did. I wondered if CJ would be mad at me. I'd only had time for a cryptic "I won't be in, will fill you in later" text in the middle of all the MDPD bureaucratic nightmare. I put the line right at 50-50. She'd have voted to let SRT do their thing. I still thought I'd made the right call, gunfire and all.

The parking garage was empty—not a soul and barely a car around. Scarce overhead lights created pools of illumination, turning the concrete into a haphazard chessboard. The building across the street shined a glow of artificial lights at the structure's edges. Their bright neon names, broadcasting their corporate allegiance in the night, were but a pale curtain seeping inside on the garage's street side.

Miami is never completely quiet. The occasional engine revved up and down the street. Cab and Uber drivers angled for fares and treated the speed limit as purely advisory on account of the hour. A horn blared in protest.

And it was hot. It's always hot, no matter that this was the witching hour. The concrete still radiated heat from fourteen hours of tropical sunshine.

I'd have patted myself on the back for spotting the two men's shadows behind a column on my way to the CR-V if they had made any effort to hide. They hadn't. They were just waiting for me. They turned to face me when they heard my footsteps approaching.

I recognized Dunn right away. He only had one goon with him this time. I hadn't met this one yet. He wasn't one of the two that broke my car window. He was bigger, broader in the chest, with arms so big around there was probably more fabric in his jacket's sleeves than in my shirt.

I had heard people talk about the weight of emptiness before, and I was never quite sure what it was supposed to mean. It took a new meaning now. I felt the great weight of emptiness at my hip, where my .45 was supposed to be but wasn't. It was still in the loving care of MDPD for ballistic testing. I had fired it and killed a man. I was a civilian. I acted in self-defense, and SRT would have my back. I wasn't headed for the slammer. But my gun was in a damn evidence locker all the same until I was officially cleared.

I kept my eye on Dunn in the dimly lit garage and waited for him to talk.

"You truly don't learn, do you?" he said.

That didn't rank a reply, so I didn't give him one.

"I told you to drop the case."

"You have a point to make, Dunn? It's late. I've got places to go."

"And you didn't drop the case. In fact, you made a rather malodorous mess of things. I suppose asking you nicely to leave this alone would do no good, would it?"

"If you're asking me whether asking me to stop doing my job will get me to stop doing my job, the answer is no. Now, get out of my way."

"How unfortunate," Dunn said. He turned to his goon. "Break him," he told the man, then walked away, patent leather shoes echoing on the concrete floor, headed out toward the stairwell and the street below.

The gorilla in front of me took his jacket off. The sleeves turned over as he peeled them over his arms. The T-shirt underneath was two sizes too small. Maybe he thought that if the fabric molded to his steroid-enhanced muscles, I would be impressed. Or scared. That didn't work, but the gun in the shoulder holster . . . now, that had my attention.

The man noticed. He dropped the jacket on the filthy floor, shrugged off the holster, and laid it on top of the jacket. He grinned at me.

"I won't need that."

I watched him move as he took a couple of steps toward me. I was a soldier. I was an operative, or at least I had been not that long ago. I was trained in the art of hand-to-hand combat. The way he moved, he was not all muscles and no brains either. He assessed me even as I did the same to him. Then he started moving on me.

My eyes flitted between his eyes, his hands, and his legs. I needed to anticipate what he wanted to do, to know his move before he decided on his blow himself. I needed to watch the parts most likely to hurt me. His eyes were alive, hopping in their orbits much like mine were. This was not going to be a walk in the park.

There is a rhythm to the way trained men fight. He took the few steps that separated us, light on his feet despite his bulk. He started jabbing at my face. I parried and jabbed back, each of us trying to see if we were quick enough, quicker than the other, more attentive to when a blow came. It soon became a flurry of blows, coming faster and faster, but neither of us landed a good one on the other's chin.

We couldn't have been at it for more than a minute when he parried a hair too wide. I went for a one-two punch and slammed a fist into his cheek. It wasn't a meaningful blow, but the first blow was mine.

It was a trap. He dropped his arm before I could get a third jab in and slammed a massive fist into my chest. Chest blows are usually useless. This one was different. It was like I'd been hit by a sledgehammer. It sent me reeling backward, puffing air out, awkward on my feet.

I pivoted and regained my footing just in time to duck a fist the size of a meteorite aimed right at my temple. It would have knocked me out if it had connected.

He swiveled on his feet just as quickly and squared to me before I could jab at his ribs. He was smiling. He was enjoying this. The pleasure was all his.

"You're pretty good for a skinny fucker," he said.

Nobody had called me skinny before, best I recalled anyway. Amusing as it was, I didn't let it distract me from the problem at hand—all 250 pounds of muscle problem.

He came charging at me, fists in front of his face. I dodged the first volley, bent my knees, and sent a short kick into his shin. It was hard enough that it should have cost another man his balance. I might as well have kicked a statue. He barely stumbled, then used the momentum coming back my way to swing even harder. His fist glanced past my arm, aimed straight at the head.

I ducked, but not fast enough. He connected with the top of my head. My brain rattled inside my skull—an instant concussion with the headache to match. My vision blurred. My knees threatened to buckle under me. I put every ounce of energy I had to launch myself at his ribs, leading with the knuckles, half seeing and half guessing at where the soft spot would be.

I hit him before he could land a second, final blow. His ribs cracked under the impact. He yelped, moved back a step. I took a second to blink, recover some vision, take a breath or two. It was a second too much.

The giant of a man rushed me again, but, instead of trying for another blow, he threw himself at me. He was too heavy for me to push him back. He grabbed me in a bear hug and started landing blows on my back and my sides. I did the same to him, but his sheer physical strength was greater. I would lose if I kept playing this game, his game, even with his cracked rib. He absorbed my blows without flinching.

I chanced being able to hold him back with only one leg and slammed my foot into his ankle with a strength born of desperation, the last-ditch burst of power of a wounded animal. It forced him to step back and find his footing again.

There were no more jokes from the man now, just a nasty snarl on his face. He'd been told to break me. Now, he wanted to. Good. Emotions get in the way. They make you rush into moves you shouldn't make. I needed him angry. I needed him to make a mistake. I wouldn't be able to hold him back much longer. Every part of my body was screaming in agony.

He charged again, a blind, rageful charge. That was the mistake I was waiting for. I ducked to the side and landed a kick to the side of his knee. That dropped him to the floor, face in the concrete. I jumped on top of him and straddled his back, showering blows into his kidneys, looking for the cracked ribs, even if fatigue and a shorter swing kept me from inflicting much damage.

He roared, rolled under me, and managed to send me flying. I hit the floor with all the grace of a drunkard falling off a mechanical bull—except that I didn't have padding under me, and all the air left my lungs as I hit the floor.

He tried to jump on me, but fatigue was getting to him, too. I rolled away, and he kissed the pavement.

It was time to end this. His ankle was next to my face. He brought his leg back to kick my head right off my spine. Before he could, I grabbed his ankle, held it in place, and jabbed at the side of his knee. They're fragile little things, knees, just a couple of sticks and a ball held together by rubber bands. His shattered, and his leg bent sideways at an unnatural angle.

He only screamed once. Then, even as I was busy catching my breath, he started crawling, pulling himself by his hands toward his jacket—and the gun.

I scrambled, put my feet back under me. My body, bruised and exhausted, fumbled in the effort. I half ran and half crawled, racing him for my survival. I had one more useful leg than he did. He was still a foot away when I grabbed the gun.

I rolled away, took stock of my body, and carefully stood up. My legs and my aim were steady—steady enough in close quarters, anyway. I pointed the gun at him.

"We're done," I said.

He propped himself up on an elbow and looked up at me. There was no fear in his eyes. There was no loathing anymore. There was no pleading, either. There was nothing but a certain calm. He expected me to kill him, and he was at peace with that. He had fought. He had lost. He was going to die. That was the way things went in the life he had chosen, and he was okay with it.

"Slide your phone this way," I said.

He reached for his jacket, pulled out a phone, and threw it toward me.

"That's the only one?" I asked.

He nodded.

I lowered the barrel of his gun from his chest to the phone and fired one bullet into the device.

"I'm not going to kill you," I said. "I'm going to leave. You're not going to do anything to stop me, then you're going to leave. I suggest you get that knee looked at. I don't care what you do after that, but if I ever see you again, if you're ever within a hundred feet of me, then I will kill you. Do we understand each other?"

He nodded again. There was no more relief on his face now than there had been a plea for mercy earlier. He remained impassive, his features only distorted by the pain. I'd changed the rules, he'd live by the new rules. That was it.

I walked backward to the CR-V. When I got in, I put the gun on the seat next to me. I started the engine and exited the parking ramp at a crawl, barely touching the accelerator. My adversary still hadn't moved. He may have played by a weird set of rules, but he played by them to the end.

I stopped at the first spot I could. My hands here shaking from the adrenaline—better safe than sorry. I'd had enough excitement in one day without adding a car crash.

Thoughts flooded my brain as I worked on slowing down my heart rate, and the rest of my body with it. I thought about bringing in Rodríguez and using what just happened to go after Dunn. But Dunn was slippery. Going after him on a simple assault, no matter how vicious, was more likely to poke the bear than trap him.

I wondered, too, if the goon he'd just unleashed on me was the same guy who talked to Scum and his gang of human waste. Maybe he was, maybe he wasn't. Dunn probably manufactured clones in his basement.

I squirmed in my seat as I slowly pulled onto the road again. My head throbbed and my sides ached no matter how I tried to sit. It all hurt like hell. That didn't bother me too much. My mind was stuck on one last thought about tonight, one that hurt a lot more than my body: at least they'd come after me. I could handle that. There was no telling what they'd do next. I'd only panic CJ or Courtney if I called now. I'd wait until I saw them in person. But we needed to have a talk.

CHAPTER 30

I still managed some sleep after all that. I didn't get much—it was the wee hours by the time I got home, and every part of my body hurt—but I got some. I even managed to make myself presentable after a good shower. Or so I thought. I took one step into the office when Courtney looked up from her desk and asked, "What happened to you? You're walking funny."

"Long story. Or maybe not that long. Where's CJ?" If she were in, my sharp-eared partner would have appeared as if by magic upon hearing Courtney's question.

"She's out re-interviewing Linda Mayak," Courtney said.

"Okay." I sat in one of our waiting room chairs and took a load off. "Do you mind if I give you my report verbally, and you type it into the file? It will go a hell of a lot faster this way."

"Of course not, go ahead."

I gave Courtney my report while staring at the wall, going through the previous day in my head, speaking in short sentences that Courtney typed into the computer. I felt bad using her as a typist, but I only had two days left, and it would have taken me half the morning. Yet we still had to maintain the file. We solved cases because we did things like that, because every fact was in there. Now was not the time to be sloppy.

I got to the part where I pulled an undercover to draw out the three gang members, and the sound of Courtney's typing stopped. I looked over at her. She was staring at me with wide eyes. She was forgetting to blink.

"You did what?" she asked.

"It was the right move," I said.

"CJ will kill you. I may kill you. You guys are investigators, not a private SWAT team."

"It was the right move, and there was no time to debate the merits with CJ."

Courtney eventually blinked again. "So, what happened?"

"I was about to tell you."

"Right, sorry."

With Courtney focused on the task again, I finished my report. It didn't go a hundred percent smoothly. There was another interruption with Courtney being mildly horrified I killed someone, and more than a little worried I was in the middle of bullets flying to start with. I revised my odds of CJ getting mad at me and moved on.

"So, are they going to arrest Dunn?" she asked when I got to Scum's testimony. She nearly jumped out of her seat, looking at me over her monitors.

I stretched my legs, lounging in the chair. The thought crossed my mind that those chairs were too comfortable. It was good for my back and ribs at the moment, but we didn't want clients overstaying their welcome.

"Will they?" I asked Courtney.

"They should, right?"

"On what evidence?"

"That guy saw him!"

"He saw someone that might look like Dunn sitting in an SUV. He saw him from across the street. The guy he saw may or may not have instructed the linebacker-looking dude, the only person who actually talked to Scum, to order a hit. Not to mention that Scum himself does not exactly shine with credibility in a courtroom."

"I see what you mean," Courtney said. "What do we do now?"

"Same thing we always do. We keep working the case. We just work it faster."

"Right," she said. "Two days,"

"Two days," I echoed.

"So, what else happened? None of this explains why you're walking funny."

"It was a long day." I went on to tell her about the ambush last night—make that this morning. I pre-empted her question by telling her that, no, I wouldn't ask Rodríguez to arrest Dunn over it. Serving thirty days over a simple battery was not worth the paperwork, not to mention that MDPD probably had just about enough of me by now. That, and I had a more pressing question than hers.

"Dunn crossed another line going after me instead of the car's window. He may just decide to go after you or CJ next if we don't drop this."

"You think I should carry my gun?" She sounded awfully calm, asking a question like this.

"At all times—if we keep the case."

"Don't drop it, Coop! CJ and I will be fine. I'll carry, and I'll be careful. I'm not a delicate flower, you know."

"I'm starting to get the idea."

"Don't drop it. Don't give Dunn the satisfaction. Plus, I want to know who killed Morrison."

"I hear you. I want all that too, but I don't want to risk your safety in the process. I'll talk to CJ, then we'll decide."

"Okay. But we keep working on it until you two talk, right?"

I extricated myself from the chair a little gingerly, took two steps to Courtney's desk, and laid my cell on it between us after I put it on speaker.

"We do. Let's start by making more friends."

Courtney looked up at me with a questioning look and leaned closer to the phone.

The person I called picked up on the first ring. "Special Agent Locke," the voice said.

"This is Cooper Malone," I said.

"What can I do for you, Mr. Malone?"

"It's what I can do for you. I told you I'd share if I came across information that may be relevant to you." I was leaning on the desk, over the phone, looking sideways at Courtney with my best conspiratorial look. There was a momentary silence while Locke shuffled some papers.

"I appreciate the call," Locke said. "What do you have?"

"MDPD arrested three gang bangers for Morant's murder."

"Is that what got SRT out of their bunker yesterday?"

"Could be," I said.

"Do you know how strong their case is?"

"My source says they have a confession." Locke did not need to know I was my own source.

"Okay, thank you," she said after another short silence. "I appreciate the call."

"One more thing," I said.

"Yes?"

"Unofficially, it may have been murder for hire."

"That complicates things," Locke said. She sounded pensive over the speaker.

"Yes, it does. And speaking of which, I realize we have two murders and enough drugs on the *Rio* to rename it the *Medellín*. I get your interest, and I promised not to screw with your case, but I'm asking for some courtesy. One of those murders is my business. Please don't make a nuisance out of yourself by keeping me in the dark."

"I'll do my best, as I promised, but this is the Federal Government, Cooper."

"Friends call me Coop, remember?"

"Okay, Coop. This is still the Federal Government. Sometimes, my hands are tied. I will do what I can."

"I'm counting on it."

"You can. And thanks for the call."

"No problem."

Courtney took a few seconds to finish typing a summary of the call. She sensed me hovering and looked at me.

"I need the forensic report yesterday," I told her.

"I talked to Hank yesterday. It will be in today," she said.

"Has everything else been uploaded?"

She nodded. "Everything's in the file."

"Thanks. I'll be in my office."

Going through the file was only making me mad. I was angry that I wasn't seeing "it," whatever it was, that one piece of information that would unlock a door or three and put me on the trail of whoever killed William Morrison.

My sinking mood lifted with a call from CJ. She had her all-business voice on.

"Did you see cameras on the VIP floor?" she asked without preamble.

"No. There was this patched up area on the wall, but it was in a corner. It wouldn't fit a camera, not one of the ubiquitous black domes that are all over the rest of the ship, anyway. I didn't see anything else, either."

"I was talking Linda Mayak through a day on board," CJ said. "All of a sudden, her body jerked erect like she was being electrocuted. She shouted even though I was right next to her. 'Cameras! There were cameras!'"

"Is she sure what she saw were cameras?"

"She is. She examined them because she considered protecting her clients' privacy a secondary objective after their physical safety. She didn't quite have time to find out more about them, and you're right, they weren't the half-dome kind. It was something more discreet, but definitely cameras."

"This makes no sense." I was not angry. I was not even frustrated. I was definitely not yelling at CJ. My tone was composed. I was working the problem with her, and the problem was that it made no sense. "If there were cameras, they would have shown the killer leaving the room. Then Morant would have known. Ruiz would have known, too," I added, thinking of Morant's deputy who had escorted me aboard the *Rio*.

"What if Morant played you? It's possible. He could have had his own agenda. Think about it. He was investigating the drug trade on board. He may have wanted to shield that investigation. He couldn't risk his secret surveillance system being exposed. He may even have nudged you in the right direction but wouldn't come out and say whom he thought killed Morrison."

"It's possible." I hated to admit it, but that was the kind of stunt I might have pulled in his place. Still, I offered an alternative. "Or someone else installed them, and even Morant did not know about them."

"That's possible too," CJ said. "He was running things at a distance. Just don't discount either possibility."

"I won't. Let's start by getting more facts. I'll call Ruiz and call you right back."

"Coop, just ask Courtney to conference all of us in," CJ said.

"Courtney!" I called across the office. "Come help out this dinosaur. And bring your tablet."

I brought her up to speed and handed her my phone. She had the decency not to laugh too openly.

"Hi CJ," Courtney said. "I've got you on speaker, and I'll work the conference. You'll be on hold for a couple." She tapped on the screen in a few places then clicked on Ruiz's number, who answered with a friendly "Hello."

"Hi, Marco. This is Coop."

"Hi, Coop. How are you doing?"

"Not too bad. You?"

"Can't complain."

"Do you have a moment for a couple of questions?"

"Sure."

"And do you mind if I conference in my partner? She's the one who brought the issue to me. Her name is CJ Beck."

"Yeah, no problem."

I pointed to the likely icon on my screen and arched my eyebrows at Courtney. She nodded. I tapped it, made all the necessary introductions, and motioned to Courtney to stay seated and listen in.

"Marco," I said, "are there any cameras on the VIP deck? Specifically in the passageway? Maybe a parallel system to the network of half-dome cameras throughout the rest of the ship?"

By the sound he made, he would have spat out his drink if he had been drinking.

"No, of course not! I wish. Then we'd have a pretty good idea who offed Morrison since we would have seen the perp come out of the cabin. We'd have a prime suspect at least."

"StarQuest had a bodyguard on board. She had eyes on the wrong exec at the wrong time, but she noticed the kind of cameras I'm talking about."

"Impossible!" Ruiz said.

"Could Owen have put something in place for his drug op without telling anyone?" I asked.

"I try not to think too much of myself, but Owen and I had a good relationship, and I oversee at-sea security. Since the *Rio* is my turf, I'm pretty sure he would have told me about something like that."

"CJ?" I prompted, having run out of questions. I could hear her wheels turning for a few seconds.

"Assuming the bodyguard was right about the cameras," CJ started, "do you have an idea who could have installed them?"

"Coop probably told you about Brett Dagheretti, the ship's Chief Security Officer. He's not my biggest fan, and I return the favor, so I'm biased, but he's a prime candidate. If there were secret cameras, they would have to have been put in by someone aboard, probably high up, so Dagheretti fits."

"That's helpful, thank you, Mr. Ruiz."

CJ disconnected. Courtney looked up and pointed to the door. I nodded, and she headed back to her desk even as I said, "Stay on, Marco, will you?"

I took the phone off speaker and brought it to my ear.

"What's going on, Coop?" Marco asked.

"With the cameras, I don't know. That's not why I asked you to stay on."

"What is it, then?"

"Don't tell Owen's kid yet because there's more to it, but, between you and me, we got the bastards who killed him."

"Are you sure?" I could hear something in his voice, a strangled hope he did not dare let loose yet.

"I was at the arrest and the interrogation. I'm sure."

"This is great news! Why not tell Ollie?"

"The perps swung the bats, alright. We have them dead to rights. But someone paid them to do it, and I don't know who yet. I think it will be better for Ollie if we can tell him the whole story at once."

"Hmm. I agree. Anything I can do, you just say the word."

"You got it."

"And thanks for letting me know."

"Sure thing."

I hung up and closed my eyes for a moment. I was letting the morning's news seep in. That's when it hit me. My eyes opened with a start, and I slammed my fist on my desk.

You're an idiot, Malone!

CHAPTER 31

had neglected one piece of evidence long enough to curse myself. That's all the self-pity I allowed. I power walked to the front desk, making it there in three long strides.

"I want to see everything you recovered from the hard drive I snagged from Morant's office," I said. "I don't care how little it is. I want to see what we have now."

My barking didn't faze Courtney. She was used to my outbursts, especially in difficult cases. She did not take them personally. She picked up the hard drive and the air-gapped laptop.

"I'll meet you in the conference room," she said.

We took seats side by side. The old computer started its boot-up routine. Courtney was looking at me. She made sure she had my full attention.

"Okay," she said. "Let me tell you what you'll be looking at."

"Go ahead."

"A video file is just that," Courtney said. "It's one file. If it's corrupted, it's corrupted. The bullshit in movies where they recover random blocks of images, that's just what it is—bullshit. You'll see dozens of file icons on the screen. Don't get excited. Ninety-nine percent of them are corrupted.

"That said, there were a couple of things for us to try. One is, even though it's one file, it contains code for multiple data streams. There are tools out there that recognize healthy data streams within a corrupted file and extract them. They're not cheap, not the good ones anyway. I talked to CJ, and she talked to Heather, and I bought two that work using different methods.

"Then there's one other thing." She looked up, looking for a way to explain it. "You know how I defrag your computer once in a while?"

"Yes."

"Normally, fragmentation is bad. It slows down the machine, uses memory that could be free, all kinds of things. Here, it can help. If an old file fragmented, maybe we can find uncorrupted fragments."

"Smart," I said. It sounded smart anyway. Courtney didn't disagree.

"Thanks. But even with all that—well, I warned you that the drive was in an awful shape when you first showed it to me. Turns out I could see the directory, and that was a minor miracle in itself, but a lot of the files were too damaged, physically busted, to recover anything, even with all the tools and methods and stuff."

Courtney pointed to the screen, which had come to life. She had divided the files into two folders. She clicked on the first one. "That's the original directory," she said. There were dozens of files. "Nearly all of those are dead. Useless."

She backed out and opened the second folder. There were only a few files there. Courtney pointed out that they were only fragments of files. This was all we'd been able to recover. The cameras had evidently been basic, filming on a continuous loop, not the motion-activated kind. With all of Courtney's work, most of what we had were a few shots of an empty passageway.

Two files surrendered only an audio track. One had sounds of footsteps and people laughing. The other only had a thump. I looked at Courtney from the corner of my eye. "Let me guess," I said. "You've listened to that noise about twenty times already."

"More like two hundred," she said with a sign. "CJ too. The noise originated near the camera, I think. It sounds close. Maybe someone drunk-slammed into the wall. Or it's a shred of a fight, someone being knocked into the wall by someone else. But we have nothing around it to tell. God knows I've tried."

"I know you did," I told her. Her disappointment at not finding anything more was palpable, even painful.

Courtney then opened the only file with a picture of more than a bare, fancy carpet.

"This is a fragment from one of the older files. It may even have been taken at install or during tests right afterward. It's as I told you. The file fragmented, and we managed to find an undamaged fragment. The picture is still distorted, though, for some reason."

My hands clenched into fists. I stared at the screen for a long time. "The picture is not distorted," I said. "That asshole is just that fat. You're looking at Brett Dagheretti, ironically enough, the *Rio*'s Chief Security Officer."

I mashed a name on my smartphone's contacts as if pushing harder on the screen would make the call go through any faster. It didn't, nor is it what made Special Agent Sally Locke answer on the first ring, but she did.

"I need everything you have on Brett Dagheretti," I said. I wasn't asking.

"Where did you hear that name?"

"Never mind where. I need to know. That's assuming you're still interested in sharing information."

A long silence followed. I pictured Locke rubbing her temples like I was giving her a headache. *I am a headache*, I fumed in silence.

"I'll call you back," she said, and disconnected the call. That did not help my mood. I sat in the conference room, grinding my teeth, pummeling a punching bag in my head with the words "federal government" printed in blood-red letters on it. *Maybe I should install one in the office*, I thought. I hated the damn bureaucracy and all the self-righteousness bound up in it.

Courtney was on the way out of her seat to escape Hurricane Cooper when I stopped her.

"Wait a sec," I said, hoping my voice was a hemisphere cooler than how I was feeling. "What about the warehouse angle, your pics against the spreadsheets Morant had? Is that yielding anything?"

"CJ started on that," Courtney said.

It made sense. Tracking white-collar criminals through number trails was CJ's forte. She had an eye for detail that did not miss a decimal or a comma. She could look at rows of numbers and it would mean something to her, create a picture in her mind.

"She'll find whatever there is to find," I said.

"She will," Courtney said. "So far, she found a discrepancy between the number of linen pallets I photographed and what's on the forms. Kind of what we noticed at your place last weekend."

"Like you noticed," I said. "You noticed it looked like there were too many, party boat or not, not me, not us. Don't give away credit, not when you've earned it. You're the one who picked up on it. Now, it looks like the numbers bear it out."

Courtney looked a little lighter on her feet. "Thanks, but what does it mean? It's just sheets and stuff."

"Keep digging. You'll figure it out."

Courtney forced a smile and left the conference room.

It took two hours and a lot of self-restraint, but I heard back from Locke before I punched a hole in the wall. She sent a text inviting me to a downtown coffee shop. It was close enough for me to walk there. It was farther for her, at least if she was coming from her office—DEA's Miami Division was at the edge of town. Maybe that was the point.

I used my walk to clear my mind. I thought about coffee shops. People used to gather in coffee houses and saloons. Now they're called coffee shops and bars. There are cafés in France, Chaguan tea houses in China, and Bierstuben in Germany. People always seem to congregate where they can hold a drink in their hands.

The moment I walked in, the familiar coffee-shop feel hugged me. I relaxed at the smell of brewing coffee, the warmth that seemed to kick up a degree from the hot coffee pots despite the air conditioning, and the din of conversation. Locke was already there. I nodded at her and went to order a black coffee before sitting across from her. She was wearing a pantsuit today, with the jacket on despite the heat. It was serving the same purpose as my overlong T-shirt. It concealed her gun.

I winced as I sat down. The chair caught my ribs the wrong way. Locke gave me a sideway look.

"Don't ask," I said, "and thanks for meeting me."

She smiled at me. She was looking down, just a bit, just enough that it gave her a tired look. "How could I refuse? You're just this side of making a nuisance of yourself again."

"It's a talent I have."

She kept her smile up. "Yeah . . . I'm not sure whether to cuff you or pin a badge on you."

"I don't do too well wearing badges. Something about not liking to be told what to do." There was enough truth to that, and I was in no mood to say more, even if I could have.

"Structure and support can be good things," she said.

I doubted she actually meant to recruit me. I shrugged. "Sometimes, sure, but not always." *Sometimes, all that "support" gets you killed.*

"Alright then," she said. Her voice dropped just above a whisper. "Dagheretti."

"Yeah, him." I leaned forward, elbows on the table, gingerly keeping both hands around my coffee mug. The coffee shop served for-here brew in reusable ceramic mugs. I'm sure it's great for the planet, but it burnt my fingers.

Locke spoke slowly, as if she was weighing her words.

"We suspect he plays a key role in the illegal drug trade on the *Rio.*

"Key role as in ring leader?" I asked.

"Possibly."

"Tell me about him."

Locke gave me the main parts in the slow monotone she had adopted for this conversation. "The county where he was sheriff had a huge drug problem. His successor seems to have cut it off, or at least a big chunk of it. Then Dagheretti works up to Chief Security Officer on the *Rio*, and, just like that, drugs flow on the ship like the waters of the Mississippi."

"He could just be incompetent or corrupt enough to look the other way," I said.

"All good points. You know how we work, though, with our structure and support." She was smiling again. "Part of the good that comes from it is we keep stats on everything. We determine how to measure a problem, then we start measuring it everywhere, obsessively. Same thing with measuring how and how quickly things get better. It creates institutional knowledge. Bottom line, when we look at the amount of drugs in both places and how quickly things improved after he was no longer sheriff, my money is on something more than incompetence or petty corruption."

I was squinting at her through her speech. She did not like that.

"I get it, Malone," she snapped. "You don't like how we work. You're a mighty seat-of-your-pants kinda guy. But good intel works. Good analysis works. It's all part of good police work."

I smiled. I liked that she cared enough to be riled up. "Fine with me," I said. "My only thought is that, sure, you know, but can you prove it?"

"No. Not yet, anyway." Her posture remained straight, defiant. "It doesn't help that the man's at sea six out of seven days and stays on the ship on the seventh. And he takes his weeks off more rarely than he's entitled to, and completely at random, which makes it hard to set up good surveillance. That's suspect behavior right there, by the way."

"Did Morant give you anything more than statistics?" I asked. I raised my hand preemptively, regretting the way I'd phrased the question. "And before you say anything, I'm not quite a caveman. I know how big data works. I wasn't dissing it."

She gave a short nod before answering. "Nothing concrete, no. There were some discrepancies in the warehouse but that could have been a corporate snafu. He also gave us Dagheretti's time-off schedule, which is how we know it's messed up. We keep getting grounds for suspicion, but nothing we can act on."

I kept our own findings about the warehouse under wraps. Locke had warned me to stay out of it—I wasn't about to throw my team under the bus. The conversation paused. Movement through the window caught my eye. Crows were screeching, fighting for a scrap of lunch someone had dropped. In here, Locke and I were the crows, fighting for scraps of information.

"What about Dunn?" I asked.

"What about him?"

"What's his connection to Dagheretti?"

"None that we know of," Locke said. She'd answered a fraction of a second quicker than the rest of our conversation. I took it to mean it had not been a topic of discussion inside the halls of the DEA. The federal machinery had nothing.

"How did you know about Dagheretti?" Locke asked before I could put another word in.

I hesitated for a New York minute. You've got to give something to get something. "Someone may have rigged a surveillance system on top of the ship's official one," I said. "I say 'may' because I did not see it myself or receive tangible proof, but I trust my source."

"And you think it's Dagheretti?"

"I thought the ship's Chief Security Officer with a questionable past is a good candidate to do something like that and do it undetected."

She nodded. It made sense. "Did your source say what the surveillance was aimed at?"

"Not overall, no, but it may have targeted places where the official cameras do not look, like the VIP deck."

"Where Morrison's cabin was," Locke said. This circled back to my case and tied it in a neat little bow for her.

"There's one more thing," I said. "And I'll need a favor from you." Her eyes narrowed with a hint of suspicion. I jumped in. "The arrest in the Morant case toppled some dominos. MDPD is on to the Morrison murder. They'll be boarding the ship on Sunday."

"Fuck!" Locke said.

I wasn't surprised to hear a DEA agent swear, but it was the first time I elicited that kind of reaction from her. I talked over it. "Whatever you decide to do," I said, "get your own warrant or work with MDPD or something else, I need you to wait until Friday."

"Why?"

"Because I have a duty to my client to find out what happened to Morrison before two police forces, well, make a nuisance of themselves, to use the saying of the day. I still have that duty now, even if my chances dwindle with each tick of the clock."

"Why Friday?"

"Because I can count on MDPD for that much."

Locke started muttering to herself more than she was talking to me. She whispered very fast, eyes in the distance, hunched over the table. "I can still get a warrant on Friday. AUSA may hate us, but they do half the time anyway. We'll need time to plan, too. I don't even know if we'll want to work with the locals or preempt them . . . ." She trailed off and looked up at me. "Okay, Coop. On Friday at 8:00 a.m., it's my show. Until then, you've got Morrison to yourself. You gave me the info to start with, so it's fair. Now, we're square."

"We are square," I said. "And maybe even friends." I was grinning at her as she stood up.

She grinned back and pushed past me, swinging her hip into me. "Don't push it," she said.

She'd had the bright idea of ordering her coffee to go and walked out with her cup in hand. I stayed at the table with my thoughts and my mug. You don't waste good coffee. This one wasn't half bad. I looked around the coffee shop crowd. Two old men were playing cards. The red-haired barista was smiling at her customers. A long-haired kid with a T-shirt from a rock band I'd never heard of was hunched over a laptop. Outside, a man down on his luck was nursing a cup of water at the same table he had occupied when I walked in. For just a few minutes, the world felt normal around me.

It was nice while it lasted.

CHAPTER 32

I called CJ on my walk back from the coffee shop. I couldn't wait any longer to see her in person to talk about Dunn. I kept walking, going around the block as we kept talking. We seriously considered dropping the case. We had a duty to each other and to Courtney not to take stupid risks. Even Heather would probably wish us to drop it rather than see any of us getting hurt. But in the end, we only had two days before two police forces took over. And we were stubborn. We'd work the hell out of the case for the time we had.

It was past closing time when I got back to the office. Courtney was still there. She stood up when she saw it was me walking in and pointed both index fingers at me. "I put the tech report on your desk," she said.

I went straight to my office. I could hear Courtney's heels behind me. There was a doorstopper volume on my desk. I sat down and pulled it closer. I opened the forensic report. Courtney sat across from me and swiped at the tablet in her lap. She had it all in that six-by-ten piece of plastic. Her dexterity with it made me feel old.

I leafed through the report. Every page had a "preliminary" watermark on it, and every page sounded the same. "We obtained this sample using that method and performed these tests in accordance with that protocol and found absolutely fucking nothing."

I looked up at Courtney. "Have you looked at this yet?"

She nodded and avoided my eyes. "They cleaned that cabin pretty good," Courtney said. "There's only one sample that returned something. Some vomit crusted in the bar sink's plumbing. It's toward the end of the report, before all the addendums. Page 185."

I turned to it. That was not particularly exciting. All the partiers were drinking too much. Then again, with all the interviews we did, no one mentioned people racing to the porcelain goddess. It could be. It could be that the sight of brain matter seeping from a caved-in skull, bone fragments on the carpet, and blood oozing everywhere sent the perp to the closest sink.

I texted Amy before returning to the report. "Quick work question: William's parties, how much of a drunken binge? Did they turn into a barf fest? Not work question: I keep thinking of our time together. All parts of it. See you again soon?"

She answered right away. "Re work, no. Booze flowed freely but more fun, less barf. Re not work, you know, I really don't think I'll fuck this up. I don't think you'd let me. So soon, very soon." She punctuated it with a kissy-heart emoji. I sent her one back, and it did not even feel weird.

I shook my head like a wet dog and shot an if-looks-could-kill glare at Courtney to wipe the stupid smile off her face. I turned to Hank's report on the vomit. My heart beat faster at the thought it could yield something. There was no guarantee it was the killer who vomited or that some trace remained that would help. There was not even any guarantee it was from the week of the murder. But if they did not run water in for a few days after the murder, enough might have crusted up that some remained when we went aboard. It could be irrelevant. But then again, it might not be.

I mumbled as I read through. "Biological material insufficient or too degraded for DNA testing . . . okay . . . fine . . . blah blah blah . . . traces of food were found and tested . . . protocol blah blah blah . . . method—get to the point! Fish . . . ."

I froze. Fish. I squeezed my eyes shut and reached for the deepest recesses of my brain. Something about fish. My head snapped up, and my eyes popped open.

"Cooked or raw?" I shouted.

"What?" Courtney asked.

"The fish Hank tested. Was it cooked or raw? Could he tell?"

Courtney's fingers flew over the tablet. She could get to the right endnote much faster than I could. "Raw," she said. Her voice was hesitant, nervous in the face of my frenzy. "Multiple species. One likely tuna, others undetermined."

The temperature in the room dropped below freezing. Goosebumps appeared on my arms. An icy lump formed in my throat. All I could hear was Jen's voice, Heather's friend, echoing in my head.

Walt wouldn't touch meat but would eat sushi like it was one of the Rock's cheat meals. Walt Rosling, who founded LandQuest before it was StarQuest. Walt Rosling, the oldest of the three partners, who still ran the real estate side but wouldn't admit to working with Morrison, only in the same company. Walt wouldn't touch meat but would eat sushi like it was one of the Rock's cheat meals . . . . He'd been an asshole in the Keys, and . . . ,

"CJ!" I barked. Courtney jumped in her seat, and I realized I was yelling. I calmed myself down and asked my question in a more measured tone. "Courtney, where's CJ?"

"She went to meet Walt Rosling. Why?"

I clutched my phone the way a drowning man holds on to a buoy. "Is she in Key West yet?" I was surprised I could force the words through my throat.

Courtney had turned a shade paler. She stammered through her answer.

"She didn't go to Key West. Rosling said he was looking at property he owned here in Miami, and they met in town. Why? Coop, what's going on?"

I rasped mine. "Walt Rosling eats sushi like every fish in the sea is about to go extinct tomorrow. And I'll bet dollars to doughnuts he barfed half of it after killing Morrison."

Courtney turned whiter than a ghost. Her hand flew to her throat. She was blinking back tears. I'd already tapped CJ's name on my phone. It went straight to voicemail. I tapped the contacts page and found Rosling's number. This time, the call when through.

"What do you want?" Rosling's voice came through weak but angry.

"I'd like to talk to you," I said, doing my best to keep my voice even.

"Talk to me? It's a bit late, asshole. You just couldn't leave it alone, could you?"

"You're a smart guy. You probably knew I wouldn't. You and I are the same. We're men who do what we have to." I kept up a mantra in the back of my head while talking to him. *Keep him talking. Compliment him. Build him up just enough. He'll respond to you. Build a rapport.*

"You screwed everything up," Rosling yelled into the phone. "Alan should have killed you. He had you twice, and now's the time he goes soft on me!"

"There's nothing that can't be fixed, Walt." I said. "Do you have CJ with you?"

"You bet I do, and you *are* going to fix this, all right," he said, still angry and loud.

"I can come to you, Walt. We'll figure it out. Where are you?"

There was a couple of seconds of silence. Rosling hesitated. Then a female voice rang out, echoing slightly. "A warehouse in . . . . . "

The call ended. I smiled through my fears. *Good job, CJ.*

Courtney clamped her hand to her mouth to keep from crying out. Tears were flowing freely.

I looked at her and spoke, my words calm and firm.

"Courtney, there will be time for emotions. It might surprise you to know I'll need time for those too. But right now, I need the woman of action. I need the woman who broke into the Mardi Gras warehouse. Are you in?"

She sat up straighter, set her jaw, and wiped her tears. "Yes. What do you need me to do?"

"Good." I was half talking to her, half lost in my phone. I slammed it on the desk. I'd never been so damn angry at myself. "I can't find CJ's phone on that find-my-phone app you installed. I can't tell where she is. Walt must have busted it. I should have checked earlier. I'm a fucking idiot."

I was reeling—which would help exactly no one. I took a deep breath, then another, and focused.

"Okay. It is what it is. That makes it your job, Courtney. Start by finding out where Rosling owns a warehouse in Dade or surrounding counties. Mainland only. Greater Miami stuff. Unless you can still ping CJ's phone somehow."

"Done."

"You can use my computer." We switched places. I wanted her to feel we were in this together. Physical proximity helped.

I fought the urge to serially call Rosling's phone. I needed to be patient. It was best to let him stew. He was a tough guy, but he was new at the outlaw thing. It's not as easy as they make it look in the movies.

There was another reason. I had a feeling I'd need all the time I could draw out of this. I already knew CJ was with Rosling in a Miami warehouse. She was most likely kept against her will. I needed time to think through my options. There weren't going to be many. Right now, my thinking time was worth more than Rosling's. Time was on my side.

I reached for a pen and a piece of paper, folded it, and wrote a list of people to call. It was short. Courtney was working furiously on my computer. I reached for my tablet, pulled up the manifest, only half looking as I worked out scenarios in my mind. I went back to the name I noticed before. It was right there, next to Rosling's on his reservation. It nagged at me, peeking out from the dungeon of my memory.

"Shit," I mumbled. "Could it be that simple?"

Courtney didn't hear me. She was in the zone. A few minutes later, I heard her whoop. The whole building probably did.

"Got it," she said. "Fuck you and fuck your shell companies and fuck your bullshit. I've got you, you evil son of a bitch." She turned the screen toward me. "They're here. No ping, but that's the only warehouse tied to Rosling in the area."

"You're sure?"

"As sure as I can be."

I took a long look. It was one of several identical warehouses set in two neat rows in an industrial area near South Miami, like a fairy tale giant had planted a breed of square corn on either side of the street. The one where CJ was held backed up to the water.

"Is it active, I mean, commercially active?" I asked.

Courtney reoriented the screen her way. "Hold on," she said.

I went back to my list and crossed some names off. Time would be tight. I sent a few heads-up texts so my calls would be answered later. Special Agent Locke was not one of the names on the list, but she'd been right about one thing. Support could be good. I'd be needing it.

I kept thinking back to the satellite picture Courtney had shown me. There'd be few options. I would have to be creative, and I would need to sell it.

"It's active," Courtney said, interrupting my thoughts. "Multiple companies ship to it."

I acknowledged her with a nod. It was time to make a move. Time had been on our side until now. This was the tipping point. I had done my thinking. That meant Rosling got no more. I dialed his number.

"What?" he snapped in answer.

"You said you wanted me to fix this, then you hung up," I said.

"So what?"

"So, I honored that, but I still want to work this out with you, Walt. I kinda need to see you for that, speak to you face to face, man to man."

My subconscious kept sending me instructions from the Way Back machine. *Stroke his ego. Acknowledge him, but don't look weak. He's not the type to respond to weakness.* I kept my voice firm. I was not yelling at him, but I was not pleading with him either. We were talking. Two guys, talking. I needed to keep it that way. I closed my eyes and pictured myself in that warehouse with him. I gave him time to answer.

"I just needed time to think," he said.

Bingo. You're justifying yourself to me. I've got you on defensive. Now don't overplay it, Malone.

"I get that," I said. "What do you want, Walt? Let's work this out."

He gave the warehouse address before his demand. Courtney had been right. I had never dreamt of questioning it.

"You'll pick me up in a large sedan with a big trunk," he said. "Then you'll take me where I tell you. Make sure you have plenty of gas. You do that, your partner lives. You don't, she dies."

"I don't own a sedan. I can find one, but it will be a couple of hours before I can be in South Miami with it."

"One hour, Malone."

"It will take two. I am not playing you. I want CJ back and safe. You want something too. We'll both get what we want, but it will take a couple of hours."

I held my breath through endless seconds of silence.

"Make it quick," Rosling barked, then he hung up.

I opened my eyes and fixed on Courtney. "I need you to go home. There is nothing you can do here right now. I will pick you up on the way. You won't be left in the cold. You'll be there."

"Promise me, Coop!"

"I promise you. And, Courtney, I'm pulling this shit together as we go, here. I don't know what it will look like. It could be I'll ask things of you I have no right to ask."

"To help get CJ back?"

"No other reason. That's why I need you to go home and be ready."

"Anything you need, then," she said, holding my gaze. Then she stepped away, and I dialed my phone. The call picked up before Courtney was out the door. I blurted out my question.

"Are you still in Miami?"

CHAPTER 33

I paced and fidgeted while I mulled. I put the Glock I'd separated from Dunn's goon in the office gun safe and swapped it for the short-nose .38 revolver that fits in a holster clipped against the small of my back. Then I sat back down.

I prefer action. Sitting down does not agree with me, not often. I am neither proud nor ashamed of it. It's part of who I am. Right then, I didn't have a choice. I had calls to make.

I stared at the phone like it was radioactive. Then I picked it up and dialed Detective Rodríguez. "I know who killed Morrison, but I'm going to need your help bringing him in," I said.

"Where are you?" he asked.

"Not just you. I need Tommy Wood and his SRT team."

"What the hell is going on, Malone?"

"It was Rosling, one of Morrison's partners. But he's got CJ hostage, and he's armed."

"I'll call you back."

He didn't. Wood did. I gave him the brass tacks.

"Okay, Coop. We've got this," he said. "Where are they?"

"Tommy, I'd like to handle this a certain way. It's my partner in there."

"That is not how we do things, Coop. You know that."

"Yeah, I do. But it's my partner in there."

"It's always someone's partner or spouse or son or daughter. SRT and MDPD hostage negotiators still handle those situations. Every time."

"Sure. But I think there's room for an exception here."

"How do you figure?"

"Two reasons. One is that I'm not 'someone.' I'm an operative, or at least I was. I know what I'm doing in those situations."

"No disrespect, especially since you handled the takedown at the bar like a true pro, but you used to be, and we still are. Your second reason better blow me away. We're wasting time here."

"What's the first thing the hostage negotiator will do?"

Wood saw where I was going before I could answer my own question. "He'll make contact and establish a rapport—which you've already done," he said.

"That's right. You've got someone with experience in hostage rescue and a rapport already established with the hostage taker. I want you guys there, or I wouldn't have called. I want your M4s at the ready and all your gadgets to take a good look inside, and your people behind them. All of that. What I'm asking is, let me take point."

His sigh was audible on the other end. "You're a pain in the ass, anybody told you that before?"

"That would be Rodríguez, ten minutes ago."

"He was right, but your approach makes sense, so long as we can build a solid plan around it. Let me talk to my team and run this up the flagpole. I'll call you back."

We talked several times in the half hour that followed, refining a plan in the time we had. Slowly but surely, SRT was coming around to me taking the lead. They weren't going to let me go in alone though, which raised its own set of problems.

"I can walk in overtly," I told Wood in our last call. "I'll be there to talk to him. I don't know how you get anyone in covertly. There are no windows, just the one door, and it will take too long to disassemble the HVAC for a roof entry."

"Then we'll need a distraction."

I gave it a moment. I had a thought, one I did not like one bit, but it was the only one in my head that even had a chance to work.

"I have an idea for that," I heard myself say.

"I'm not going to like it, am I?" Tommy asked.

"No, you won't." I told him anyway.

"You're coloring way far outside the lines here, Coop," he said when I was done.

"It wouldn't be the first time."

"Fuck! Fine, because I don't have anything better right now. I may still change the plan before we execute—my discretion—but I'll back you on this for the time being. We're going ahead with your op in mind."

"Thanks. I owe you."

I hung up and went down to the garage. I got on the road and made the call I had least wanted to make, dialing Courtney from the car.

She answered with an uncharacteristic "Talk to me, Coop." There was no hello or cheerful banter.

"I'm going to need your help to pull this off," I told her. "But before you say anything, you need to know it's not safe, and I've just been reminded it's way outside the lines. You can say no. Hell, CJ would want you to say no. We'll let SRT storm the castle. They're good at it. Truth be told, they're not all that happy with my alternate reality, but they're indulging me."

"Is your plan better? To get CJ back unharmed, I mean?"

"I think so, yes. Marginally, but still better."

"Then, I'm in."

"CJ may kill us both if Rosling doesn't get a shot first."

"I think she may let this one slide." Courtney was falling into using bad humor to handle the tension. That was a good thing. It works. I should know.

"Alright, then. I'm on my way to your place now. I'll be there in ten. I need you dressed in the most outrageously provocative outfit you can come up with."

A pause followed. "Why?"

"Because I need a distraction, a compelling one, and I need it from someone who can sell it, not to mention someone I trust. And if it's someone CJ recognizes, all the better. It will be good for her morale. She's in shit land right now."

There was another short pause while what I said sunk in. "From how far away will I need to be distracting?" she asked.

I thought about that. "Call it . . . about halfway through a dimly lit warehouse."

"Okay. See you in ten." She hung up before I did.

I parked by the door of her apartment building and waited a few minutes before she came out. She opened the back door, threw in a backpack, closed it, and sat in the passenger seat. She was wearing hooker heels, a skirt barely wider than a belt, and a see-through blouse on top of a black bra barely holding her big tits in.

"For the record," she said, "I bought the skirt on a dare and never wore it outside the house until today, and I wear this blouse over a cami. I'm class, not crass, even when I go out clubbing."

"I know you are. Duly noted all the same."

I drove off, eyes on the road, my mind on what I was about to ask of Courtney. It felt hard to breathe. I opened the sunroof. The feeling of extra room made it easier. I took a deep breath and started talking as I guided the CR-V south.

I spent the rest of the twenty-five-minute drive explaining the plan to Courtney. We rehearsed, went over her part over and over again. When we were done, she had the good sense to take a couple of minutes and think about it. I was proud of her for that.

Then she said, "Okay, let's do this."

We parked two blocks away, at the back of another warehouse. An SRT truck and half a dozen cars were already there, people spilling out, putting on vests, inspecting M4 assault rifles. I put the car in park and dug into the center console. I handed Courtney a small box.

"Coop, you shouldn't have," she said.

I flashed her a big smile for still having her sense of humor. She opened the box.

"The earbud is for you to hear us," I said, "the microphone for us to hear you. I already synced with MDPD. We're all on the same frequency." It's not like she did not know what she was looking at. I was nervous-talking.

She put the bud in her ear and twirled the mic around her fingers. It was about the size of a marble at the end of a two-inch pin. She pinched her lips.

"Try and pin it somewhere where it won't rub on clothing but he won't see it," I said.

She nodded. After another second, she opened her shirt and pinned it between her breasts on the inside of her bra. The black fabric hid enough of it that Rosling wouldn't see it even when he stared. Courtney rebuttoned the shirt and took a deep breath. The gear was making it real. I handed her the last prop, squeezed her hand, and we got out of the car.

Detective Rodríguez was standing outside. He squared up to Courtney.

"I'm sure Coop asked you already, but I have to ask for myself," he told her. "Are you willing, able, and ready for this?"

"I am."

"You're fully briefed on the operation and your role in it?"

"Yes," Courtney said.

Those were things he needed to ask, but you could also hear the concern in his voice. He dropped out of bureaucratese. "Are you sure you want to do this?" he asked. "It's no joke."

"I'm sure."

Rodríguez nodded and waved to the group of officers next to us. A shadow fell as a giant of a man approached. Alberto Villadeste introduced himself to Courtney, then turned to me.

"Tommy is on covert entry," he said. "I'm tactical lead."

"I'm glad to have you, brother. Sit rep?"

"We have low light cameras inserted through the HVAC, and infrared pointed at the building. It's giving us a fair picture. They're in the middle of the place. Crates are all over the floor around them. It's a low-light environment.

Your partner appears to be tied up to a chair, and the perp is sometimes leaning against a crate, sometimes pacing in front of her."

That was meant for all of us. He turned to Courtney next. "If you see something the cameras missed, by all means let us know, but don't worry about it. Your mission is diversion to facilitate insertion of the cover-entry team. Keep your focus on that. You good?"

"I'm good to go," Courtney said with a nod.

Villadeste looked at Rodríguez, who gave him a nod. Then he looked at me. "Our bosses are not happy with you taking lead and your team all over this. Too many civilians. They may not be wrong for a change, so be careful. Be smart. Don't fuck this up!"

"That's the idea."

Villladeste clicked his mic. His voice took an official, authoritative tone.

"Cut the chatter and take your places. The word is execute, execute, execute."

CHAPTER 34

A **hush descended on the staging** area. Footsteps and whispers faded as everyone took their places. Then the hush became silence, save for the flies and the mosquitoes.

I gave Courtney one last look before the big show. "You've got this," I told her.

I went to Rodríguez's red Taurus, leaned on the roof, and tried to stretch without being too obvious. My bruised ribs were still bugging me.

One of the SRT men tapped me on the shoulder and handed me an earwig. I put it on. I had nothing left to do but to watch and listen.

Courtney went back to the CR-V, sat down in the passenger seat, and closed the door behind her. Rodríguez took my spot behind the wheel. Then the CR-V drove away, leaving a big empty space and a knot in my guts.

The radio net came to life in my ear. "Final scan," the voice said. I recognized Villadeste.

A different voice came in, reporting back. "No change. Infrared and low-light optics still show two people inside, one likely sitting, one likely standing and occasionally pacing, both roughly at the center of the structure. The one standing appears to be armed. No movement outside the structure."

"Diversion team, please acknowledge," Villadeste said.

"Driver acknowledges." That was Rodríguez's voice.

"Yes," Courtney said, "I acknowledge. I understand."

The CR-V was nearing the warehouse.

I pointed to the mic of the officer standing next to me. He handed it over, and I cut in on the radio. "Courtney, this is what we call the last abort point," I said. "No shame in that if anything feels off, anything at all, including you."

My earbud carried her voice back to me. "I'm in. I'm doing this." I wasn't sure if I should have been proud or terrified.

"Point Bravo," Villadeste said, keeping track of the op for his team. "No abort."

Now we waited. It would be thirty seconds more before Rodríguez and Courtney reach the door. It might as well have been thirty years.

I rested my chin on the Taurus's roof and watched others go into harm's way, including one who had no business going. A faint smell of diesel permeated the air, a thoughtful gift from convoys of leaky big rigs. The night was clear, but there were no streetlights in the area. The smells and darkness threatened to take me back to other warehouses in other places in my past. I focused on the moment, on Courtney in the car.

I unclipped the night-vision binoculars I had brought with me from my belt and glued my eyes to them. There'd be little to see, and not for long, but it made me feel better to have a bead on Courtney while I could.

The place was thick with nervous energy. Some people were adjusting their NVGs. Others were squinting into the darkness. One chewed gum like it was alive and his sacred mission was to kill it with his teeth. Another kept clicking from mode to mode on his goggles.

The CR-V covered the last hundred feet to the warehouse with its engine revving, making a lot of noise, then stopped right in front of the door. The passenger door opened, and Courtney got out, a half-empty bottle of vodka in her hand.

The radio came to life. "Point Charlie. No abort. Breaching Team, negative on entry. Hold position."

"You coming or what," Courtney asked, her words overlapping with Villadeste's. She was loud. Her voice sounded happy and ever so slightly slurred. Hand the lady her Oscar. I breathed easier—just a little bit. She had this.

Detective Rodríguez's male voice rang out. "See you never, bitch!"

Courtney's voice again. "What the fuck, asshole?"

Tires screeched. Courtney shouted, "Don't you dare drive off!"

Tires burned. Courtney got even louder. "We're in the middle of nowhere. Don't you fucking drive off!"

The engine noise grew louder, then it receded. Courtney yelled at the top of her lungs. "Asshole!"

This was the next node in the plan, but Villadeste would not be calling it on the net. He would not risk distracting Courtney until she was out of there and out of danger.

Courtney walked in circles, looked around, faked a swig of vodka, acting the way someone stranded in the night might do. There were no windows on the warehouse, but acting it out created the right time frame before the next act.

Nice job, Courtney, I thought. I felt silly, like a proud parent at their kid's play. Except this play could get her killed.

Courtney stepped to the warehouse, opened the door, and disappeared inside. I put the binoculars down and held my breath. The silence lasted a second that stretched into an eternity. I did not know if the next sound I'd hear would be Courtney's voice or a gunshot. Bile burnt my stomach, threatening its way up into my throat. Beads of sweat formed on my forehead even though the day's heat had left and a cool night had descended.

"Oh, wow," Courtney's voice said in my ear. I exhaled. Her voice was a beautiful sound. "Oh, thank God," she said. "I didn't think anyone would be in here. This is great. I need help."

"Get the fuck out!" Rosling's voice came through loud and clear. My breathing eased another notch, in and out. Two voices, zero gunshot.

"No, no, you don't understand," Courtney said. Her voice was higher pitched than normal, and she kept up slurring her words a little. There was a valley girl affectation to her speech that she was probably borrowing from one girlfriend or another.

"I need help," she said. "My loser boyfriend threw me out of the car. We came here to have sex, and he left me stranded. I mean, seriously? Can you believe it? Who doesn't want to have sex with this?"

I smiled and shook my head. I could picture Courtney running her hands in front of her while saying that. The sounds of her heels on the cement meant she kept walking. She was moving, keeping Rosling's attention fixed on her, distracting him. She was playing everything out just like we had talked about. This was not talking, though; this was doing, and Courtney had it. She had guts, and she had skills.

She was talking a mile a minute now. "I trusted him, you know. My boyfriend? And he just drove off. Like, this is crazy. I don't even have my phone."

"Out!" Rosling yelled.

Courtney's heels clunked. Her voice changed and rocketed into high soprano.

"Is that a gun? Shit, mister, you don't have to be like that. I'm going, okay?"

The bottle of vodka crashed on the floor. Her steps quickened. She was running. She had known he had a gun. Her character had not, and she was playing it flawlessly. She reappeared through the door, half falling all over herself. When she rounded the entrance, she downright fell, ass over tea kettle. I wasn't sure if she did that on purpose or not, but it portrayed a panicked drunk to a tee. She got up and kept running down the street, heels and all. Rosling appeared for a half second and slammed the door shut.

"Door's closed," someone announced over the radio.

Courtney slowed into a walk, taking a straight line in long strides. Her voice came through loud and clear, even if she was breathing heavily.

"Did it work?" she asked.

"Covert team is in place," an anonymous voice responded.

"Yes!" Courtney said.

"Point Foxtrot," Villadeste came in, back on the line.

Courtney cleared her throat and came back over the air sounding calm and collected. "Okay, I didn't see too much. Rosling kept his body in front of CJ the whole time, but I made sure she could see me, at least for a moment.

Rosling is armed, we knew that. I'm pretty sure he has CJ's gun. I didn't see any other weapon. It's pretty dark, though, but your eyes adjust pretty quickly. Oh, one more thing. It looked like Rosling was limping. He did not move enough for me to see how badly, but there's definitely a limp."

Her report was crisp, spoken in tempo with her steps. She'd heard CJ's all-business voice often enough and was putting it to good use. If I had had time to think, I'd have reflected on how good an investigator she'd become with proper training. She may be better than me one day.

But I didn't have time to think. It was time to act.

Courtney's voice cut off my train of thought one last time.

"And if I flashed anyone falling down, I hope you enjoyed the show, and please remember to tip your waitresses." Stifled laughs rippled through the staging area. Good for her.

We waited another minute until she cleared the area, out of sight and out of danger.

"Point Golf," Villadeste said, unfazed. "Overt team is go for entry. Breaching team, hold your position and stand by."

Overt team was me. Courtney was out of the woods, now it was my turn. I nodded to Detective Rodríguez, who'd circled back around, and to the SRT team around him. They were ready. I got into the Taurus's driver's seat, then I counted to thirty-four because it was a random number, turned on the engine, and drove to the warehouse.

I got out of the car and slammed the door shut. I stormed into the building. I allowed myself to sound and look pissed. I was pissed. It wouldn't take my inner Hollywood to sell it. It just wasn't for the reason I was about to say.

CHAPTER 35

stomped around a crate and bellowed, "Who the fuck was that?"

I pointed in the direction in which Courtney had run out. It deflected attention from me and had the additional benefit of setting him on his heels. It also gave me three seconds to take in the lay of the land. A few isolated bare bulbs provided the only light, and half of them were obstructed by crates piled high throughout the warehouse. Odd shadows filled the place. Light tried in vain to find a foothold in the darkness.

I managed to make eye contact with CJ. She was tied up to a simple wooden chair and gagged with a strip of fabric tight across her mouth. She had a black eye and was down to her jeans and bra. That made no sense. I hadn't pegged Rosling as a petty sexual offender. Then I saw her T-shirt, torn into strips at Rosling's feet. A broad swath was tied around his thigh. Even through the dim light, I could see a blood stain. He had a hundred pounds on CJ and had subdued her, but the tigress had gotten a shot off. I held back my smile.

Rosling was standing next to her, with her gun in his hand. He extended a stiff arm toward her head. He was sweating. His shirt stuck to him. The vest and coat of his trademark three-piece suit were long gone. His hair was matted to his skull. He was shaking, maybe with shock, moving in jerky motions. The problem was that this was all happening while he had his finger on the trigger and the barrel pointed at CJ's head.

"Who the hell was that?" I asked again before he could recover from my bursting in yelling. I enunciated every word, still pointing to a spot through the wall where Courtney had disappeared a minute earlier.

"You tell me," he said. He was yelling back, but his voice was weak.

"How the fuck would I know? I don't like surprises, Walt. I said I'd come to you, just you, get things sorted out, not you and some tramp and my partner without her shirt on. What the fuck is going on here?"

A good offense was the best defense. Rosling backed off like a rookie coming face to face with an all-pro linebacker.

"Never mind that," he said. "She's no one. I made her leave. And your partner, she's just too fucking nosy is what, and she likes her gun too much." He lowered the pistol toward her middle. "Maybe I should put a bullet in her for good measure."

"You do that, and you die a very slow death," I said. I meant it, and he probably could tell, but that didn't matter. He didn't want any complications. He wanted out of here. Everything else was bravado.

He changed the topic. "You have the sedan?" he asked.

I didn't answer him. The situation was fluid. The little voice in my head was back. *Get him talking, Malone. Time's on your side. Make him feel important, worth listening to. Show him he matters, that what happened matters. People want to be heard.*

"What happened, Walt?" I asked. "How did we end up here?"

He started shaking harder. I was terrified of an accidental discharge that would hurt CJ—or worse. He wasn't answering me either. I needed his attention on me and on what I was saying. I played my trump card. There had been two names listed under Walt's cabin number in the manifest. Two.

"Is it about Claire?" I asked.

He swung around and pointed the gun at me. He was shaking like a leaf. Sometimes the barrel pointed right at my chest. Sometimes not. I didn't like those odds if a shot came off. I tried to remember how hard a pull CJ had set her trigger at.

"Don't you say her name," Rosling yelled.

He took a step toward me. He had his back to CJ now and she made eye contact with me. She silently mouthed two words through the gag: "Kill him."

Rosling's aim was getting wilder, but he was getting more and more tightly wound. His finger was taut on the trigger. There was still a chance this could end up very badly for me.

"What happened, Walt?" I asked again. *Keep him talking. Drain him. Drain him emotionally, physically. Keep going.*

"He took everything from me," Rosling said.

"Who? Morrison?"

"Of course, fucking Morrison. It was my company. Mine. Then this . . . this . . . this playboy comes in with his boy genius. Says he wants to partner up, grow the company, expand, diversify. Sure, why not, right? Then all of a sudden, the company changes its name. It's LandQuest, damnit. LandQuest, not StarQuest. What the hell does that mean anyway? We're building rockets, now?

"But you know what? I didn't even care. He could have it. I didn't care." His voice dropped. He faltered just when I needed him to keep talking the most.

"Because you had Claire," I said.

"No one knew about her," Rosling said. "She was . . . she was everything to me. She was fifteen years younger, but so what? When I was with her, all the bullshit, all the haggling, Morrison pretending he was the face of the company, nothing mattered. Just her."

"Why bring her on the cruise?" I asked.

"Stupid cruise was Morrison's idea. A break, he said, a reward for all the hard work. Reward, my ass. Reward for him, maybe. He's the one who wanted to go. That's all he knew, booze and drugs and whores. That was how he brought in those people he called 'investors.'"

"And you didn't want to go," I said. *Tell me your story, Walt. We have a rapport, you and me. I understand you.* I was willing it to him, one word at a time. "You didn't want to go without Claire."

"Want to? I couldn't. I couldn't stand the thought of spending a week on a ship with Morrison. Not without her to keep me sane. And she agreed, you know. She'd go with me."

"What went wrong?" My training was still there, urging me along. *Don't let him pause. Keep the pace, even if he talks about the bad stuff.*

"What went wrong?" Rosling was yelling at the top of his lungs now. Spit flew from his mouth. "She betrayed me is what went wrong." His voice dropped. "Morrison is what went wrong. He got her drunk and he got her high and she went to bed with him."

"Is that why you killed him?"

He barely heard me, but he kept talking.

"I would have forgiven her. I would have. It was Morrison's fault. I confronted him after everyone left. I told him he couldn't have her, to keep his hands off her. And you know what he did? He laughed. He couldn't stop fucking laughing. He said I was too old and stupid for a woman like that, and then he doubled over laughing, saying something about how deluded I was. He had taken everything from me, and he thought it was funny. So, I grabbed that ugly centerpiece from the table, and I swung it at his head as hard as I could. Then he stopped laughing."

He still pointed at me with his gun hand, but he was barely keeping the pistol upright.

"Why don't you drop the gun, Walt?"

He stared at me, lifting the gun. "You said you'd fix it. You made a mess of it poking your nose in it. Now, you're going to fix it."

"The only way to fix it is for you to drop the gun."

"Where's the sedan?" he asked.

"Right outside the door." I let that sink in, then I tried to replicate CJ's all-business voice. "But you're not getting in it."

His eyes narrowed like he couldn't understand how stupid I was. He'd explained everything before. "Either I do, or your partner dies," he said. He spoke slowly, like he was explaining something to a kid who was having a hard time getting it.

"No, Walt," I said softly. Then I lifted my head and shouted into the warehouse. "One, please."

From the dark recesses on my right, where crates were haphazardly piled on top of each other and light did not reach, a red laser beam shot across the warehouse, seemingly out of nowhere, landing on a spot on Rosling's sternum. He turned to it in a wild, uncontrolled motion. He pointed his gun all over the righthand side of the warehouse.

"That's my friend Danny out there in his sniper's nest," I told Rosling. "We served together. He's the best sniper I ever saw. He could take your belt off with one bullet right now without grazing your belly. But he won't. He came a long way to put a bullet in your head."

When Danny had insisted on going on the motorboat with CJ while I boarded the *Rio*, he'd told me he needed a week in Miami anyway. I had no clue whether he meant it or was shutting me up. Turned out he meant it, and his answer to "Are you still in Miami?" was "Where do you need me?" Man had my back. Always.

The jumble of crates and containers on my left offered just as many hiding spots. Rosling's hands had barely stopped swinging around when I called, "Two, please," and another red laser pierced the darkness and landed right next to where Danny's had, but this time from the opposite direction. Rosling turned around, yelped his panic, and nearly fell over.

"And Tommy over there behind his sniper rifle," I said, "he's Miami SWAT and a former Marine, if there were such things as *former* Marines. He's very good at killing."

Rosling kept pointing his gun back and forth in the darkness, left and right and left and right. I kept talking. "See, while you were busy staring at the hot chick looking for help, just a phone call, really, those two snuck in. It's over, Walt. Drop the gun."

He stopped moving the pistol around. He cocked his head and hunched over, looking at me from the corner of his face. When he spoke, the words came slow and slurred. "Youuuuuu fucked up."

He swung his gun toward CJ.

A deafening gunshot echoed in the warehouse.

Rosling collapsed, screaming in pain.

The shot had come from the left. Tommy Wood had taken out the same leg CJ had shot earlier, and he'd saved Danny from having to explain a civilian shoot for good measure.

I had my gun in my hand before Rosling hit the floor. "You move, you die," I shouted over his screams. Behind me, all hell was breaking loose. The door flew open, nearly coming off its hinges. Men in helmets with assault rifles in their hands spilled in, yelling orders. Within seconds, cries of "Don't move!" and "Show me your hands!" changed to "Medic! Medic!"

Rosling had to have half a dozen M4s pointed at his head. I holstered my pea shooter and hurried to CJ. I pulled the gag out of her mouth and started working at the knots tying her to the chair.

"Will you be okay?" I asked. I looked at her while I worked on the ropes by feel, digging my fingers into the knots.

Tears in the corners of her eyes that she couldn't completely hold back belied that infernal calm in her voice. That was CJ, always in control of herself.

"I will be," she said. She yanked at a rope still attached to the chair and kept talking. "In spite of all this, I will be. I could deal with it because I knew you were coming to get me. I knew."

She was still managing to keep all emotions out of her voice. She was stating a fact with as much composure as if she was reporting on the agency's monthly profits.

"Anyt—" I started.

She interrupted me, trying to sound pissed off, of all things, trying to hide all the other emotions so she could deal with them later, privately. "You were supposed to kill him."

I barely could open my mouth, let alone make a sound, before she kept going.

"And you were not supposed to involve Courtney. Courtney, Coop! Courtney! You have to be certifiably insane. You lost your mind if you ever had it."

Even if CJ was done, I still could not talk. Alberto Villadeste, aka José, the oversized and over-tattooed SRT officer who had walked in with me to arrest the thugs who had killed Morant, had just knocked the wind out of me by slapping me on the back with a whoop. He managed to bend low enough, knife in hand, his rifle slung over his shoulder, to cut what remained of the ropes tying CJ to the chair. Paramedics joined the fun, jostling us around as they tried to get a look at CJ. They were jostling me around, anyway, since Alberto was something of an immovable object.

Then we were all slammed on our asses and out of the way by an F5 tornado. When I recovered, Courtney was glued to CJ. She had covered up in an SRT windbreaker and was shaking with all the emotions CJ was still keeping inside. Even the medics and Alberto's tree-trunk arms could not tear her away.

CJ hugged Courtney back and looked at me. "I'm okay, guys," she said, "I'm okay. And thank you."

I could swear I heard her voice shake a little. I put a hand on her shoulder. "Anytime, partner."

I stepped away, taking in the scene. Rodríguez had come in on SRT's heels and was directing the chaos. He made sure that Rosling, though in pain, could understand him, then he read him his rights. He would need to read them to him again later, before any formal interrogation, but getting them in now couldn't hurt.

An SRT officer eyed CJ, who was still a little shaky on her feet, a blanket over her shoulders. "Fucker has no right," he snarled under his breath, just loud enough for a few of us to hear. We all nodded, and we all knew it was wishful thinking.

I squeezed CJ's shoulder one more time. I whispered in Courtney's ear that I was goddamn proud of her, then I got out of the warehouse and let everyone else do their job.

The rest of the night was a blur of statements, lights, rides, and a lot of deep breathing trying to keep everything in check, taking stock of all that happened. Dawn was breaking by the time they released CJ from the hospital where the paramedics had taken her, kicking and screaming. Ironically, it was the same hospital where they'd taken Walt Rosling. I was looking at him through a window. He was handcuffed to the rails of the hospital bed, leg in traction. Here was the guy who killed a man and led to another's death. He looked pathetic.

I was lost in thoughts when CJ and Courtney appeared down the hallway. CJ had inherited the SRT jacket and Courtney had changed into the jeans and T-shirt she'd stuffed in her backpack before coming down to meet me.

"Even if they save the leg," I said, "he'll never walk right again."

"Then I may forgive you for not killing him," CJ said. I wasn't sure if I was supposed to laugh at that, so I kept my poker face.

"Speaking of which, how is Danny?" she asked. "I owe him big time."

"He's good." I stifled a laugh. "He's pissed Wood took the shot before him. I told him we'd all get together before he leaves—you too, Courtney, the four of us."

"The sooner, the better," CJ said. "I can use one."

Silence fell. CJ broke it before I could suggest we get out of there. "I'm sorry I let him jump me," she said.

"What? That's nonsense." The look on my face must have been priceless as I turned to look at her. I couldn't believe she was apologizing. She'd got off a shot that crippled him. Things could have turned out a lot worse without it.

"I mean it," she said. "You've been trying to tell me to trust my gut more. When Rosling agreed to meet right away after all but kicking you out of his property on Key West but asked to meet at some warehouse, my gut told me not to go alone, that something wasn't right. I didn't listen."

"CJ, come on," I said.

She kept talking over me.

"We met outside. When I started asking questions, he became agitated. He started pacing back and forth. He sounded more and more upset with each question. I could not figure out why. But instead of following my instincts to get the hell out of there, I kept analyzing his answers, trying to figure him out like he was a spreadsheet. Looking back, he had probably convinced himself we knew everything. Maybe Claire called him after we told Courtney to direct message her, and that sealed it for him, but that's only a guess."

"Could be, and that's on me," I said in a tone that suffered no debate. For one, it was on me, and, for another, I wasn't going to have Courtney feel guilty over doing her job.

"Either way," CJ continued, "he must have thought I was pushing for a confession, for something incriminating. He probably thought he was done for. At some point, he lost it completely. He took a few steps like he was leaving then snapped back and stormed toward me with his hands balled up into fists. I got my gun out. I put a warning shot in the pavement. You know me, CJ Do Right. You've got to fire a warning shot first. He kept coming, and I put one in his leg, but he was already on top of me and knocked me out cold. So, yes, I'm sorry."

Courtney took CJ's hand in hers and looked at her. "You're being dumb," she said. That probably meant more than anything I could have said. I put my arm around my partner and Courtney squeezed her hand.

"Time to go home," I said.

CHAPTER 36

Wait, wait, wait, wait, wait. I've got questions."

Amy was sitting next to me in the booth at a nice chophouse. She'd put her glass down long enough to raise both hands in the air.

It was Friday night. The gun-shooting part of the case had closed just over a week before. This was our first real date. We'd seen each other earlier in the week. That had been a rip off our clothes, pent-up passion sex marathon. It was good. This was better.

We had Ubered here, and we would Uber back to her place or mine. We had drinks, then we had appetizers and wine and dinner and more drinks. We knew where the evening would end, and we had no reason to rush it. We chatted about nothing and everything, and I told her all about the case—or, apparently, not quite *all* about it.

"Ask away," I said.

"So Morant's and Morrison's murders were not related after all?"

"Oh, they were, but indirectly. Rosling's been singing like a canary trying to save what he can of his hide, and the Feds got quite a bit from the *Rio*'s hidden surveillance system—they had a lot more to work with than Courtney. We've been able to piece the story together."

Amy was windmilling her free hand in the air like she was signaling a home run. "And . . . ."

"And we learned that Dagheretti was in fact the *Rio*'s drug lord. He had a deal with the cartels. He's also the one who set up those cameras. Most of the security staff on the *Rio* was working for him. It paid better. When Morrison was killed, Dagheretti went to his secret cams and saw Rosling leaving Morrison's cabin right around the time of the murder. He was looking the worse for wear, jumpy, seeing ghosts behind the walls. Dagheretti could have arrested him and found a way to make himself look good, but he had a bigger problem."

"Morant," Amy said.

"Exactly. Morant was working on shutting down Dagheretti's drug business. Eventually, he would have succeeded. So Dagheretti blackmailed Rosling. He would rat him out for the Morrison murder unless Rosling killed Morant."

"And he introduced him to Dunn for the dirty work."

"No," I said. "The DEA was right, for once. There was no connection between the two. Dunn was Rosling's man all along."

"Huh? How?"

"Well, 99.9 percent of land deals in the Western Hemisphere are boring. Buyer and seller quibble, lawyers bicker, and the only thing to die are trees, sacrificed on the altar of the mighty red tape. But that last tenth of a percent might as well be deals for poppy fields in Afghanistan. Dunn was Rosling's muscle for those."

"This is incredible!" Amy said. I rather liked the way she looked at me right then. I rather liked any way she looked at me so long as she did. I took a sip of my rye. A layer of warmth added itself to what I was already feeling. Amy looked incredible in a silky blouse open just enough to tease. Maybe I didn't want to wait too much longer after all.

"But," Amy continued, "how did Morant get the hard drive to start with? You know, the one you—hmm, how should I put it—*stole* from his office?"

"Oh, that hard drive," I said, scratching my chin. "It all goes back to the Sunday when you, Heather, and Jen came back from the cruise—when the *Rio* docked with a body on board. Dagheretti could not quite hide that a murder had happened, and Morant had come down to take stock of the investigation. He noticed the hidden cameras, knew they weren't supposed to be there. One of Dagheretti's henchmen saw Morant checking them out. They managed to hide most of it—cameras, hard drives, all that—for use later. That's the part the DEA found. They tried to destroy what they couldn't hide. Morant found one of those—the hard drive he took back to his Miami office."

"You mean the hard drive you stole?" she said with a grin.

"Yeah, that one."

Amy wasn't done. Her curiosity was not yet satisfied. "And the linen? All that work on the warehouse angle? Did it have anything to do with this?"

"I knew you'd ask." I pulled a small packet of white powder from my back pocket and handed it to her. "It's not cocaine."

She opened it right under her nose. Her whole face puckered, and she recoiled into the far corner of our booth. She frowned at me. "It smells . . . clean, in a way, but so intense it's like acid. It burns your nose."

"It's concentrated commercial detergent. Shippers sprinkle it in between sheets to keep them smelling fresh in transit, especially in tropical climates, but here it has a dual purpose. It's so strong it masks cocaine, even from drug-sniffing dogs. Law enforcement found crates with that detergent and cocaine in them in every port the *Rio* stops at."

Amy handed me the packet back. "Wow. You know what?" she said. "Whoever thought of that should get their drugs back."

Who was I to disagree?

"And the bad guys are all in jail," Amy said, concluding the story.

I breathed through the heat rising in me, the same heat I'd felt when Detective Rodríguez had called me last Monday.

Amy saw it right away. "Coop?" It wasn't a question.

"Rosling has been transferred to a prison infirmary," I said. "And Dagheretti was arrested in the Caribbean on an Interpol Red Notice—an international arrest warrant—trying to leave the ship. He will be extradited in a matter of weeks, if that long. But Dunn is in the wind. Assistant State Attorney Tippins obtained a warrant for his arrest right away, and MDPD fanned out with lights and sirens, but they were too late. Somehow, he got tipped off and scrammed."

"I'm sorry."

I smiled and took her hand. "Don't be. Sure, it pisses me off when I think about it, but this was a good two weeks' work."

She squeezed my hand back and beamed. *Damn that unfair million-dollar smile!* "I'm glad you see it," she said. "You and CJ and everyone did an unbelievable job."

"Speaking of everyone, did you talk to Heather?" I asked.

"I did." She leaned against me and put her hand on my shoulder. "She called right after you gave her the closed-file report. I told her she'd been right to call you, and you in particular because she'd be seeing a lot more of you and me together. She did not process that for about twenty seconds, then she stopped mid-sentence and asked, 'You mean together like *together* together?' I told her 'Yes,' and she proceeded to tell me that, well, of course, she should have seen that coming because you and I are basically the same person except I have boobs."

I wrapped my arms around her, and she melted into me. "Popping the champagne with us. That's good."

"Yes."

That was the first time I'd truly shared the story of this case, even though I had told it or part of it before. But as close friends as Heather and I were, and as grateful as she was, that part had been a PI/client report. I'd also called Linda Mayak, the bodyguard. "One-third," she'd whispered. "I had to have my eye on the one out of three protectees not involved in this. Rotten luck." Then she'd hung up. And I'd sat with Ruiz, who'd been promoted to Morant's job, and Ollie Morant, the man's son. The kid could see the big picture, that his dad had died fighting drug dealers. His chest had swelled with pride, and tears had rolled down his cheeks. I'd given him Owen's badge from his days in the Jamaican Constabulary, the one I'd retrieved from his office desk. Ollie had taken it, then he had taken my hand in both of his and walked away without another word, clutching his dad's credentials against his chest.

Now I could finally share it all for me—for Amy and me. I pulled her closer to me. "Ready to go?" I whispered in her ear.

"More than ready."

I signaled for the check. We raised our glasses before draining the last of their content. "To our future," Amy offered. I was pretty sure I was looking at it right there before my eyes.

To our future.

ACKNOWLEDGMENTS

It is the nature of writing books that only the author's name appears on the cover. But no person is an island, and I am no exception. A great many people had a role in bringing this book to you. If you enjoyed it, please hang on for a few more words and join me in thanking them. (If you did not enjoy it, it's on me.) And to those not on this page, please blame my scattered brains. It's a real problem.

Penny, you are my alpha reader, beta reader, omega reader, first editor, greatest cheerleader and most honest critic. You are my best friend and the love of my life, and I still can't believe you agreed to marry me all those years ago. Without you, this book would not exist.

Mom and dad, a lifetime of love and support are worth so much more than a line at the end of a book, but there it is anyway. Thank you.

Emily (ladies first, and because radars emit waves, not beams) and Nick, beta readers extraordinaire, I am in your debt for making this book better.

Thank you, Lauren. Your coaching helped me see the possible.

I am forever grateful to the team at Indigo River and the splendid job everyone did through editing and publishing.

And let me say a word for all the people we never think about, those who toil in paper mills, work magic behind a computer screen, spend hours behind the wheel of delivery vans, and everyone with a job to do between the author writing a book and the reader holding it in their hand. We may not know your names, but know that I am immensely grateful to every one of you.

WATCH FOR COOPER MALONE'S NEXT ADVENTURE!

The Fourth of July in South Florida is a fun and crazy time when everything goes well. This year, it didn't.

Someone is dead. Others are missing. But not to worry—Coop is on the case.

www.ingramcontent.com/pod-product-compliance
Lightning Source LLC
Chambersburg PA
CBHW051629260626
47170CB00004B/1096